SHADOWS ON THE HILLSIDE

A WEIRD LANDSCAPES ANTHOLOGY

SHADOWS ON THE HILLSIDE
A WEIRD LANDSCAPES ANTHOLOGY

Edited by Storm Constantine

NewCon Press
England

First edition, published in the July UK 2021
by NewCon Press
41 Wheatsheaf Road, Alconbury Weston, Cambs, PE28 4LF

NCP 259 (hardback)
NCP 260 (softback)

10 9 8 7 6 5 4 3 2 1

ISBN: 978-1-912950-96-6 (hardback)
978-1-912950-97-3 (softback)

Text layout by Storm Constantine
Cover by Danielle Lainton

CONTENTS

BETWEEN SKIN AND SEA

Cat Hellisen

I moved here to escape the ocean. That makes no sense, you say, as we leave my stone-walled cottage, its garden swamped by lapping dunes, fig-marigolds in pinks and purples, creeping cape rushes and heath ericas. The sea batters at my door, fish reeking, iodine tailed.

Not all oceans are the same, though all oceans are one.

Again. I see you, daughter. You roll your eyes, mutter under your breath. You check your wrist and pluck excuses from the carcass of our visit. Chicken feather lies, white, choking the air around us.

Three years have passed since you last visited. I understand. You hate the smell of magic, and you hate the hush of water, the suck of grains of sand swirling away from your feet. It reminds you of what we are, and what you pretend not to be.

It's raining. I'm making you walk with me along the water's edge where tiny jellyfish have come to die in translucent pink mounds. We are trapped waterwise, between the drizzle and the salt sea.

There is no escape.

Rain runs down my head and back and I long to stretch out my arms and fly between these worlds of water. We walk from river mouth to river mouth, white sand turning golden beneath our naked feet. In silence I gather fallen feathers, green and black as oil, and put them in my woven bag.

"I'm thinking of moving," you say. The secret you have been sucking between your teeth – sour and pebble hard – you spit it out so that it lands between us. It takes root in our churned footprints.

"You're not thinking." I will not ask where you're going. It will be far from waves and the rotting carcasses of stingrays, from the ash-black wheeling of the gulls. Back bowed, I dig a fallen cormorant feather out of the muddy sand, my long skirts pulled by the endless Cape winds. "You've already packed your things."

You shrug in response. I was never the best of mothers, but you were never the best of daughters. A fair trade then, both of us awkward and ugly in our different ways. "It's not the end of the world," you say. "You can visit."

We both know I won't. I am tied to the water. "Hmm." We have reached the boundary of the river, and while you stand on the crumbling sand bank, I step into the swirling estuary, brackish brown, thick with broken stems of water hyacinth, and look upriver to where the flamingos stand at sinuous attention. They gabble at me in their harridan goose voices and I step back out. It is time to go home. I shrug out of my sodden top and let the rain soothe my ruined skin. Already the clouds are thinning, and the wet sand smell of witchcraft and promises will dry up under the returning sun.

When you were born, I made you a tiny coat. It was green and sharp, a poisonous baby jacket of nettles and thorns. I thought it would keep you safe here with me. The world is no place for women like us. Our bones are wrong. People want to cage us. They see only beauty that they must own. The grace, the bright eye, the pointed nail, the curve of a neck or arm, so wing-like. Delicate.

I thought if I stopped you from growing up and becoming like me, that I would have done my duty as a mother. Instead, you screamed every time I made you wear the jacket, and one morning I found it torn to pieces in our front room. A display of temper and self.

When you turned teenager and the landscape of your body began to transmute, I knew that no coat of nettles would ever help. I left my ocean shores and limped inland, trekking to the garish city shops, the hordes of people who stared at my dowager's hump hidden under a thick coat, my scarred face, my beakish nose, my too-black eyes. There I bought you creams and silver tweezers, depilatories, unguents, suicide-sharp razors, glitter and oil. I taught you how to pluck and paint, to redraw your personal topography. You dyed your hair cadmium like a flag of war. We learned to keep secrets from each other, burying ourselves in separate graves.

This is not the first time you are running from me. "Do you remember…?" you say, as we take the winding paths back to my home, past your father's empty cottage where the lampless lighthouse stands in solemn erection, convinced of its mastery over the slick rocks and wanton water.

"Yes."

When you left home, I gave you the skin you were born in, stripped while you were still bloody, rinsed and dried and folded away. It had grown as you had grown. I wrapped it in brown paper and tied it with salt-grass.

"Did you ever open it?"

You look to the sky, now mussel-shell blue, dragged with wisps of white, the sun extending grasping golden anemone tentacles. You laugh. "What did you want me to do – wear it?"

Perhaps. I wear what's left of mine. My husband pulled all the feathers from my true skin and burned them in the lighthouse fire that warned ships of danger, told stories across the darkness. *Stay Away, Stay Away.* There is no safety here. The sea will eat you.

My skin is pebbled and stretched saggy, but it still fits. Sometimes I dream that if wear it long enough and keep it warm with blood heat, the feathers will grow back in; bright darts piercing outward, their barbs tight, oil-preened, black and glossy. Instead, all I have now are nudified wings, draggled with stolen plumage, pathetic and ugly as uncooked Sunday roast. I stretch out these raw, hideous limbs, and you curl your mouth in disgust.

"Hide them."

"Why should I?"

"Because they're disgusting. You look like a freak. Do you want people to know what we are?"

"So?" You make me childish and petulant. I want to stamp my feet and throw myself down on the ground, scream. I taught you to hate yourself. To hate me when I should have taught you to hate the men who trap us in these stone cages, who trick us with pretty words, beams of light, safe harbours, then steal who we are from ourselves. "This is me," I tell her, but it is too late to unpick the work of twenty-three years.

When I was married, I lived in a lighthouse cottage. I fished from the slippery rocks, gathered periwinkles, white mussels, oysters. I burned home fires on bleached driftwood, the flames blue. Skinless, I swam the whale-roads, swallowed brine. I could not drown.

After your father died, I left the lighthouse and walked down the coast, my palms beggars' bowls, until I came to the place I live now. Small and broken, sand carpeted, the windows empty. I claimed it and filled it with flotsam and jetsam salvage. All I took with me when I escaped the lighthouse were you, and our skins. And the ring around my throat, brass and heavy, placed there on my wedding day. No will in the world will break it.

You and the ring and the empty skin. We lived on loaves and fishes. I cooked flatbreads mixed with oil and sour milk, the fire tonguing the black-burned pan. We drank from empty shells and ate from plastic lids. Gift by gift, I built our house anew, furnished with the sea's leavings deposited at my door with each spring tide. I walked miles every day with you strapped to my back, a digging stick in one hand, my woven bag slung about my chest. For years I wore no broken wings, just the weight of you.

Now you are too big to carry. You stare down at me, and I, in my turn, have shrunk in on myself, collapsing around a heart that beats too fast. My bones have turned light and hollow. All the better for flying.

"I have to go," you explain, when I invite you to stop at the house you grew up in. I have made supper. Sullen-mouthed fish resigned to their deaths, starchy tubers dug from the estuaries, little shrimp like fat glass monsters, wild garlic, bitter herbs. You have the look of someone who wants to tell a relative about a death in the family but cannot think how to begin. "We – I have plans."

You don't share your plans, so I wave you away and pretend not to watch you walk out across the fynbos-covered dunes, disappearing between the green hearts of the arum lilies, their slender white trumpets, the powdery yellow phalluses of spring. I wonder if you've found a man. If you think some sly smiled demon is going to rescue you from poverty and from the ignominy of your mother, your mother's house, your father's pitiful little death. A slip on a rock.

I had nothing to do with it.

After I've eaten, I trim the soft woven wicks on the paraffin lamps, fill and light them. The dark comes later now, but I am far from the helpful glow of street lights and even I cannot do fine work by moonlight. The day's gleanings are cleaned, the feathers carefully pulled between finger and thumb. I set barb to barb, brush the sand to the floor, until each cormorant feather is straight and black as a well-told truth. When I'm happy, I stitch them in place, threading through the calamus with the sinews of Southern Right whales as I add the plumage to my skin.

It has taken many years, many nights sat with my skin spilled over my lap, painstakingly pinning feather after feather. The bright glossy wing feathers, the brown coverts, outlined in black, that scale breast and crown. The tiniest, softest ones that are so hard to find and collect. It is not unlikely that I have added the lives of others to my own. Here a flight-feather from an oystercatcher, here a tertial from a tern. Perhaps I have shaped my new throat with the pale offerings of pelicans.

Fingers shaking, eyes squinted in the weak orange light, I stitch the final feathers into place and oil them flat with my palm. It is done. I am too scared to move. I promise myself I will look at my finished skin in the morning, and instead of retreating to my bed, I curl into the contours of my worn armchair, and let its broken back and arms cradle me. Head tucked, heart frantic, I breathe with the roar and hush of the waves.

Seven mornings pass, and my skin lies crumpled on the kitchen table. I eat around it, I push it aside, I pretend tomorrow I will fit it on, and see if I should still believe in magic.

It is finally, on a day when the spring mists have cleared, and the sky is bare and blue and dried to a powdery softness, that I scrape together the courage to shake my skin out, to let the light catch on every plume. There are no gaps I can pretend to fill. My skin is finished.

Under a bright sun, on a beach that is empty but for the rotting humps of baby seals and storm-washed kelp, I strip myself down, and redress the wrongs my husband burned onto me. The skin fits. It closes around me, a warm fist, squeezing me out of the shape I have known for so many years, that I have become accustomed to. Wife and mother and servant and gatherer and lost thing. I am reformed, the pressure cracking my skull, pulling bones askew, rearranging vertebrae like a string of misshapen pearls.

The heavy ring that has choked me for decades does not transform with me. It falls to the sandy carpet with a dense thud, the exterior scratched and scarred by my fingernails, the interior shiny as potential, polished against human skin. The neck ring crumbles and turns to ash and the last link to my lighthouse years is finally loosened. It cannot shackle me to the earth.

I want to scream my joy to the sun and silvering water, but no sound comes from my freed throat. My voice is gone. I am made silent but given wings.

A fair exchange. No one ever listened, anyway.

I fly once across the waves, testing my freedom. I skim the green glass shallows, dip over the deeper blues. The waves roll beneath me, shaking their shaggy heads and laughing. Schools of fish skitter under the ocean skin, and a great white shark moves like a slow and patient ghost, hunting the bay. I flit between air and water, a slick dive, fill my belly with eels, fish small as fingers. I swallow and swallow and swallow.

When I am tired and glutted, I sit on the rocks to hold my wings open, welcoming the heat of the day. I forgot what living feels like. I forgot the truth of myself. This is who I am; sea-raven, bird-girl, water-woman, wife-of-the-sea.

If only I could have shown you this when you were younger and taught you to love yourself. Perhaps you would have worn your own feathers and stayed by the water. Perhaps you would not have gone chasing some man in an apartment in the city. So eager to scrub the salt from your skin. Perhaps there is still time to give you this blessing, mother to daughter.

I wait for you to visit, eager now for one of your rare ventures home. Usually I both crave and dread them. There is a soft armed, milk-breasted part of me that longs to hold you close and whisper to your crown, how you will rule the world, crush monsters beneath your chubby rounded feet. A louder voice tells me that you will pull faces at my meagre offerings of fish stew, of redbush tea, stamped grains. That you will pace my cottage and turn it from a sanctuary into a cage. That with your pennants of war you will remind me that we have never been at peace. That these visits are part of the expected traditions of cease-fire. You are merely going through the motions, stockpiling your weapons.

But you do not come. Too busy moving from your beach-front rental into a city loft, I suppose. Putting miles between you and the tang of sea. Exchanging the crash and roar of storms for the crash and roar of traffic.

So I gather my skin around me, gather my armour, and go to you. I'm not sure what to expect. After all, you left me an address, and the intimation of an invitation – but what if it was merely the distant politeness of a stranger bound by blood? And what of this man? Will I have to peck out his eyes in order to save you from your willing blindness?

I follow the river, the serpent winding its way from the sea, threading inland. The little seaside village gives way to suburbs, sand dunes rolling into over-grassed golf-courses, houses rising regal and all matched up. Planned. Developed. The stink of magic recedes. My feathers are coated with the gritty exhaust of trucks, trains. The miasma of humanity. The city seethes below me and I bank, catching the heated updraft. It's harder to fit the human map of lines and letters over my avian view, but finally I land on a wrought-iron balcony, barely wide enough for pigeons to nest on. The glass doors are closed against the smog, but I crook my head and peer in.

At, first, the flat appears empty. Oh, there are furnishings, clean and neat and soulless as a catalogue, but there is no sign of your mark. The curtains are limp and pale, the sofa a creamy brown, a facsimile of nature. I know these shades. Oat and mushroom, slate and heather. They assume the names of living things to mantle their deadness. Then I see you. You're curled on the small armchair, your head cradled in your arms, your red hair loose. You have fallen asleep, perhaps while reading, and he has taken the trouble to fold your book closed, to drape a greyish-blue throw about your shoulders. You are smiling in your sleep.

My beak raps unexpectedly against the glass and I jerk back against the bars of the balcony.

For a moment, I wonder why I am here. It is too late to teach you freedom.

I take wing, circle the building, then stand sentry on the jutting ledge of a nearby building. I watch the apartment entrance far below, beady eyed, waiting to see the one who's trapped you here in comforts and cushions.

The day drags, and I am tired. I almost miss the moment a little laughing dove swoops past your balcony to land on the bathroom windowsill. The glass pane is partially ajar, just wide enough for the little pinkish bird to squeeze through. The invasion is so unexpected that I almost topple from my perch, only realising I am winged at the last moment, snapping pinions in fright.

Through the window, at an angle only a bird could see, I watch the dove shake free of its skin, and hang the feathered cape neatly on a peg. Next to it, yours hangs, black and green. You did not move here to escape the ocean.

I send you an invitation. It takes me three months to write and post it, because I do not know the words. I know only that my own sour past has made me assume your future could hold nothing good.

Bring your skins, I tell you.

You arrive on a summer Sunday, and the beach – even this far out from the village – is hot and crowded. The air smells of sunscreen and children, chips and vinegar. You emerge from the knot of humans, your red hair bound up against the sandpaper wind, your hand in hers.

I open my door and spread my arms.

ALL THAT DEAD BEAUTY

Andrew Hook

Blake had almost forgotten his connection to countryside during his second year in the city. A punishing workload from dawn to dusk together with a parallel social life at weekends had served to sever any ties he'd once had with birdsong, marsh and meadow. This paring of existence to its extremes extended to the interior of his apartment: minimalist, modern, mechanic. On the third floor there was neither garden nor window box. Nor even an imitation plant gathering moisture in the bathroom.

Arriving from a farming background Blake had been glad to shed his past. Whilst his parents continued to toil amongst swill and mud, rising in pre-dawn light, their silhouettes forming against a close background of trees as though being revealed through scratchboard art, Blake found mornings in music, through the cacophony of his radio alarm clock through to headphones as he walked to work culminating in elevator muzak as he ascended to his office. He held no time for extraneous sounds. Initially repudiation in the manner of a surly teenager – albeit older than those years – this lifestyle grew around him as readily as ivy twining a tree. The dissolution of the natural environment *became* his natural environment. Those brief journeys to visit his parents were marked out with disdain, as though there was something backward about the backwoods, as though his rise had been wholly intellectual and not restricted to the height of apartment and office.

If he had paused in his whirlwind city life Blake might have reflected that his parents weren't of the idiot template that his dismissive mind required them to be. He was named after William, and a reproduction of *Adam Naming The Beasts* had adorned the head of the stairwell in the family cottage. The serpent was entwined in a surprisingly friendly fashion around Adam's left arm, whilst the animals behind him grazed in a pastoral landscape, unscathed by man's transgression in the Garden of Eden. Additionally, Blake's family were prolific readers, and he owed his youth to them in books held near riverbanks and in woodland. Perhaps it was unsurprising that they had continued with literature as presents, despite Blake not owning a bookcase in his sparsely furnished apartment.

The distillation of his life to modernity was not unheeded. Paper was anathema to a paperless office. On his twenty-fourth birthday his parents bought him a Kindle – the name of the item almost scurrilous to those who favoured print – whose contents contained two single books: *Drive Your Plow Over The Bones Of The Dead* by Olga Tokarczuk and *Animalia* by Jean-Baptiste Del Amo. *The latter book is us,* they enthused, *a powerful novel about man's desire to conquer the natural world harnessed to a background of pig farming.* Blake eschewed the opportunity to engage in what he wrongly dismissed as his parents' biography but found himself drawn to the former novel with its murder mystery conceit. Finding himself stuck, however, after a handful of rather dour pages, yet considering an obligation to the thoughtfulness of their choice, he nevertheless allowed the Kindle's battery to wind down once he realised the novel had become a movie. He might engage with the story in an almost multiplex setting and gain enough insight to converse and thank his parents as though he had taken the trouble to read it.

So it was that during his viewing of *Spoor,* a Polish film which didn't make the busier circuit and which he had to go somewhat out of his way to view, that Blake witnessed the contrast that would start the revolution in his life.

The Polish-language title, *Pokot,* was a hunting term that referred to the count of wild animals killed. The English title *Spoor* referred to the traces and tracks left behind by hunted game. If Blake was struck by the main character, an elderly woman who surrounded herself with detritus amidst her remote mountain cabin, he did not realise how fully immersive he had entered the story until the scene switched to that of the antiseptic apartment of the younger police IT expert and systems whizz, Dyzio: minimalist, modern, mechanic. Blake paused in thought whilst the movie played on. In one fell swoop his dissociation from his parents was made evident. He found he paid little attention to the remainder of the picture, where nature cast a wide net and drew a deserving audience inside. Instead his mind conjured with other things.

Returning to his apartment, Blake walked with headphones off.

Night patterned distilled images in roadside puddles teeming with invisible life. The aura of streetlights attracted bugs and moths, drawn to the glow as false navigation. Whilst his fancied fox was no doubt of feline persuasion, Blake still found himself open to a form of urban regeneration, concrete reclaimed by persistent tufts of green, walls decked with moss, car noises underscored by the sounds of persistent night birds. On one occasion he stopped. Glanced up at the sky which dominated both city and field. He began to wonder how sly his parents had been with their bookish gifts, how loving they were when it came to tendering his happiness.

What once appeared to be an anti-something-statement, his apartment now felt barren. Blake glared at the pristine fixtures and fittings just as the unadulterated light from their surfaces glared back. He examined corners and crevices for cobwebs and spoor. Finding none, he slipped naked between his crisp white bedsheets, a packet of poppy and sesame seed crackers in his hand as he re-entered Tokarczuk's eco-terrorist world through illuminated pages. The crackers turning to mush in his mouth, coating his tongue like mulched leaves against damp ground, until eventually he rose and pried a few of the seeds apart from the crackers' hold, placing them on moistened cotton wool on top of kitchen towel and wondering if – like the cress he had once grown on his bedroom windowsill – these seeds would take and cultivate and flower.

Blake's dreams that night were infused by the wood. Miscellaneous birdsong couriered a backdrop of memories: dappled light reflected in a brook, the soft plop of a watervole seeking sanctuary, leaves variegated according to shadow and sun, a burst of wing from a disturbed blackbird, the presence of man defined by the absence of man, the warm buzz of insect hum, that summer glow perfected through the closing of one's eyes.

Saturday saw Blake at Woodwose Garden Centre. His arms replaced by a shopping basket replaced by a trolley. s*pider plant / wandering jew / satin pothos / mistletoe cacti / fishbone cacti*. Blake chose generously and well, guided by name rather than experience, intuition over methodology. *triangle fig / rose of china / radiator plant / false shamrock*. He picked up an indoor water feature: a bearded man carrying a club presiding over a scene of deer and rabbit. *golden jade tree / hare's foot fern / zebra basket vine / lipstick plant / aloe vera.* Instinct coursed his body as though sap ran through his veins. Positioning his purchases on tabletop and kitchen counter Blake realised he required more surfaces than his apartment afforded. He lined them against the walls, bordered his living room and bedroom. The tinkling of the water feature splashed moisture onto his black tiled floors.

During the course of the evening Blake faltered in his exuberance. The sterility of his apartment dominated the flashes of green. What had initially appeared exciting now seemed punitive. He deliberated calling his parents but had nothing much to say. Cancelling an arrangement with friends he settled for a quiet night in. Ordered Indian takeout that would accompany a fridge-chilled beer.

When his food arrived, Blake chose to stream a film. A comforting favourite, *Tetsuo: The Iron Man,* where a magic metal fetishist inadvertently killed by a couple stalks them through their dreams. The not-so-innocent salaryman becomes dominated by visions of industrial machinery until he is himself transformed into the *Iron Man* of the title, becoming an unstoppable mass which absorbs the fetishist's attack, until the two are combined into a single monstrosity which charges through the streets, promising to burn the world and return it to nothing more than a rusted ball in space.

Blake used to masturbate at the conclusion of the movie, finding solace in a vision which eradicated nature and projected man's development to a logical end; however, as the light of the film faded to black and he closed his laptop screen, the ensuing darkness brought the plants around him that much closer and instead he held his breath, all too aware of their shadowy presence.

This time during the night the figure from his water feature prowled through the greenery. Not limited to the plants lining the walls, the figure patterned the tiles with grass and foliage in the taking of each step, like a monarch unfurling a red carpet with each forward stride. Blake attempted to focus on the figure's face, but the features were indistinct: covered in hair which seemed almost alive in the intensity of its depth. The figure held the club high, and Blake held the sensation that something was tied to it, however he couldn't focus in the soft fluidity of dream. He heard the songs of nightingale, blackbird, chaffinch, surprised by the realisation that he could identify each bird. Part of his dream-self wondered whether he was ascribing names to *any* birdsong, it wasn't as though he could check veracity in sleep. But these were sideshow aspersions compared to the full force of the dream, which rolled him over in the bed and pushed his face into the pillow.

Sunday saw a return to Woodwose Garden Centre. Tape measure in hand Blake bought wood panelling which adhered to the measurements he had made that morning, a bowl of cereal forgotten and soggy as he concentrated on his task, mapping the four rooms of the living room with numbers on a piece of paper. At the till he eyed the pallet trolley heaped with wood, paid extra for home delivery, and extra again for that afternoon. The boy who took his order fresh-faced, barely out of school, yet was the same person who pulled up outside his apartment and assisted Blake to manoeuvre the items inside. The metal floor of the lift subsequently speckled with shavings, with a warm and comforting odour.

Late afternoon and evening were spent fixing the panels to the walls. The sales clerk had warned him wood glue contained formaldehyde, had persuaded Blake to buy gloves and goggles and a respiratory mask. He layered the glue with a trowel directly onto the wall and then onto the wood, pressing them both together until his fingertips went numb, before gingerly standing back and expecting the panel to peel forwards like Eucalyptus bark, although it appeared he had judged the mixture well.

Opening the windows created airy ventilation the like of which his apartment hadn't previously experienced. At dusk he could hear starlings and he paused in his work, leaned on the open windowsill and watched them flock together, wheeling and darting through the sky in tight, fluid formations. A murmuration.

Despite an incoming chill he kept the windows open after dark on the sales clerk's recommendation to avoid headaches and breathing problems which might be associated with fumes in a confined space, but Blake was aware there was more to it than this. He dragged his mattress from the bedroom and placed it central in the wooded place. When he slept he didn't so much as dream, but simply existed within the environment. Oxygen generated from the plants rejuvenated his thoughts.

Whilst he called in sick on Monday, Blake had never felt so healthy. He forwent his usual shave and lay on his back watching the ceiling. He created a Spotify playlist out of birdsong and woodland noises. Scrolling through his choices he discovered *Snapped Ankles* who dressed in foliage and played log synthesisers, who described themselves as channelling forests of a pagan past sent to remind mankind that trees were watching and judging dance moves. At lunchtime Blake again found himself at the Woodwose Garden Centre, barely recognising his movements, buying woodchippings and more plants with which he latterly decorated the tiled floor around the mattress, manoeuvring the water feature so that it aligned with his feet at the foot of the bed, finding an allegiance with the wild man figure despite the certainty that it was a child which had been tethered to the club.

Waking the following morning Blake walked barefoot to the window, chippings sticking to the soles of his feet. As he watched the sunrise pick out each and every windowpane, he imagined taking the chippings and using wood glue to adhere them to his skin, covering each bare space until he became the opposite of *Tetsuo, The Iron Man*, until he was transformed into a creature born of forest and flesh, until buds began shooting from his fingertips, until his gait became wooden in more ways than one.

After washing his face in the water feature, Blake dressed for work. Leaving headphones at home he became attuned to the outside world. The city held more nature than he had previously been aware. An oasis of a park contained both rabbits and squirrels. Birdsong vied with traffic noises separated by concentration. Even carefully tended gardens were only a handful of days away from wilderness. Blake turned one hand over and over creating a perpetually moving landscape for a ladybird which had found its way there, its legs tickling the soft hairs on his skin, smelling his woodchip aroma, ready to ooze a poisonous gel should Blake become something other than what he appeared to be.

When his work colleagues bantered over his unshaven appearance Blake responded with a smile. He performed his tasks mechanically, instinctively, without much understanding. For the first time since arriving in the city he understood the term autopilot, his work and mannerisms no more than a typically fixed pattern of behaviour in response to certain stimuli. He viewed both this and the remaining days of the week as a period of hibernation, of withdrawing from what he now considered to be his real world into some aspect of dream. It was when he was in his room that he was wholly alive, when he would converse with the woodwose of the water fountain, who had manifested himself as a logical and permanent partner.

At the weekend, whether in vision or blurred reality, the woodwose took Blake on a tour of local Norfolk churches. He pointed out a 15th century font in Ludham, where a male and female woodwose mingled with lions; the misericordia at Norwich Cathedral depicting two hairy woodwose fighting each other with cudgels held in one hand whilst clutching at each others' faces with the other; the nonchalant woodwose posed on the spandrels of the pulpit at Felmingham's St Andrew's Church, his hand on his hairy hip.

Blake segued from one scene to another, at times feeling the woodchippings hard against his back, at others noting spray from the water feature dew his beard. When his mouth became dry, his thirst became quenched. When his stomach signified hunger he found that he was full. His personal woodwose proved an excellent guide, club raised to indicate he had not been subsumed by Christianity.

And there were more: St Botolph's Church in Trunch with its carved column of a woodwose attacking a dragon, his club thrust deep inside the beast's mouth, and one fighting another dragon at St Agnes' in Cawston. There were woodwose on the baptism font of St Mary at Happisburgh, in the crest of the Woodhouse family at St Peter in Kimberley, on the font at St Edmund's in Acle, on the end of a pew at St Peter and St Paul at Tuttington, and in the chancel at St Margaret's Church in Hapton.

Blake felt himself freewheeling, immersed and entranced, entrenched within a folklore that time itself hadn't quite forgotten.

His father's voice was so quiet on the line it might have been the case that the telephone were not invented.

Ah, the woodwose. It wasn't all fun and games, you know. Some said they had superhuman strength, were deaf to the word of God and would think nothing of snatching a child and eating them. A medieval bogeyman, if you will. Others warned of them seducing wives, Pan-like characters, although not Pan himself, and occasionally female too, present in carvings, whose appetites for men were equally voracious. Sometimes they were a sideshow, mostly not to be trusted. Why do you ask?

Blake was barely cognisant of his reply. He had nothing to fear from his companion, who might fit within the crook of his arm. If anything, he was the adult and the woodwose the child. He watched as the figure froze in the pose of club carrying, flanked by rabbit and deer, as water coursed out of an aperture from a *rock* on the right of the feature into a small pool from which it was sucked back and recycled.

Your mother and I have been thinking of paying a visit, just a day or so. Do you have any plans this weekend?

Blake made excuses: to his parents, to his work, to himself. Within two weeks under extended sick leave he wood-panelled his remaining surfaces: the kitchen, the bathroom, the bedroom. Plants with greater reach trailed across woodchippings: heartleaf philodendron, ivy, pothos, creeping fig and hoya. As humidity rose, Blake disconnected electrics, the gas. He reduced himself to underwear, continued to grow out his beard. Hours were spent at a time examining foliage, marvelling at intricacies of pattern, of reproduction, of silence only broken by birdsong and traffic noises, the latter rendering themselves as background, as though the humming of cicadas or the more British grasshopper or crickets. Hubbub was augmented by constantly running water. Blake alternated between the rooms in his apartment, making trails, leaving spoor.

He reasoned that he hadn't lost his senses: in fact, they were heightened. The woodwose directed him to tinned meat and peaches, supplies which Blake assumed had been bought in anticipation, with foresight. Sometimes he sat with the woodwose before him, playing simple games such as rock paper scissors. Other times Blake allowed contemplation of how his previously minimalist life had facilitated the transformation. There was little to be shot of other than his laptop containing digital collections of music and movies, and his Kindle with the two unread books, items which could be deleted with only the barest of fingerstrokes. If he saw no irony in cutting up clothes to wind the shreds around himself for warmth, then neither did he consider the troubles of complete isolation. The woodwose, having made its point through the journey of Norfolk churches, seemed content, having proved its existence to simply coexist with Blake without further demands. Blake didn't consider a motive. Unless the woodwose's purpose was to prompt the watering of the plants, a task that Blake neglected as he became further withdrawn.

Give it a good push with me, Mother.

Blake's parents forced the door into the apartment, woodchips and soil on the interior side bunching up in little hills, festooned with a brown topping that was once greenery.

His father squeezed himself through the gap, in two minds as to whether to allow his wife to continue. It was as he feared. His son's dissociation in the big city had adversely affected his mental health. The spare key in his hand was the only sign of humankind. Almost every inch of the apartment was covered with foliage, but nothing healthy, nothing that couldn't have been tendered had Blake sought his father's advice. The entire apartment was symptomatic of their relationship breakdown.

When mother entered, she clasped her husband's arm, eyes wide at all the dead beauty. Unwatered plants wilted, the tips and edges of leaves dried out and turned brown. The panelling on the walls was no substitute for the rich texture of tree bark. She knelt to the ground, partly in distress, partly in supplication, her fingers reaching out for brittle stems, mushy roots. Frost had caught some of the plants near the window. There was no logic or reason as to placement. She felt both angry and annoyed at her son's behaviour, as though no thought had been given when creating this wilderness.

They moved gingerly through the landscape, calling Blake's name, their voices as dry as the vegetation, unsure whether they were more fearful to hear a reply or to hear none.

Once they were satisfied the apartment was empty, they tugged two kitchen stools away from the entwined clasp of ivy then sat, side by side, in thought.

Before them was a water feature, at the foot of a mildewed mattress. Rabbits and deer sat around an empty pool, which was discoloured from the evaporation of stagnant water, their expressions ignorant to the lack of moisture. Between them, two stunted circles denoted something broken at the base, the resin white, in contrast to the surrounding grey, indicating that the damage had been recent.

Blake's father's fingers reached for his wife's.

They remained in contemplation, in silence, breathing softly as though not to disturb the vegetation. As though not to disturb their thoughts.

Aye, Blake's father finally spoke, his fingers gently squeezing those of Blake's mother. *Seems there's more than one way to lose a child.*

Camouflaged, Blake disagreed.

THE WHITE WOOD

Sarah Singleton

Marcel dragged the chains across the yard and hooked them over the tow bar at the back of the tractor. His father Lucien was sitting on the tractor's curved metal seat, one hand on the steering wheel, the other resting on his thigh. A thin cigarette trembled on his lip as the engine vibrated. The rusty red bonnet shook when he pumped the accelerator. Marcel dropped the tails of chain in the metal skip behind the driver's seat and jumped nimbly onto the tractor, one booted foot on the tow bar, the other on the back of the skip. Lucien shoved the gearstick and the tractor jumped forward. One of the farm dogs gave a single bark and raced after them, as the tractor bounced along the stony track from the yard along the edge of the home field towards the clump of trees at the top of the hill.

Marcel stared at the top of his father's cap, once dark blue, now greasily smooth and black. The old man was near seventy, but he'd changed little over the last twenty years, becoming only more obdurately thin, more hardened, as though time was paring him down to his essence – tough, spare, laconic. Well, it was impossible to talk over the rumbles and snorts of the old tractor anyway.

The dog fell further and further behind them, but still it ran. Ahead, beneath a vast blue sky, the little wood drew into focus – the tight space of it, the narrow blackthorn trunks, the puffs of white blossom. Not a big place, *la Foret Blanche;* less a wood, more *un bosquet.* A grove. A hectare perhaps, a spillage on the top of the green hill.

Marcel had returned from Paris three weeks before, after walking out of another job. His father hadn't said a word when he heard the news, but Marcel observed an alteration in his aspect, a kind of tightening in the face. The family was failing, slowly. Marcel was an only child, born when his father was over forty, and Lucien himself had no brothers or sisters either. And this

25

after centuries of farming, when young wives had birthed a dozen children and three or four generations crowded the long stone farmhouse at once. Marcel's grandmother Mathilde had blamed the war – the Great War she meant. That was when it had started going wrong.

But Mathilde had died years ago, before Marcel was born. Just the two of them left now, of this farming dynasty. Father and son.

At the top of the lane, Marcel jumped down and lifted the gate open. His father drove into the wood, leaving him to follow on foot. The dog caught up, panting, and slunk past him to the old man. Harder for the tractor here – slogging over the steep banks and plunging hollows, whipped by thorny branches. Marcel could hear the engine labouring. A breath of diesel hung on the air amid the falling petals. The tractor's engine quietened to a low rumble as Marcel stepped into a clearing. His father jumped down and lifted the chain from the skip.

The two men worked together, wordless, wrapping the chain around the trunk of the largest tree. This was not a hazel or blackthorn, but an old apple, torn on one side where a bough had broken. Brackets of fungi spiralled the trunk. One black apple sprang from a high twig, but no blossom, no leaves. As Marcel fixed the chain, Lucien dug around the roots with deft chops of a spade, the cigarette still gripped between his lips.

When Lucien nodded, Marcel took the driver's seat. He put the tractor into gear and moved slowly forward, taking up the slack. The chain tightened. Slowly, slowly. The soft, ridged tyres gripped the clay. The engine's rumble deepened.

A cloud of exhaust and the first creak and snap of roots.

Marcel looked to his father, who nodded again and raised his hand in encouragement. Marcel pressed more heavily on the accelerator and the tractor began to strain. The tree resisted. Beads of sweat popped from the skin on the back of Marcel's neck but any apprehension in his father was indicated only by stillness – that hand still raised in the air.

When Marcel was a kid, he'd played war games here with boys from the village. The hummocks and dips under the trees had made perfect trenches and shell holes. As the tractor pulled the tree, he remembered those days, hiding on his belly under the blackthorns at the edge of the woods, surveying the long slope and the fields of yellow and green below, the pylons crossing the plain, the distance blurring into blue – and then some friend or other dragging him out, leaping on him with a shout and a delicious frenzy of fists and kicking. Happy times, at least in recollection.

Moments passed. Engine, noise, chain, tree. Then a whip crack, the ripping of wood.

The tractor jumped forward and all at once the tree was out of the ground in an explosion of soil. It fell in a rain over Marcel and his father, clattering over the metal surfaces of the tractor. Lucien had stepped back, out of the way of tree. Its exposed roots bounced in the air. The old man was looking at something. Marcel couldn't make out what it was, but he saw his father push his hat back off his head, and stare.

"Pa? What is it?"

Lucien didn't answer. His gaze flicked briefly to his son, and he gave a barely perceptible shake of his head. Marcel cut the engine and jumped down. The dog, close to Lucien's legs, began to bark. Then Marcel saw what it was – hanging in the roots of the tree, suspended in the sunlight after a hundred years in the dark. Ribs, long bones, the puzzles of hands and feet, the skull with tendrils sprouting through clay-stuffed eye sockets. Though soft tissues were long gone, the roots held the bones together.

The two men stood side by side and stared. The dog kept barking, till Lucien shouted and it dropped to its belly on the ground. The old man threw his cigarette to the ground.

"Another one," he said. "I thought we'd seen the last."

The White Wood was marked on the 17th century parchment of an old *seigneur*. The map was now hanging in a frame on the wall of the mayor's offices in the village, among photographs of the Great War. When Lucien was a child, his mother Mathilde had told him tales at the hearthside about the Great War and the battle that had raged here for most of a year, when she was a only little older than he was. But Lucien preferred her stories of *les dames blanches*, the white ladies, who haunted crossroads, and holy wells, and the places where streams ran over roads, or ponds where their children had drowned, or quiet paths where they looked for lost lovers. One might imagine these lonely ladies lingered in every quiet country place, during the hours of twilight or just before dawn, long hair unbound, tears always falling from their eyes, always looking for someone they loved. And the White Wood, of course, had its own *dame blanche*, the young wife of a long ago *seigneur*. In traditional fashion, she had fallen in love unwisely and, while waiting to meet her lover in the White Wood, was murdered by her enraged husband as she ran through the trees in the moonlight. The story thrilled Lucien. He remembered gripping the fabric of Mathilde's skirt as she described the white lady, running, always running through the trees of the White Wood as the hooves of her husband's horse thundered on the ground behind her. And this in his wood! On the land his family had farmed for generations! Mixed with the pleasurable tingle of fear, he felt a proprietorial pride.

Lucien's mother was older than most mothers – having been obliged, she said, to spend long years caring for her younger brothers and be the woman of the house. Despite the white that marbled her dark hair, Lucien could see she was the most beautiful woman in the world, and the kindest, and the best at story telling. And those brothers she had cared for, all had gone off into the world, to America, to Paris, to drink, to ruin – so the farm had, unexpectedly, fallen to her, and the kindly but not particularly competent husband she found, just before turning forty.

Some moonlit nights, little Lucien would climb out of the high wooden bed, in his pyjamas, and walk on cold feet to the landing window, drawn by the view of the wood at the end of the long lane, at the top of the hill. He would stand on tiptoes to stare through the high window to see the wood and imagine a brighter glow on the hilltop. The too-big house was never silent. As the temperature fell at night, its timbers shrank and creaked, doors shifted on their hinges. Above his head, in the long attic, small creatures scratched. Was that a horse he could see, galloping up the hill? If he stared hard enough, he could imagine it into being, and the wood would glow brighter, especially in April when the blossom was out.

The power of the story faded for a time, but in adolescence, Lucien's feet often took him to the privacy of the White Wood and he recalled his mother's story of *la dame blanche*. He liked to be alone, to escape the long list of jobs to be done. The farm was slowly failing. The fields on the far side of the hill were soon to be sold, but still, the work never ended. Already he knew he was a better farmer than his father. It was in his blood, Mathilde said, with a rare smile.

But that day, in the White Wood, his blood felt overheated. It was April, blossom white on the blackthorns, spring flowers shivering in the thin grass. On the wood's far side, the world beckoned, the road leading to the city, to the world. Behind him lay the lane to the farmhouse and the village. His limbs itched to move. He ran up and down the hollows, swung around the taller trees in the middle of the wood, whacked at the fresh nettles with a stick. His brain seemed to fizz, a chaos of thoughts and images that rose up and popped in his mind. It wouldn't stop. He kicked at the trees, threw his stick away with a swing of his arm, then stood with his eyes shut, burning up, his hands clenching and unclenching by his side.

Lucien lay on the ground, in the shadow of the wood's only apple tree, a *Reinette* – the little queen. It was not yet in full blossom, but tight, white buds, touched with pink, covered the branches. He looked through the swaying twigs to the blue sky. He could feel the beating of his heart, as though his pulse came through the ground, the Earth's rhythm hammering through him. He drummed his heels on the grass, then covered his face with his arm, to shade his eyes from the sun, and sleep overcame him.

When Lucien awoke, the moon was hanging over the apple tree, criss-crossed by twigs. He was cold and stiff. A lump of grass pressed into the small of his back. Thoughts galloped through his mind – the cows, the chickens, the firewood waiting to be chopped. He jumped to his feet, rubbed his face and turned towards home.

But something stopped him, in his way, something moving through the blackthorn trees.

The boy stared. White light shone on the blossom as it passed, this undefined being among the trees. But he knew what it was at once. The half-forgotten stories assembled in his mind, the evenings by the fire gripping his mother's skirt. It was the white lady, with her long hair loose, and tears unravelling from her eyes. Lucien stepped towards the light, and the light resolved itself, a young woman walking with a long, swinging stride. But she wasn't crying, no. When she saw him, a smile broke on her face and she held out her hands. The air around her seemed perfumed with flowers, with the scent of apples, and warm, as her arms went around him and her lips pressed against his forehead, and he was overwhelmed, saturated, with a feeling of such intense love and homecoming, it blotted out thought.

How long did it last, this encounter? A moment?

She was gone, and Lucien was alone in the wood. A cloud covered the moon. His body was cold and bruised from lying on the ground and he anticipated an angry reception when he got home. Nothing about the white lady made any rational sense, yet indubitably, it had happened. He accepted this but put the dream to one side, asking no more about it. What else could he do? But something had changed. He ignored the call of the world on the other side of the hill, and turned home.

When his father died, Lucien became master of the farm. Mathilde remained mistress of the house and the two of them rubbed along well enough, mother and son. He didn't marry till she died and, a year later, Marcel was born. Lucien stuck to the old ways, barely turning a profit from their reduced land holding, but over the hill, a huge tractor with an air-conditioned cab pulled an eight-furrow plough through an old pasture, and there they were, the first skeletons, broken up by the blades. They were the remains of soldiers buried since the Great War, more than sixty years before. It had happened on other farms over recent years, as meadows were turned over to make way for subsidised cereal crops. At first, a poignant reminder of the slaughter, and later, a nuisance, when work had to stop and authorities were called in to take the bones away. But time passed, and everyone thought they had seen the last of them.

Father and son covered the skeleton in the roots of the tree with an old tarpaulin and Marcel made the phone call. He had not seen one of the war dead before, not close up like this.

The following day, two men in smart city clothes came from the local government office, taking photographs and notes. Marcel briefed them on the discovery, then left them to it. By evening, the bones had been freed from the roots and were lying on a trestle table in a barn by the house. They had rigged up a light using an extension lead, the bland men from the town, with their digital cameras and mobile phones – though they'd be lucky to get a signal here, Marcel mused.

He thought the investigation would be over in a day, but this was not the case. The next morning, they returned to the wood and dug the soil in the cavity left by the uprooted tree. Looking for further evidence, he assumed, in case there was any chance of identifying the deceased. Buttons, weapons, buckles, ammunition, shell casings – memories of war that persisted in the soil. They came back empty handed, except for a thin, tarnished wedding ring.

At the end of the second day, the visitors called Marcel and his father into the barn. Skull and bones lay on the table. The wedding band, tagged and numbered, had been placed near the left hand. The old man stared at it.

"Well?" Lucien said at last. He'd been told to leave his cigarette outside the door.

One of the visitors picked up the skull and gestured to a jagged hole at the back with a gloved hand.

"Two, three blows," he said, then placed the skull back on the table. "Hard to say for sure, but the level of decomposition matches the other war remains found in the area."

"Another dead soldier," Marcel said.

"Not exactly." The second man looked at Marcel, and his father. "This is a female. A woman."

"A woman? Well," Lucien said, "plenty of women died in the war too. Women and children."

"Yes," the second man conceded. "I'm sorry, there's nothing more we can tell you yet. We'll make some enquiries, and perhaps she can be buried in the village."

Marcel and his father were dismissed, and the two men from the town set about bagging up the remains and stowing them in the back of their large four-wheel drive.

Neither father nor son spoke of the bones, of the long ago past, far behind them.

The next day, Lucien began slicing up the old apple tree with a chainsaw, ready to be seasoned for the following winter's firewood. They had a mutton stew for dinner, and ate in silence, in the gloomy living room.

"You'll be back to the city soon," Lucien said, when they'd finished.

"Yes Pa. Friday maybe."

"Nothing for you here."

Marcel felt a familiar twinge of guilt. His father and mother had split up ten years before, not long after he had left for college. His mother lived in Paris, where he'd stay till he got sorted, and the old man would be alone again.

"When I die, you'll sell the place," Lucien said.

"I don't know. Why do you say that now?" The words came out more sharply than he had intended. Guilt, defensiveness. As a child he'd enjoyed working with his Pa. But another world had beckoned, luring his away.

Lucien gave a quick shake of the head and lit another cigarette.

"Sell it, sell it," he said. "It's finished. It's not for you."

Mathilde was sitting on the stone doorstep, watching her little brother throw grain for the chickens. He was two years old, with a fluff of fine blond hair, and not yet competent at the task. The grain slipped through his fingers to the ground, where the russet chickens pecked around his feet. At eight, Mathilde was the eldest. Another two brothers were playing in the barn where father was mending harness. The youngest, baby Victor, was in the kitchen, sleeping in a cradle.

In the sunshine, in a silence broken only by the chickens' clucking and her brother's exclamations, and the murmurs from her mother in the kitchen, it was hard to imagine a war was raging. It would come soon enough, in February, and three hundred thousand soldiers would die over ten long months, and the land would be carved up for miles. But not now. Not yet.

"Mathilde? Mathilde! Would you come here?"

The little girl stood up and went into the kitchen. Her mother had taken half a dozen loaves of bread from the oven and turned them out onto the table. The scent made Mathilde's mouth water. Her mother was tall and slender, with long blond hair tied up under her cap. She had married at twenty, and born five children, one after the other, but neither this nor the endless labour of caring for them and the farm had yet extinguished the priceless shine of youth from her face. And more, a kind of burning glamour these past weeks, a distraction, something preying on her mind – a something Mathilde sensed was dangerous.

"Will you go to the cellar and get some apples from the rack?" her mother said.

"Apples?"

"Yes, apples! Hurry up, will you? A dozen should do. I'll make a compote." She turned away, rocked the cradle with her foot, pushed the cooling loaves aside and took out a brown pot of sugar from the larder. Mathilde waited a moment longer, staring at her mother's back, anxious, wanting to say something, to plead – but for what?

She sighed, left the kitchen and went one step at a time down the steep stone stairs into the cellar. It was always cold, even in the height of summer. Faint light from the narrow window under the ceiling revealed jars of preserves on the shelves. The apple racks stood in the darkness at the back of the cellar. A faint, cidery perfume hung on the air.

Mathilde reached up and pulled out a slatted tray. Autumn's apples were leather-skinned by spring. Some had rotted and were removed, fed to the pigs and chickens if too far gone, but Mathilde counted out twelve good fruit and bunched up her skirt to carry them up to the kitchen.

The jar of sugar waited on the table. Her mother was sitting down, smiling, lost in thought. Baby Victor gurgled in his cradle.

"Ma. Ma! I've got the apples."

"Put them on the table, Mathilde." She picked up the largest, breathed in its scent, admired the golden green skin with its crimson stain, and picked up a knife to peel it.

"Do you know what sort of apple this is?" she said.

"A *Reinette*," Mathilde answered. "From the best tree in the orchard. A little queen."

Her mother gave another private smile, as the apple peel dropped in ribbons to the table. She chopped the fruit in half, giving half to her daughter, then eating the other half herself. Then she glanced at the clock, stood up, touched her hair and took off her apron.

"I'm going out," she said. "I won't be long. Watch your brothers, Mathilde."

"Please don't go, Ma." Without thinking what she was doing, Mathilde went to her mother and clung to her skirt.

"I won't be long, silly girl."

"Please don't go."

"What's got into you? I have to go to the village."

Mathilde stared up at her mother, still holding on. Some other, much greater communication seemed to pass between them. Her mother's face wasn't happy anymore. She saw a flash of desperation.

"Please, Mathilde. I won't be long, I promise."

"Don't go, don't go!"

"I'll soon be back!"

In his cradle, disturbed by the voices, and the cloud of emotion swirling in the air above his head, Victor began to cry. Mathilde's mother squatted, so her face was on a level with her daughter's. She brushed the hair from Mathilde's face.

"Please," she said. "This is the last time. I promise. For you, for your brothers. This is the last time I will go. It's the end, Mathilde. The end. Please. Let me go."

A tear swelled in her eye and rolled over her cheek. Seeing it, Mathilde went limp. Her hands dropped to her side. Victor cried louder. Their mother stood up, hurried out of the kitchen door across the yard, glancing around her as she went. Mathilde stood on the doorstep and watched her go, not to the village, but running, running up the lane to the White Wood in all its glorious spring blossom, at the top of the hill.

Victor wouldn't stop crying. Mathilde picked him up and cradled him, jigged him up and down, but still he howled. Then her two year old brother came in, with a graze on his knee, and he was crying too. Mathilde tried to comfort them both. She watched the door, silently urging her mother to return, to be back soon. She sensed the danger rising, the threat hanging over them.

"Where's your mother?" He stood in the doorway, cutting off the light with his strong, square body. Tough, unpredictable, her father was prone to outbursts of temper.

Mathilde didn't know what to say. The boy and the baby cried louder.

"Shut your noise!" he shouted.

The little boy did as he was told, but the baby had not yet learnt the cost of disobedience.

"Where is she?" The man pushed Mathilde with the flat of his hand.

"She's gone to the village." The words seemed to choke her.

"Gone to the village? I know where she's gone!"

The other two brothers appeared, attracted by the shouting. Their father brushed them aside, ran across the yard, through the gateway and up the hill to the White Wood.

It was dark when he returned. Mathilde had fed her three brothers a meal of bread and apples. She fed logs into the stove, swept the floor, and gave the baby sips from a cup of milk. When the boys were tucked up in bed, she took her mother's seat by the fire and waited.

Her father sat down at the table and laid his head on his forearms.

"Are you hungry?" she asked.

"No," he grunted.

Mathilde stood up and moved towards him – but not too close. "Where's Ma?"

He sighed, the square man with huge, strong hands. "She's gone. She doesn't want to live with us anymore."

He raised his head and stared at the little girl, his daughter, with his glittering, bloodshot eyes.

Mathilde could smell beer on his breath.

"She's gone. Too good for us, you hear?" He was shouting now. "Not coming back. I don't want you talking about her again. I don't want to hear her name in this house."

Mathilde nodded. Everything inside her seemed to melt and drain away, but still she stood, a brittle shell, balancing on two small feet.

Late that night, unable to sleep, she stood on tiptoe to stare through the high window on the landing.

She wouldn't see her mother again. She wouldn't even say her name.

Under a high spring moon, the blossom on the blackthorns in White Wood seemed to shine.

BOG GODDESS

Fiona McGavin

She has always been there, down on the lochside where a single stone marks her glory. She is forgotten, but not gone. Sometimes, you feel her in the dawn or the dusk when the air is thin and the mountains fade blue into the sky and the loch, when the swallows dance and swoop low over the water. You feel her despite the hum of traffic and the smell of barbecue from the holiday cottages in the next field, and you turn to search the fields and the hills, wondering who's there, who's there... and something – maybe fear, maybe wonder, maybe just the sense of something otherly prickles your skin and creeps down your spine and you leave that place thinking that there is more that you don't understand than you do.

She has always been there, though in truth, she is not there at all. They pulled her from the peat bog some fifty years ago, glistening and reeking, from the place where she had lain all those thousands of years, and at first they thought she was nothing, just wood, until someone noticed the hollows where once she had seashells for eyes and the slash of her mouth and the crude female shape of her. And then there were museums and curators and conservators. There were darkened rooms and carbon dating. Papers were written and even a book. Finally, there was a glass case in a museum in Edinburgh, where people came to look and then wander away, disinterested, to other shinier gods.

All the time, she watches, blank-faced, for she is not really there at all. She is further north and further west where the grass grows down to the shore and heather, bracken and gorse grow up the mountainsides and the swallows dart through clouds of midges and mayflies and summer evenings stretch on forever. She is there, as she has always been there, watching and waiting and remembering those long-ago evenings when she was venerated with drums and flames and dancing, and a man with antlers and a knife spilled blood on her gleaming flanks. When she was All and all adored her and feared her.

The Americans took one of the little white holiday cottages on a permanent basis. They were retired and wealthy and had some vague romantic notion of seeking out their long-lost relatives for they were MacDonalds and the land, so they had heard, was soaked in the blood of MacDonalds. After a while they found that the only MacDonalds they came across were disappointingly ordinary – the boy in the chip shop, some school teachers, a crofter and his wife and their brood of far too many unruly children – so they began to spend more time in Edinburgh and London and going back and forth to visit their children in the States. So, the cottage stood empty for most of the year, even in the high summer when the holiday families came and went from the other cottages in the field next to the standing stone where no one cared that a goddess had been found there.

It was to this cottage that Angel and Scar came. Scar crept and ducked in and out of the hedge that lined the gravel track afraid that someone might see them. Angel walked with her usual confident strut, her flip flops slapping against the soles of her feet, her legs encased in the skinniest of skinny jeans

They found the cottage empty. It was the last of the little houses scattered across the field, just as Scar had known it would be. Scar hung back, nervous and jittery, as Angel paced round the tiny garden.

'What if someone sees us?' Scar whispered.

'There's no one here,' Angel said, 'did you see any cars at the other houses? No. They're all out climbing mountains and shooting peasants or whatever.'

'Pheasants,' said Scar and giggled.

Angel had a quick glance round. No tell-tale CCTV cameras or burglar alarm boxes probably meant that there was nothing inside worth taking. The cottage was separated from its neighbours by a wooden fence, just high enough to give holidaymakers privacy when they were out on their decking, and low enough to give the reassurance that there were other people close at hand when the night came down fast.

From then it was easy. Break a window and reach inside for the latch, open the window, and Angel clambered in because Angel always went first even though Scar was smaller. Then while Scar stood shifting from foot to foot, Angel ran round to the front door and let her in.

Inside, with the door shut and the blinds at the front of the house pulled down, Angel prowled round the house opening doors and drawers and exclaiming when she found a half bottle of Scotch and an almost full bottle of Baileys gone sticky round the rim. Scar breathed out with relief and collapsed onto the futon in the living room and stared out through the French doors at the buttercups dancing in the long grass that stretched down to the loch where the midges danced over the water and the swallows swooped and screamed above it in an ecstasy of feasting. In the distance a few cows moved lazily through the grass and, further away still, houses and a hotel stood out white against the greying hills and there was a sudden peal of church bells carried down through the summer air.

'Some silly fool's getting married,' Angel said and then resumed her inspection.

Scar stood up and walked to the window and gazed out over the field to the water's edge where she could just see the tip of the standing stone above the long grass. She drew her breath in sharply and fought to resist the urge to pull open the French doors and run, arms outstretched towards it. For a moment, it was as if there were not two of them in the house, but three.

She is here, she is here, she is here…

Angel told anyone who asked that they had been friends forever. Scar could name the exact date when they became friends. It was 22 June 2007, when some well-meaning adult decided to throw them together, to manufacture a friendship, in the hope that one might settle the other down whilst at the same time bringing the other out of her shell. It worked, to some extent. Their full names were Angela Catherine Mary Woods (always Angel, never Angie and most definitely never ever Ange) and Scarlett Jones (Scar for short, and for the long scar that ran from the lower right of her stomach in a long diagonal to her left shoulder from when the Bad Thing Happened and Daddy was sent away forever).

They were here now because they were eighteen and finished with school and exams, and they had time to waste before Angel went away to university. Scar didn't have anything better to do because she had failed all her A levels and wasn't going anywhere, and now her brother had come home and was every bit as angry as her father had been. They were closer than sisters, as close as two people could be, their edges merging and blurring into one. But they were standing on a cusp now. The future, with all its unwelcome changes and strangers, stretched out before them, and neither of them wanted it. Angel imagined herself at university and had no doubt that she would excel, that she would shine, surrounded by large happy groups of friends, dazzling classmates and tutors alike with her brilliance. She pictured herself returning home two or three times a year and finding Scar grown smaller and greyer, working in a supermarket or a bank or married to some dull grey man, or worse another angry man like her father and brother, bringing up a brood of tiny Scarlets of her own. And in these imaginings, she saw herself and Scar meeting in a coffee shop or a pub and having absolutely nothing to say to one another anymore.

In the bus rattling up the twisting road between the mountains, Angel had seen this future so clearly, she'd felt as if she was falling into a void that there was no getting out of. She had thrown her arm round Scar's skinny shoulders and whispered in her ear. "Promise me you won't ever get boring."

And Scar had smiled her dreamy smile and watched the road opening up before them as they headed west towards her goddess, and said, "Maybe it's you who'll get boring, not me."

Angel laughed. "Me? Never. Don't be daft."

They were here because despite her middle-class upbringing, Angel liked to think of herself as a bit of a bad girl, and she had taught herself how to break and enter a few years ago because it was something to talk about to the type of middle class bad boy she liked to impress. Of course, she only ever broke into empty places, places that no one really cared about. She was confident that hers were victimless crimes.

They were here because, in a nightclub in Glasgow, Angel had spent the last of their youth hostel money on four green pills that a man with an accent so broad they could barely understand it had said would blow their minds into the fourth dimension. Angel had never been to the fourth dimension and felt it was worth investigating. Scar was scared of drugs and alcohol, but she knew that pills could help you see the things that were there but that you couldn't see any other way, the things that waited and watched by the lochside, for example

The thing she knew would still love her, even when Angel had gone away and forgotten all about her.

And they were here because it had rained in Edinburgh, so they had sheltered in a museum because it was free. They had wandered between cases of ancient agricultural tools, artefacts that might have belonged to Mary, Queen of Scots, or Bonnie Prince Charlie or Robert the Bruce or someone else. Angel had complained about having sore feet whilst basking in the admiring gazes of a group of German students. Scar had drifted, liking the sound the rain made against the windows and the quiet murmur of voices as other visitors passed and stopped before exhibits.

Until they'd come to the glass case where the earthly form of the goddess was imprisoned. Scar had stopped, transfixed and stared. Angel had stood beside her, frowning and cocking her head to one side and recoiling when she realised what the gashes on the wood represented.

"God," she said, "that's nasty."

She'd walked away, like so many other tourists did, but Scar had remained staring through the glass, slowly raising one hand to touch it, feeling those empty sea-shell eyes boring into her. Something, like an invisible hand, reached into Scar's chest through space and through time and squeezed her heart.

And in a moment she saw:

mountains fading grey and blue into the sky

a sky full of millions of stars

mayflies and midges swarming

the bright bloom of gorse on a hillside

firelight flickering

perfect white cottages all in a row

buttercups dancing in a field

swallows darting low over water

people twisting, turning, dancing

a road going northwards and westwards

blood on cold stone, dripping down into long unmown grass

a man with antlers

a heron sweeping over the water to meet its mate standing one legged on the shoreline

a woman pulling entrails from a calf

sunlight sparkling on water

and the bog goddess when she was young, and her wooden body was newly carved and hung with strings of beads and bones and shells, festooned with wildflowers, oiled until she gleamed and the undulating curves of her body mirrored those of the hills that sheltered the place.

For a moment, Scar felt as if a veil was pulled away and she saw the world as it really was. What was real – what mattered – was the goddess and the drums and the wild, terrified dancing in starlight; the firelight flickering and the blood on stone; the man with antlers and the gleam of his blade. Nothing else was real, not the museum, not her scars and not the last dying days of a friendship.

Scar had turned away from the case and saw that Angel was in full on flirt mode with the German tourists, flicking her hair and giggling and making sure that they could see how long her legs were and how full her breasts and how narrow her waist.

Scar had walked over to a case full of old ribbons and medals and pretended to be interested. Reflected in the glass, she'd seen a face with seashells for eyes and she'd smiled and known where they'd be going now.

I am with you, a voice in her head had said, *I am always with you.*

They'd caught the train west to Glasgow, Angel complaining good-naturedly all the way because this detour had not been her idea. Scar had tried to tell her, tried to explain about the goddess but she'd seen that Angel hadn't really understood for all that she'd nodded enthusiastically at the notion of anything strange and a little bit creepy.

"I felt something, is all," Scar had said lamely, "and I want to go there."

Angel had been happier once she had asserted her control and dragged Scar to a nightclub where Scar had seen stars and fire instead of disco-lights and Angel had bought pills.

"Maybe these will help us see your precious bog goddess," Angel had said and tucked them away inside her bra out of sight.

And now they were here.

Scar stood at the window and watched the landscape, feeling the presence of the goddess wrap around her like a cloak made of black feathers.

"You'll never guess what I found—" Angel burst into the room and stopped when she saw Scar standing so perfectly still at the window. She came and stood beside her and together they stood in silence watching the landscape, Angel exclaiming just once when they saw a bird, too small to be an eagle but huge all the same, sweep low across the loch.

And Scar knew, and perhaps Angel did too, that despite the road and the houses in the distance, that this landscape had been the same for thousands of years and would be so forever when the road and the people were all gone, when even the standing stone was nothing more than dust. But even then, when there was nothing else left, the goddess would be here for this was her place now and forever.

When the sun was setting, washing the sky with blood, they put on summer dresses and took the pills and the bottle of Baileys and walked down through the long grass to the standing stone. The swallows had reached a frenzy and there were bats, quicksilver, amongst them, half glimpsed and then gone. In the next field, the cows were meandering slowly towards their barn.

"Does Baileys go off?" Scar asked.

"I don't know," Angel said.

"Then maybe we shouldn't drink it."

"You are so risk averse," Angel said, "that's your problem, you know."

"I just don't want to get sick," Scar said.

"We won't get sick." Angel laughed. "We'll get drunk and we'll get high, but we won't get sick."

She ran ahead, lifting the hem of her dress up, spinning round to grin at Scar. "Come on," she called. "Race you." And she was off, tearing through the grass to the lochside where the standing stone was bathed in red by the sunset.

Scar didn't run. She felt the long grass against her bare legs and breathed in the warm scent of the gorse. She watched the swallows and saw that the shape of the hills, stark and black against the red sky, echoed the shape and curves of the goddess.

There were four pills.

"Two for now and two for later," Angel said.

"No," Scar said, "one for you, one for me, one for the goddess as an offering and we can split the last one later."

Angel opened her mouth to protest and then nodded. She

wrapped the last pill in a tissue and tucked it inside her bra again. Scar put one of the pills on the standing stone.

"For you," she whispered.

Angel poured the Baileys out into mugs she had taken from the kitchen. She filled them up to the brim.

"That's an awful lot," Scar said nervously.

Angel grinned. "You're being risk averse again," she said and put a pill in her mouth and washed it down with a big mouthful of Baileys. "Do you want to see this goddess of yours or not?"

Scar knew she didn't need drugs or alcohol to see the goddess, for the goddess was in the mountains and the loch and the fields, as intangible as the sky. She smiled and took her own pill.

Angel laughed and lay down beside the stone, pulling Scar down to lie beside her.

"Best friends forever," she said.

"Forever," Scar echoed.

As the pill worked its chemical magic through their bloodstreams and their brains, Angel saw a man with antlers in the field behind them or perhaps it was just a tree, She heard voices singing her name, and the voices were full of joy and adoration, soaring above the primal beating of drums, or maybe that was just her heart beating. She saw the hills move and shapeshift into the form of a woman, and the clouds bled and took the shape of the man with antlers. She felt the earth vibrating beneath her and every swallow that swept and swooped wasn't a bird at all but an angel, and each one bore her face, and each one loved and adored her forever and ever.

Scar saw nothing more than the loch and the hills and the sunset and felt nothing more than a little drunk. Perhaps her pill was a dud. Perhaps she just didn't need anything more than what she already knew was real.

She lay beside her best friend and listened to her laughing and mumbling to herself and after a while, she sat up and took a photo with her phone of Angel's beatific face to remember her by.

"They love me, Scar," Angel said, "everyone loves me. They really really do."

"Yeah," Scar grinned. "They do. I do too."

She thought of how once, long ago people had come here with the things that they loved and valued most and given them to the goddess in return for protection from evil, from the elements, from plague and famine and fire and people who sailed up the loch in long strange boats.

She saw how easy it would be to break the bottle and make a blade and she sat for a long time feeling the goddess and the man with antlers and all those who had been brought to the standing stone screaming or weeping gather round her, waiting, watching for her to do something. Once her hand twitched towards the bottle, but she snatched it back.

"You've got one of our pills," she said, "and you can have my phone with all of my photos of Angel, and you've got me. You've got all this. Don't get greedy."

She thought she heard laughter, drifting across the water, laughter laced with contempt, laughter that said, *don't tell me what to do, don't tell me I'm greedy when the whole world is mine. I will get what I want, I will get my way. Always.*

Scar shook her head and stood up and walked away, leaving her friend whispering and dreaming in the long grass.

In the morning, Scar woke up and knew at once that the house was empty. She got up quickly, pulling on jeans and a hoodie. The air was misty with a light drizzle and a greyness had washed over everything.

She pulled her hood up and walked down through the fields to the standing stone. Angel was still there, sitting shivering in her summer dress with her back against the stone and her hair lank with rain.

"Are you all right?" Scar asked.

Angel nodded. "I saw the whole world, Scar," she said, "for a moment I saw everything. I *was* everything."

Scar smiled. "Good pills, then."

Angel nodded. "I saw your goddess. I said to her, *make Scar happy*, and she said she would. Only not in words, in feelings. I think you're going to have a long and happy life."

She stood up, brushing down her dress.

"Can we go now? Back to Edinburgh? I've got the phone number of one of those Germans and he's got a friend. They were talking about a secret music festival. Can we go?"

Scar smiled and didn't reply. It was only later when Angel had packed her back pack and written 'Edinburgh' in capital letters on a piece of cardboard for hitch-hiking, that she spoke.

"I'm never leaving here."

"What?"

"I'm staying here."

Angel frowned. "Well, I guess we could stay for another couple of days but after that it'll start to get boring."

Scar shook her head. "I'm never leaving."

"But we have to go. This isn't our house. The owners will come back."

"I know. I'll find somewhere else. Somewhere close."

Angel sat down on the sofa. "But what about your family? What about getting a job, or doing your A Levels again or–?"

"I don't care about that anymore. None of that matters."

Angel was silent for a long time, much longer than Scar was accustomed to. "But what about me?" she asked at last.

"You're going to university. You're going to be a lawyer or a doctor or a teacher or something and have a big house and lots of friends. You don't need me."

Angel's eyes glistened with tears. "I do," she said.

Scar shook her head. "You're going to university, and I was going to stay at home and be a nobody with my horrible family and a horrible boring job. This is better, for both of us."

She went to the kitchen and washed up what few dishes there were, swigging the last of the Baileys from the bottle. The mist was clearing and a few tentative rays of sun were breaking through, turning the buttercups into splashes of light. The holiday makers next door were shouting to one another, slamming car doors, starting engines. A heron stood perfectly still at the lochside, and the hills looked different in this light, closer and greener and full of lush vegetation and secret curves and hiding places.

"I'm going, then," Angel said.

"Promise me," Scar said softly, "you won't ever become boring."

She tried to smile and found that she couldn't.

They walked up to the end of the gravel track together, Angel in her super skinny jeans with her flip flops and her 'Edinburgh' sign. At the top of the road they hugged, the kind of hug you give someone when they have been everything to you, and you know you will never see them again.

PARROT'S DRUMBLE

Jordan Biddulph

Out of sight, behind a veterinary warehouse,
Luscious greens mixed with black, grey and brown.
Pine pricks and veiny leaves blanket the blue ceiling
where dirt trails follow red streams, yes red.
As a child I would look at them with horror,
the earth's blood trickled in front of me
gushing towards the heart of the wood.

A small wives' tale, Parrot's Drumble,
wood with a pirate, waiting to hook prey.
Childish fancies called us to the night once,
frightfully awaiting an eye-patch.
None came, not even a flash of silver hook.
Rooted for days still, not even a peg-leg.
Forfeited the endeavour, not even a parrot took flight.

Winding wooden footpaths, vines and foliage,
overgrown and clambering towards any that
dare tread on what has now been claimed as its own,
thick sticks and brambles for each step, scratching skin.
Treacherous steps to trip up unsuspecting visitors,
surrounding their victim in sludge.
The peevish wood plays pranks, if you notice nothing.

The heart: clearing, small and sheltered.
Rotted rope swing hangs from clawed hands,
bank stretches back, twenty second climb to the top
with barbed-wire finishing line.
The flat: blackened with fire, smouldering earth and clay,
stairs leading away to one side, a bridge to another.
The water running redder still, echoes the hollow.

Jordan Biddulph

A tree that was struck by lightning became a
seat, insides blackened, its bark sickly green.
Nature destroyed itself, without the design
of humans to aid it, fashioned this scorched throne.
A cold stillness surrounds, wind and water heard clearly,
Nature is still here, it's still alive, Parrot's Drumble speaks.
Its heart pulsing with life as another resides within.

Wind brushes against branches, rattling their fingers
against one another, their leaves catching gusts.
Water, muddied with time, yellowing as the iron
that resided within stripped itself bare.
Rope swing a mangled mess on the flat, ravaged by children,
burned amongst bits of the wood.
The heart is dying, yet, the voice of the forest sings.

OCHRE AND FAIENCE

Nerine Dorman

The earth is bright red where the bulldozer chews at it, dragging its metal maw across the ground so that the stones spatter. Great gouts of black smoke belch forth every time the engine lets out a throaty growl, and even here where Gerhard and I stand on the hill overlooking the site of his new dam, the diesel fumes make me crinkle my nose.

"I'll be able to put in the Sauvignon Blanc," my brother says, gesturing to the patch of heath to our left. "And over there, just after that, where Jacob's busy putting up the fences, are our bush vines for Pinotage. They've been all right so far, but I'd like to put them under irrigation if the current weather patterns continue."

All this speaking of viticulture is foreign to me; instead I allow his proud ramblings to wash over me while I take in the view that encapsulates this river valley.

It seems a pity, somehow, that this virgin veldt is being scraped up, the ground shoved into piles so that a furrow can be diverted from the river. By the time I visit again, I might encounter a scene that could be termed pretty, picturesque, even, with the burnt orange of the surrounding sandstone peaks frowning their reflections back at the world against a cobalt sky; and not the devastation that now greets me with its eddies of dust and naked earth. There used to be a small stand of oak trees here where we played when we were little. Now the trunks are piled up, off to the side, their limbs lopped off and their foliage shrivelled in the summer sun.

I expect they'll end up firewood come winter.

Gerhard nudges me. "You'll be all right."

"Huh?" I turn to him.

"You'll see" – a smile, a wink – "a week here on the farm and you'll be right as rain. A little sunshine and good food for my kid sister."

He has Ma's simplistic view about what will heal the kinds of hurts you cannot see nor touch, and I don't have the energy to argue with him.

We haven't talked much about Ashley, about the hole she's left in my heart, and I'm sure it will come out eventually, after too many glasses of Pinot Noir with dinner tonight. Or tomorrow. Who knows?

But right now, it's all right to be away from the city, standing on the very earth that formed my bones and breathing in the bitter herb scent of the wilderness that waits just beyond the cultivated land. This, being here and *present*, is preferable to the medicated sleep sinking me into the depths of nothingness. Every day the pain will grow a little less, they say; it will become bearable, the waves smaller, less apt to knock me off my feet. I've yet to master the equilibrium of loss.

My brother and I cross the soft, turned earth, puffs of red ochre dust pluming at each footfall, and it's when we're halfway across the expanse of disturbed earth, the bulldozer worrying at a rock somewhere behind us, that I glimpse the scrap of blue. And stop.

There. Bright blue beads scattered in the dirt.

Gerhard ambles along, talking about his goats, but I'm crouched, carefully picking the beads out one by one.

I've found San artefacts here before. There are caves and overhangs all around the farm where the first people painted their little hunters, antelope and elephants in bright orange and white pigments. Gerhard and I would sometimes dig in the dirt where we imagined old campfires once burnt, and sometimes we'd uncover ostrich eggshell beads or bits of flint arrowheads. Once, we even found clay shards and flakes of rock some ancient stone knappers must have cast aside.

But never bright blue beads. Five little tubes that look as if they were once part of an intricate band. Old instincts kick in, and I hunch closer to the ground to carefully scoop away the red earth.

"What you got there, sis?" Gerhard's shadow falls across me.

"Look." I hold out my find and drop the little beads into his outstretched palm.

"Mm, never seen anything quite like this. Costume jewellery? Maybe some old trekboers from back in the day?"

"I dunno." I straighten once it's clear I'll not find anything further.

"Jane found some old china when she was digging her herb garden," Gerhard says as he drops the beads back into my outstretched palm. "People have been farming here for generations."

"But out here?" I turn a half circle and gesture about. "I can understand by the farmhouse."

He shrugs. "The workers have found some pretty strange things over the years."

The beads are each about as long as the first joint of my pinkie finger. Fine work. The markings resemble little beetles scratched into the blue glazed ceramic.

"I'll ask one of the writers when I'm back at work," I say. "There's a lady who does the weekly auctions column. She's into all that arty stuff."

"You do that." Gerhard is already walking on ahead.

We say nothing more of the find, and I slip the beads into my jeans pocket, where I quickly forget about them.

Dinner is hardly a sombre affair, for which I am grateful. True to form, Jane makes me belly laugh so much with her stories about the twins' doings that my life beyond the boundaries of Disafontein become nothing more than a mirage. The Cederberg is like that. Once a cedar person, always a cedar person, Ma always used to say. Our roots run deeper than the icy clear rivers that loop and coil through the valleys or the orange tors weathered by the elements, where lightning-struck cedars lift their skeletal branches to the sky in supplication. I may have left this mountain fastness for the city, but the mountains will always have a hold on my soul.

Later, once I am alone, I can almost pretend that Ashley lies tumbled next to me on the big double bed in the spare room. When I reach across the expanse of cold linen, that space is empty, the mattress flat. She never did like visiting here. I suppose I can do so now without any guilt.

The sky is the colour of dove feathers, a kind of slate grey that still hints at blue turned to faded peach on the horizon. Around me, the reeds are hissing, the wind shivering in waves that break the vegetation upon the weathered sandstone tors. My feet sink deep into white sand that glitters with grainy crystals, so that each step seems an insurmountable challenge, while a sickle moon gleams ahead of me, luring me ever onward with its pale sliver. It doesn't seem strange at all that I am out here, despite not having a clear idea as to why I am trudging towards the broken ridge that waits forever ahead of me.

One moment I am alone, the next there is a man. He stands tall, about twelve paces ahead of me, with skin daubed in red ochre like the rock paintings – naked but for a leather loincloth, fringed with beads and small bones. He says not a word, but then I don't expect a man with the head and spiralling horns of an eland to say much of anything. Those liquid black eyes shine with the light of infinite black suns.

Not a muscle moves, until I am right before him, and he raises a hand and points at my hip.

"What?" I ask, puzzled.

He twitches his index finger then turns his hand over so that it is palm up.

The beads. Of course. I feel at the pocket, stroke the bumps beneath the denim. None of this seems out of the ordinary, though a wriggle of discomfort lodges itself in my belly.

The eland man crouches before me, and with swift movements scoops a hole in the sand. Then he mimes removing the beads from a pocket and burying them in the hole.

For a moment this interchange enchants me, but even as I reach into my own pocket to comply, I begin to shake my head. Who is this man to tell me what to do with these beads?

"They're *mine*," I tell him. "I found them." Inexplicably it seems absolutely vital that I keep these little trifles. Who or what exactly is this bizarre creature before me?

Darlin', my sensible self tells me, you're arguing with a near-naked, eland-headed man. This simply isn't possible.

He shakes his head, an ear twitching, then points at the hole, goes through the whole rigmarole of mimicking the burying.

"No." I take a step backwards, and then another. An impossible thing. A thing that shouldn't be, as if the fabric of reality itself has twisted on itself and gained a kink that is about to trip me up if I don't flee immediately.

I scrub at my eyes, but the figure remains before me. Slowly he rises to his full height, muscles ropey beneath his ruddy skin. A living being that breathes, that has weight and agency.

Events blur around the edges then, difficult to trap between thumb and forefinger, and the wind gusts grit into my eyes. I turn around and run. And run and run and run, until my lungs and heart are near bursting, and the stitch in my side is a flaming sword twisting my innards.

Only once I spill to the ground with a stunning collision that jerks the breath out of my body, does the dream end, in gravel cutting my knees, the soft pads of my hands abraded. Moisture beads on my forehead, sends trickles down my cheek. My old Smashing Pumpkins T-shirt clings wetly to my skin around my armpits and at the small of my back.

It is simply enough to rasp in breath for my starved body, of cold, crisp air already hinting at the overture of winter. When the edges of my vision stop tunnelling, I look up to find myself outside my brother's farmhouse. Laughing doves marching along the thatch roof. The half-door is already open, with children's voices ringing from deep within.

Wide awake.

Painfully wide awake.

I am barefoot in my pyjamas in the driveway, and the sun is just rising over the mountains. And those cursed beads are most likely where I left them, in the pocket of my jeans lying discarded on the bedroom floor.

Only a dream.

Even as I stumble upright, wincing at how badly my feet hurt, and *no, no, no, don't look at how badly scratched your legs are…* I keep seeing that ochre-skinned eland-man scooping sand with his big hands.

Or not a dream.

I turn and gaze back down the drive, past the rows of sentinel cypresses pointing their spears to the sky but see only three geese waddle across the dirt drive, honking their rusty displeasure to all who would listen.

I never dream these days. That is the thing.

I return to Cape Town the very same day, having concocted an emergency at the office. I don't think Gerhard believes me, for he saw my dishevelled state as I came inside, and I had not wanted to remain long enough for him to disbelieve the story he'd drag out of me.

"Are you doing drugs again?" he'd want to know.

He won't believe the truth, that I've been clean these past five years.

Not after having seen me like he had. I can imagine now how he'll be talking to Jane in low tones so that the twins won't overhear, how his little sister has cracked again, and how he won't be paying for a second stint in rehab. Shame burns through me, makes me clutch the steering wheel with white-knuckled hands all the way back home.

Home.

The city.

Table Mountain dominates the city centre, its characteristic buttressed flanks soaring above our infinitesimal lives. Impossible to miss. Yet as I arrive back, a thick fog has washed up from the ocean, so that the dark sandstone heights are swallowed up. The sun itself gleams like an old coin rapidly sliding west. The strangeness of the fog makes it so that I can stare the sun in its single eye without flinching.

It being a Sunday, the streets are near deserted, discarded packets fluttering like spent birds hooked on razorwire fences. Vagrants huddle in doorways, their ragged blankets pulled up to their ears. The late afternoon holds a particular dimness, as if I am viewing my surroundings through a thin film of gauze. As it is, the mist steals all the colours and reduces everything to a monochrome palette cross-hatched in hard strokes.

This is hardly the most encouraging homecoming.

I park my car in the underground garage, check to see that no one is loitering – a woman was robbed in our apartment building just last week, right near the lift entrance – then I hurry inside with my things.

I've been away a week, and everything in my little loft apartment is covered in a fine coating of dust. It doesn't help that the bulbs in the primary light fitting have blown. The reading lamp by the telly, as well as the kitchenette lights do little to dispel the gloom that seeps in past the curtains.

There, a bare wall with a picture missing. Here, gaps on the bookshelf. On the floor, the scuff marks where the sofa once stood. Incompletions. I sink to the floor, and the imitation marble tiles leach the warmth out of my bones almost immediately. The double-volume space soars above me, vanishes into nothingness.

On impulse, I reach into my pocket for the beads. I've

wrapped them in a tissue and unfurl them carefully so I can study them. Scraps of red earth still cling to them, ruddy, like the skin of the eland-man. A shudder goes right through me. I can't articulate why these five beads are so important, but I am a firm believer in small signs cast up by the world around me. I even have a printer's tray on the wall (Ashley always moaned about how kitsch it is). Now I place those little beads in their own little niche, next to the tiger's eye stone I found at the scratch patch the day I graduated and just below the piece of sea-tumbled blue glass from that windswept weekend in Pringle Bay when Ashley said she'd move in with me.

Each object is a memory, tells a little part of my life story – some vague, others precious keepsakes, like the little jade bear my grandma brought me from her trip to Alaska. I have tiny pieces of the bigger world set aside. And now the beads will remind me of my first tentative steps into a new period of my life.

I ask Crystal, the auctions writer at work, about the beads. I've forgotten to bring them with me to the office, but from my descriptions, she pulls up pictures of similar beads. Faience, she says it might be. A type of ceramic. We can't find anything similar to what I describe to her, although some of the pieces the ancient Egyptians made were the closest.

"I'd really have to see the pieces," Crystal says.

"I'll bring them tomorrow," I tell her, knowing I won't.

"If they're the real deal, you really need to show them to an archaeologist. It's an important find."

"Egyptian artefacts all the way out in the Cederberg? Ridiculous. Probably just some farmer whose wife had lost some of her things a few hundred years ago."

And, because it is the office, and because we're on deadline buzzing at the same frequency as the overhead lights, and I've missed out on a week's worth of emails due to having taken sick leave, I am tossed right into a maelstrom of minor emergencies. The question of the beads becomes but a distant blip on my radar.

On Thursday, when I go to fetch the mail, I bump into my neighbour in the lift. I like old Mrs Fischer, even though her apartment tends to smell of cat pee (she claims she doesn't have a cat) and stale tobacco. The latter clings to her and remains as a ghost in her passing a while later. We're on good enough terms, though, that I am her designated spare key holder, and take on the duty to water her peace lily whenever she visits her sister in Malmesbury.

"You've got something smudged on your forehead," I tell her, indicating the centre of my own brow.

The old lady turns to the mirror – yes, our lift had a floor-to-ceiling mirror, ostensibly so we won't feel claustrophobic in the little box – and peers myopically at her forehead.

"I don't see anything, girlie."

"There." I point at the red smudge that looks almost like a bindi, but more like an afterthought, smeared by a careless thumb dipped in red-orange poster paint.

"It's right there." I even touch her forehead.

"Oh! You're just having me on!" she snaps, slapping at my fingers.

By now I am genuinely puzzled but decide not to press further. Besides, we've arrived at the seventeenth floor, and I can walk faster than the old lady down the passage. The tobacco stench of her clings to my clothing even as I hurry along to my door.

I think nothing further of the incident until work the next day, when I am called into my boss's office. I never much like being under John's scrutiny. He has that way about him that always makes me feel as though I am somehow inadequate, which is not helped by the awards and certificates he has stuck up in a row next to his desk. A tropical beach scene from his trip to The Maldives last year blazes from the oversized stretched canvas mounted on the other wall. The too-white sand hurt my eyes.

Yet that is not what snags my attention. Seemingly unbeknown to him, he has a reddish thumb print smudged in the middle of his forehead. I can't help but stare at it, morbidly fascinated, while his mouth keeps flapping and words pour out – words I forget as soon as I hear them.

"What?" he eventually says.

I blink, give a small gasp. "Sorry, John, you've got something on your forehead. Right there." I dab with my index finger on my own forehead to indicate the spot.

"Eh?" He opens a drawer and pulls out a small mirror that he uses to check himself.

Yeah, I know, he keeps a mirror in his drawer. Dodgy AF.

"There's nothing," he tells me, frowning. "You must be mistaken."

What the heck? I rub at my eyes, carefully, behind my glasses. The red splotch is still there. "Whoops!" I say with a high-pitched giggle. "Must be the light."

However, no matter how much I blink, that dot remains, and it is with great difficulty that I concentrate enough to get through the rest of the meeting. What are the chances? Is there something in my head that's broken?

I hoped to sleep in Saturday morning. I couldn't get comfortable all through the night, and kept staring owl eyed into the dark, as if my walls were crawling with black spiders that were weaving closer and closer. Eventually I drifted off into that kind of half-awake slumber that doesn't bring any rest. No dreams, of course.

A frantic knocking at my door brings me back to the waking world.

For a few heartbeats I lie there, hoping it is someone who'll realise the error of their ways and move on, but then the knocking continues for a fourth round, and I drag the duvet around me and climb down from the loft.

"Coming!" I call, then yelp as I nearly slip on the ladder.

The woman on my threshold is a stranger – short, dark of skin, her hair in cornrows. "Hi, I'm Thandeka. You're Priscilla's neighbour, you've got her key, right?"

"Priscilla?" My thoughts are sluggish as I turned over the name. "Key… Oh, wait, Mrs Fischer, right?"

The woman nods. "Her sister sent me. We need to get into her apartment immediately!"

"A problem?"

"She hasn't answered her phone the whole night. Not this morning either."

"Maybe she's gone out?"

"She was supposed to visit her sister this weekend. She never arrived."

"Oh." A small sliver of alarm twists in my belly as I duck back into my apartment and grab Mrs Fischer's key off the keyring.

Thandeka pretty much snatches the key from me before I have even extended my hand, and half bemused, I followed her across the passageway, still wearing my duvet like a cloak.

She struggles with the key in the lock, her hands are shaking so much, but she succeeds on the third attempt.

"Priscilla!" she shrills then bolts in, almost as if she expects something awful to have happened.

The stench in the apartment hits me like something solid, so thick I have to take a step back. It is more than the usual miasma of old tobacco and cat piss, something dark and foetid that speaks of things best forgotten in swamps, of skin long sloughed from flesh turned to naught but rancid fat and sinews.

Ahead of me, Thandeka is hunched over, retching, and my own gorge rises in response to the sounds of her obvious distress. The buzzing frenzy of flies that we disturb as we enter the bedroom clouds our vision, so that it takes a while for us to resolve the writhing mass of grubs and maggots that seethes in a vaguely humanoid shape on the carpet.

I am not sure if I am the one who starts screaming first.

There is no accounting for the advanced state of decay, I hear later from Clinton, who lives in the flat two numbers down. It is all rather bizarre. I last saw Mrs Fischer the Thursday. We discovered her badly decomposed corpse during the early hours of Saturday.

The police come around to ask questions, yet they don't seem too fazed, and after the pathologists and other officials are done, a company specialising in the removal of medical and biological waste finishes the clean-up.

It is all rather perfunctory and depressing, and I can't help but wonder what will happen to me one day when I drop off. Will I be found rotting in my apartment or will I drop dead in the toiletries aisle in the supermarket? Or the bathroom, with my panties around my ankles. How undignified.

But that is human life for you. While the world slowly erodes around us, concrete crumbles, tiles crack and glass shatters, our bodies bloom and wither, like some sort of exotic fungus, leaving no trace save for a smear of fluids or a few bits of bone.

On Monday I go to work, with nothing out of the ordinary until I get out of the lift at the third floor. A handful of my colleagues are all glumly sitting in front of the glass doors of a darkened office.

"Hey, what's up?" I ask.

Rencia, the lady at the front desk, says, "John's not in yet."

"And he's not answering his phone," Claudette from accounting adds.

"Maybe he's caught in traffic?" I ask.

"He lives in Green Point," Rencia says. "That's what, like jogging distance if you're feeling fit. And you know he's never late. Even if he's half dead from the flu." Her face is pinched.

"Then maybe one of us should go fetch the key," Claudette says.

"Doesn't anyone else have a key?" I already feel uncomfortable, drawing conclusions. That tell-tale smudge on his forehead, so like Mrs Fischer's...

The only other person who has a key for the office is Marlise, our COO, but she is on leave, so it falls to me and Rencia to drive over to John's when by nine-thirty we still can't get him to pick up his phone.

John stays in one of the older spots, which is just up the road from the office, but we get stuck in the traffic, so it takes a bit longer to reach the place than it should, and our tempers are considerably shorter. Then it is a case of trying to find parking in High Level Road, which means we end up parking at least four or five blocks from our destination.

"What a crap way to start the week," Rencia mutters, her heels going *tap, tap, tap* along the pavement.

It is misty too, like wading through cotton wool. Cars' headlights barely penetrate the gloom, and my ears hurt from the cold.

John's house is situated on such a steep incline that he had a lift installed. Except the lift is at the top, so we have to take the stairs, which are the type you don't want to tumble down as they're a few degrees shy of being called a ladder. The house crouches beneath two venerable coral trees, their branches skeletal this time of year. It is an odd-looking place, with crumbling redbrick walls and a slasto-paved porch where rusting patio furniture huddles and bleeds trails into the stonework. Fascia boards of pine panelling complete the picture. So 1970s. Typical John.

No one answers when we knock, and the curtains are still drawn.

"Doesn't look like he's home," Rencia says.

My teeth are chattering by then, and thanks to more than just the cold.

That's when I notice the flies. Hundreds and hundreds of flies crawling on the inside of the windows, against the glass, knocking themselves silly.

"Rencia..." I say. All the blood in my body rushes to my feet.

She turns to me, frowning. "What?"

"Call the cops."

Rencia and I are booked off for a week, given the number of a counsellor we go speak to. I'm not sure if talking to anyone will help me. Instead, I entomb myself in my apartment and kept the curtains drawn, all the lights blazing. Except for the main lights. I still haven't gotten the electrician to come in to repair them.

Maybe it is just coincidence. The red marks, the gruesome deaths. What if I am going mad? What if that eland-man dream has something to it? No. Preposterous.

So, I drink what red wine I have – several bottles of Pinot Noir from the farm – and binge-watch through seasons two to five of *Supernatural*. Not the best choice, but there is something to be said about Sam and Dean fighting monsters and overcoming evil.

I don't think I sleep.

After three days, I am down to one tin of chickpeas and wheel of feta cheese, and it is time for me to leave the apartment, do something. Everything feels jagged; if I move too fast, objects stutter, the light refracts at the edges and splits into its constituents of red, green and blue. Sleep deprivation.

I must be cursed. That can be the only thing.

If I go out now, everyone I see will end up with a mark, and they'll die, horribly. Yet I can't remain in my apartment indefinitely. I'll starve. Come Monday, I'll have to go back to work.

It is 7pm, there is a miserable drizzle, and I could walk down to the Eastern Bazaar for tikka chicken. The eatery isn't far, and it's Ashley's favourite. I'd like to go for old time's sake where I can wallow in my self-pity. So, I grab my coat and my purse, shove my feet into my Docs, and take the elevator down to the entrance.

Solly, the security guard at the front desk, waves and gives me a cheery hello. No red mark. The couple who come up the stairs as I go out, they're fine. Unmarred foreheads. I allowed myself to breathe.

See, it's going to be all right.

The pinpricks of moisture on my face are fresh, pleasant – cleansing rain, water gurgling in the gutters. The particular scent of wet tar with the orange streetlights making oily smears in the puddles. After sunset, the city transforms, its grid work of streets becoming canyons slicing between the squared-off bulks of buildings. Shopfronts mostly dimly lit, save for the odd hole-in-the-wall pub where voices spill out onto the pavement, dancing with the gentle strains of intertwined saxophone and walking bass. The susurrus of snare softly shaking.

My destination announces itself with the scent of curry and spices, and tawdry Turkish music twining through the air long before I round the corner. The Eastern Bazaar is a bright, shining beacon in the gloom, where people step out of taxis holding the hands of small children. Though I search, I see no telltale red thumbprints standing out on any foreheads.

Relax.

It's over.

Yet I can't help but feel as if the part of the story where bad things happen in threes holds some truth. It is something my mother always said, and those words press a shadow on my heart even while I place my order and take momentary fright at the bindi of the obviously Hindu woman ordering chana masala with garlic naan at the counter next to me.

My meal – chicken tikka with rice – is tasteless. I find a table in the corner near the washbasin, and slowly chew mouthful after mouthful, but I may as well be eating paper pulp. The mango lassi furs my tongue with a bitter aftertaste, as if it is slightly fermented – I won't be able to finish it.

All around me, families are chattering, mothers wiping babies' faces with napkins, fathers laughing, children trying to save space for their dessert. And there am I, in splendid isolation among the masses, sunk in my own private hell. I am not hungry, but I must eat, and all the while I keep watch, fearing what must come.

Presently, I discard more than half my meal, my stomach twisting in on itself. No one looks at me as I stick my hands in my pockets and prepare to plunge back into the drizzle. My face is too warm, my chest too tight, so I feel as if I am not drawing enough air into my lungs.

I am not certain who is more surprised: As I step into the chill, damp night, still dazzled by the bright interior, I nearly run into a couple dashing along the pavement, clearly keen to get inside. Within an instant, recognition sets in on both counts – I've nearly bumped right into Ashley and her partner.

Jean is a big, rugby player type with close-cropped brown hair and florid complexion, and next to him, Ashley seems doll-like, her hand clenched firmly in his fist. Her mouth is set in an 'o' of surprise, and Jean nearly falls on his arse, so suddenly does he come to a halt.

Except that is not what makes me cry out – there, in the centre of Ashley's forehead, is a red thumbprint, lurid against her skin.

"I'm so so—"

"Get away from us!" Jean roars as he throws his arm around Ashley and yanks her along with him.

I consider calling after her, warning her, but all the sound I can make is a strangled croak. A hollow ache begins in my chest and gradually starts chewing at the rest of me. Where will this end? Until everyone close to me is consumed by the decay? Or am I imagining things? Yet that startled face with the hectic mark. Blue eyes wide. I know what I've seen, and there is nothing that I can do.

I'm unsure how long I stand on that pavement, getting rained on, while I flex my hands and concentrate solely on inhaling and exhaling. Until a gang of teenagers swarms past me and heads inside the bazaar, the girls flicking their long hair, the boys joking, calling out to each other. Bragging about inconsequentialities.

I could go in there now. Could walk to where Ashley and Jean are ordering from the shawarma counter, their backs held stiffly to me. And what will I tell them? Her?

Ashley, you're going to die, horribly, and there's nothing you can do about it?

What will that achieve?

Nothing.

Who'd believe me, anyway?

I'd only cause a scene. Merely seeing the two of them together drives that rusty blade in deeper, until I want only to fold in on myself and slip between the cracks and be washed away along the stormwater drains. Eventually I'll reach the sea, where I'll dissolve, and the fishes will drink me. And no one will speak my name, and that will be all right.

So, I walk back, the nausea churning up my innards until I eventually stop by a dustbin and vomit up what I've eaten. By the time I unlock my apartment door, I am feverish, heartsick, and curl up on the armchair with the last of the red wine.

Sleep rises on a black tide and—

Stones press into my bare feet, and around me the reeds hiss and shiver, like clumps of dull green wires, but it's the ridge of red-orange rock that draws my attention. It's familiar. I've been here before, only now the sky is boiling with heavy cloud, and white-violet flashes of lightning illuminate their swollen bellies.

By all rights, I should be freezing, but my sense of my body is dulled, and the environment seems curiously indistinct at the edges of my vision, as if it is creating itself only when I turn my head to look.

The eland man is waiting for me once I reach the top of the ridge, in a hollow surrounded on all sides by weathered pillars, cracked and flaking, and contorted into fantastical shapes that make me think of emergent chthonic creatures captured in stone, forever threatening to come to life in a heartbeat.

The red ochre of the paint coating his skin flakes off in parts, rubbed away, cracking, and his unfathomable gazes draws me closer until I eventually come to a stop about a car's length from him. I can't bring myself to go any closer, despite this overwhelming need to go kneel at his feet.

How long we watch each other, I don't know. The wind is mourning between the rocks, but the sound is as if I'm hearing it from a great distance. A living thing, like some sort of hound, hungry and prowling.

The eland-headed man holds out his big hand, palm up, and I know he wants the beads. This understanding is laid upon my heart in the solidity of stone and earth and the heavy tread of thunder that shakes the sky.

"I don't have them here," I tell him, and open my empty palms.

I jerk awake with the suddenness of someone who has had her feet knocked out from beneath her before she can prepare for the fall, and for a while all I can do is lie there, half sprawled off the armchair. My heart thuds as if it will explode out of my chest, it's beating so hard against its prison.

It all started with the beads, didn't it?

I'm not superstitious, am I?

Yet there is something to be said for a conscious laying to rest of the past. We scatter the ashes of our dead loved ones. Sometimes we hold onto things of the past that were never meant to be collected and displayed in the first place.

Surely not...

My head throbbing something fierce, and that dream of the eland man so tangible I find myself glancing about the room just in case he's physically manifested (stupid, I know) I make my way to those five cursed beads.

They lie there, bits of red ochre soil still crusting the holes.

Tiny little faience tubes. So, innocuous.

Oddly, they're warm to the touch, as if they've been lying in the sun the whole time.

What I'm intending is absolutely irrational, I tell myself time and again as I nose my car out onto the N7 for what will be a three-hour drive at night. I've never enjoyed road trips after sunset, following the hypnotic white line as it stutters between a solid and staccato. Or the occasional flash of rabbit eyes in the headlights. The grinding of the tar vibrates through the steering wheel, until my hands are numb. The only radio station is RSG, and this late – or early, I can't tell, the car's clock is bust – they play obscure music. Stuff that sounds as if it crept out of its grave during the 1960s and slid along gutters, collecting bottle caps and cigarette butts, until it has summoned the power to drag itself through the air.

If I were in a better mood, I might laugh, but now the music with its mawkish flutes, vibraphone and trite conga drums makes me grit my teeth. Too goddamned cheerful. Yet when I try to change to another channel, all I get is static. It's either white noise, bloody Les Baxter or the grind of the car's tyres.

I suffer through this obscene soundtrack, and all the while I feel the hard press of the beads through my jeans pocket. Burning.

The night's bleeding away in the east by the time I pull over at the side of the road, on the hill above where they've been building the dam. When I wipe at my eyes, my fingers come away gritty, and no matter how much I blink, my lashes are all gummy, my vision blurry.

The earth is still raw and red, but since I was last here, my brother's diverted a channel from the river, by the looks of things. Water as silver as the sky is dimpled with cat's paws in the chill dawning. Maybe by the time spring comes, they'll have planted lilies. I'd like to think Jane will do that. She has a thing for Monet. And maybe in a year or three, the dam will seem as if it's always been here, and the children will come ride on their canoes here, and patient herons will spear luckless frogs and fish.

On clear days, the water will be a mirror, holding up the sky and the mountains, and clever photographers will position themselves just so, to make viewers wonder which is the real mountain, and which is the reflection.

The beads are hot in my hand, my skin slick and clammy as I step through the wire fencing and make my way downslope, past humped termite nests and piles of shale that slide with my footfalls in a loose clatter. This entire venture is foolish. An ill-considered whim. Yet there's a rightness to it too. Call it catharsis, perhaps, in which I ascribe meaning to a seemingly random object and project my own pain. That's what Ashley would say, playing Jung to my psychosis.

Except Ashley's been marked, and it's my fault.

I don't even know if what I'm about to do will be enough, because the spot where I uncovered the beads is now covered by a gradually growing body of water. My Docs sink toe deep into the mud that slips and slides beneath my soles.

It would be nice to imagine that I've been mistaken all along, yet I can't get the droning of the flies out of my head. I know what I saw. People are dead, and I'm the plague carrier.

The beads grow white hot in my hand, and without further preamble I fling them into the water. *Plop, plop-plop-plop. Plop.*

Just like that, the water swallows them up.

There is no crack of thunder. No lightning bolts.

Just a small spotted bird making the sound of rusty hinges from the top of a protea bush off to my right. The air is cold, laden with moisture, and judging by the clouds smothering the Sneeuberg, rain is coming, and soon. What sunlight pierces the gaps is weak, soon swallowed up as the cover crawls across the sky.

By the time I'm back at the car, the first fat drops spatter on the bonnet, make dusty tear trails down the windshield. Me – I'm empty. All the fire has sputtered to ashes and I'm wrung out, exhausted, and there is only one place I can go – back to the farm, where I was born. The prodigal sister. As always.

The seat creaks as I put my weight down in it, and it's when I check in the rear-view mirrors as I'm reversing, that I see it – a red mark like a thumbprint, right there in the centre of my forehead.

A HARD COUNTRY TO DIE IN

Paula Wakefield

Georgie Zakiros wasn't found until the snow thawed, when her body looked like wet bloated cardboard, and the foxes and the birds had already made a meal of her. Unusually though, they'd left her eyes alone, and Llewelyn, the postie, who found her, said it was as if she was staring in fear, still not believing what she'd seen. Mrs Williams at the undertaker's said it was a look of horror as well as shock and she doubted very much whether 'that woman' was at peace, chapel of rest, or no. They had to sew her eyelids shut.

In the village the event was chewed over without much surprise. She wasn't liked down there either, and Olwyn was the first to predict no good would come of her. There's just the one shop and Dr Zakiros, though she was no medical doctor, had upset Olwyn the first time she visited with her nicer-than-nice disappointment over Olwyn having only a bit of nylon wool on the shelf. She'd decided to take up knitting while she was 'in the country'.

"I'd assumed you would have the real thing, living here." Ha-ha. "And, only store cupboard food... What a pity." It was clear she could only be a stranger.

"She still wants her milk, though, and there'll come a time when she's glad of a few tins of baked beans or a microwave ready meal!" Olwyn told Mam. They had a good laugh about it.

The weather and the land are bad enough down here in the valley, but it's worse up there, and besides that everyone round here knows it's a dangerous game to get on the wrong side of Olwyn; her generations are deepest rooted here.

We knew before Olwyn did that Georgie Zakiros had started visiting. To get up there you have to start off on our track and there's no choice but to go right past our front door. Not that she bothered to knock and introduce herself. Not until she wanted something. It's a long trek, even in a 4x4. In wet weather the ground slithers away from you, when the track disguises itself and shifts direction without warning. The rain and the run-off burden the ground until it's too heavy to support itself and so it gives up, falls away, amputating bits of itself, and where once you thought there was a firm foothold there's only mist. One wrong turn, one slip and you've got a broken leg, or neck, or else you're being sucked down in the bog. When it's dry, the track outruns your feet with hissing pebbles and shale so you can't stand still even if you want to. The earth cracks and opens up and finds different ways of hurting you, not that she knew that, nor would she have listened if told.

But, as I said, there's no other road so we knew straight away when she arrived, though it wasn't until after all the re-building and clearing up was done, when I suppose she thought it was safe.

Chris Zakiros had spent months overseeing everything. There was no doubting he'd got plenty of cash, but that's neither here nor there except to say he'd got enough money to feed into a place that nobody had wanted since, well, since any of us can remember, and we're born with memories as long as the weather. But the land's memories are even longer. The land never forgets – and it never forgives, as your great gran always said. Nobody local was interested in the work up there, obviously, that was why they had to bring in builders and landscapers from some way away.

But not all the money in the world could ever master that place, and there are some who can never escape it, and I reckon Georgie Zakiros has become one of them. That land's vengeful, you see. But people are misled because the ground flattens into a plateau, and when you're up there you've got hills and mountains behind you, and you can see down into the valley, all around, so for a while there's a false sense of security. Our ancestors must have felt safe there once, when it was a hillfort but not even we remember as far back as that; that's why the stories remember for us.

There're plenty that tell of how if strangers linger they'll start to feel watched, especially on bright blue days when the sky's innocent of hawks and carrion crows, when it's least expected. It might have taken a while to realise there's nothing ordinary to be heard, just the groan of land shifting, and the leftovers of those it won't let go of. Incomers and strangers don't realise what the sounds are; if they don't dawdle it all seems innocuous. They might think it's only the wind that has nothing to stop it honing the rocks with its voice because most of the trees were felled ages ago. There's plenty of scrub up there, Blackthorn, some hawthorne, but it is bleak, though outsiders think there's a beauty to it. That wind scathes even on warm days so most hillwalkers get a move on, and nothing more is thought about any of it. But when you're born here your ears are tuned and you know the wailing descants and the baritones – nothing like you'll hear in the kirk – aren't the wind's voice; but it is carrying warnings. Sometimes even we say that it is just the wind, after all, but there's only so long you can fool yourself.

When they're up there, hikers who hang about start to feel the hills closer than when they first arrived, out of breath, as if the mountains behind are pushing at the rocks, and at them, forcing them back, down towards us and the valley. While their hearts still pound after the climb, the waterfall looks like it was set there specially for a water colourist or a postcard photographer, but when the sweat starts to cool on their backs they might swear that the water that churned with froth has become a sheet of glass, a mirror, and they fancy they see Agnes falling over, and over, (strangers have no idea who it is), down onto the rocks that she thought would break her body so badly it would be the end of her. It wasn't. She was crippled and went mad, and death only came to her years later in the asylum, long after everybody who'd known her, but had refused to speak to her, had passed peacefully on. There was a young couple, a few years ago, who called the air ambulance out so certain were they that somebody must be lying injured.

And then there's Widdwer's Jump – it's not called that for nothing. It's mainly men who see in that spot. The lads I was at school with did, just like their dads and uncles and older brothers before them. One boy said it was Iyain, but the others argued it must have been Sir Geoffrey, because the man they saw resembled the portrait that still hangs, mildewed, in the kirk. Sir Geoffrey had built a hunting lodge and taken Lady Matilda, his new wife, to chase and hunt. When her horse lost its footing she fell, and her spine snapped like a dry twig.

Sir Geoffrey killed twelve stags and had the antlers hung in the kirk, then he went back up to the lodge, without his servants, and threw himself off the crag, joining his new wife in death. Of course, she was buried at the kirk but he couldn't be, so he has no choice but to wander around up there, grieving her death and his own stupidity, even though his nephew, who inherited, had his battered remains scooped up and interred back at their other estate.

The battered oak is all that remains of the proudest trees from Sir Geoffrey's time, when this was famous as hunting country and nobody would ever dare hurt it. That tree is left alone to break off its own branches when it's ready, but we used to dare each other to see who could sit under it the longest. Nobody had ever tried to do it alone but even in summer, in little gangs, and with plenty of cider inside us, we couldn't keep our backs to the Hanging Tree's bark when the darkness started to thicken. I hold the record for sitting there until dusk, but I shifted like a bat when I saw her.

Iyain built the first proper house and lived up there with his wife Branwynn, and they were happy and thankful that she had survived so many childbeds and that not one of the children had been taken from them. Husband and wife had never spent a day or night apart since their hand fasting but then news came that Branwynn's family in the next county were sickening and wanted her, so off she went with her bundle of blankets and herbs, despite the blackness of the season. Iyain couldn't leave the animals, you see, and there were too many children to take if husband went with wife. Besides, if it was a plague outbreak she was heading for, it was no place for the children.

Branwynn was gone a long time and, after a year and a day, hope of seeing her again was given up and Iyain and the children worked on in their woe. Little did they know that Frances Fullford had made up her mind that she would have Iyain. He hadn't forgotten Branwynn but he wasn't so old that he'd forgotten his need for a woman either, and once Frances had got her claws in him, she was relentless and would not let go.

Later, but not 'til after she was married to Iyain, it was discovered that when Branwynn had gone off to her relatives' in their sick beds, Frances had secretly ordered the boundary stones to be moved, knowing that if Branwynn wasn't already dead of a fever, coming back without the stones to mark her way she'd be lost. Her bones and rags were found sticking out from the last of a snow drift where the boundary should have been. The shepherd who found her said that her arms were outstretched, the palms held up, at right angles, so she must have gone around in freezing circles searching for the stones that would map her way home.

The children were sent to the relatives after all, because Iyain was broken by his guilt and fury at being tricked. He was a widower, but he needn't have been, not then, not in that way. He could not bear the sight of Frances and took himself and his remorse off to the crag, taking the leap that Sir Geoffrey had.

It's possible, though doubtful, Frances strung herself up; more likely it was Branwynn's relations who made the long journey to avenge their kinswoman. That's always been the dare, you see, because for years Frances and the shame she never felt in life, have been spotted swinging from the oak. But I know it wasn't Frances I saw, although I expected to. It was Branwynn, arms outstretched, stumbling towards the wreck of her home.

The men have destroyed themselves up there, but the land can't abide women who are unjust to other women. Althea and Emmalina, the twins in your granny's days, were cruel to their cousin from the time they could walk and talk. They were nine when they told Beth they'd teach her to swim and then tried to drown her in the pool. Beth was all right. The water coughed her up and straight out onto the bank but those two ended up crippled by polio, prisoners for fifty years in the iron lungs that did their hard breathing for them. Beth lived happily 'til she was ninety-three without a day's illness in her life. She died in her sleep, sitting in her chair at the back door, where she liked to look out at the fields, and the mountains in the distance. She died easy, and smiling.

The children whose bodies are buried somewhere out there, on the moor land, so the wicked murderers claimed, are never told of. We know the land holds them tight and safe in its rage, and we say nothing to the walkers who have stopped off at the pub to reward their thirst after their descent and then remember the news headlines. Sometimes one of them might say they thought they heard something, but we turn our talk to foxes, how they can get through twenty lambs a night.

You'll learn all about that soon enough – how their tiny teeth leave those lethal love bites, to the heads as well as the necks. Even if the young sheep carry on for a few weeks, they drop eventually, as if vampire foxes have drained them.

The badger, he's got a couple of ways: there's the way he does it with two piercing wounds at the back of the head, then the liver snouted out – skilful like a surgeon. The second – that's more usual – the whole lamb peeled from its skin, smooth as a sleeve pulled off a shiny wet arm that steams in the air.

But the crows… they don't wear those black death hoods for nothing. You see them drop out of the sky aiming at the fresh eyes or stabbing at the young tongues, but it's worse when they open them up with their beaks and then, bored, fly off leaving the lamb panting through what's left of its lungs.

After a few pints, and listening to that ordinary talk of ours, the pub visitors think they've heard the worst of things, so they move out of the bar to go and tuck into their steak and kidney. They don't know the half of it because they don't live with the land the way we do, as parts of the one story that shifts, just like the land does.

Which brings me back to Georgie Zakiros. Olwyn had told Mam that although she and Chris got on well, they were, as it happened, divorced, but nothing had ever interfered with Georgie's hold on Chris's life – least of all, Chris. But then he told her about Seren.

Seren, Olwyn's daughter, lives on the other side of the valley. You've already met her, so you've seen she's lovely to look at, and that she's a loving, laughing soul. A bit wild, like the land, and that's why Olwyn has always been more protective about Seren than her other children.

So…what can be said about the way Seren and Chris loved each other? Well, it made us feel, even on the greyest and wettest, even on dangerous days that the land – though not ready to forgive – might not lash out quite so often. We felt that if the two of them were up there it could make a difference.

When Chris told Georgie that he was with Seren, Georgie knew what he meant and to say she wasn't happy, well… She started spending more and more time visiting, knowing that Chris wouldn't see Seren while she was staying with him, up there.

She was marking what she thought was her territory. First of all, Georgie said she wanted a 'proper' garden and an arbour built in the rock face at the back. Your granddad told them it wasn't wise, and they'd be bringing all sorts of trouble down by disturbing things, but she went on with it anyway.

You see Chris Zakiros had seemed ready to plant himself here, with Seren; he loved the wildness, but Georgie wanted to tame it.

She wanted a conservatory, but she didn't make Chris get it rebuilt after the rock fall smashed it. She wanted the oak felling, because she said it blocked out too much light, but we knew the real reason; she'd already caught a glimpse, and of course she would refuse to believe it. The builders drew the line at touching the oak, anyway, and gave her a straight 'no', and I bet they wish they had said the same to draining the pool.

Work on that had to stop when they found the leathery head. Then the experts from the county were called in and they found and removed the rest of the body that the peat had preserved. By then it was full autumn – the weather had been wet and dismal all summer – getting more stuff up there was a fool's game before the spring. The builders had already started coming down at lunch time and not going back until the next morning, because the days were so short.

Ignorant as they were when they arrived, they had never been easy working up there but work's work, so they carried on. And even before Olwyn and Seren – though Mam and me never took to Georgie Zakiros – we couldn't afford to say no to the pay for cleaning the house and hanging curtains for her. At first, we tried chatting a bit, friendly like, thinking we might give her a bit of warning, like your grandad had, but she'd have none of it. 'I don't do small talk,' she said, obviously thinking she was putting us in our place.

Without having to say anything to each other, your gran and me knew we wouldn't go back, whatever the cash-in-hand, because that's the way invaders talk – all of them, thinking they're a cut above, believing they've the right to decide what's small talk and not.

Not long after that, she drove her bony-self round to see Seren and, in that haughty way of hers, she told Seren that she wouldn't let anybody come between her and Chris. "Besides," she said, "you only want him for his money."

Can you believe it?!

Seren couldn't.

We could.

Olwyn did, and she spit feathers: "In this day and age – and probably calls herself a feminist!"

For once, and because Georgie had said all this to her face – rather than to her city friends that Mam and I had heard her talking to on the landline – Seren stuck up for herself, "If it was Chris's money I wanted, there'd be an easy way to go about getting it, Georgie."

Seren was a good bit younger than Chris or Georgie but even so Georgie must have looked puzzled. "I could get pregnant," Seren said, and closed the door on her.

Olwyn and Mam laughed 'til they cried when Olwyn told us, and I chuckled until my belly shook, and you were rolling and kicking to keep us company. We don't abide bullies.

The more Georgie Zakiros came up here, the more time Chris spent away and Olwyn said Seren's heart was breaking because she hadn't heard from him. Olwyn didn't need to say anything. I'd told Seren I was worried about the weight she'd lost. 'Love hunger', Olwyn called it. "Gnawing away at my girl. I won't have it. That woman – trying to make out Seren's been abandoned – claiming the land like she claims him."

The last time we saw Georgie Zakiros was in the shop. She'd arrived with her car rammed with posh food and even posher duvets, but she needed firelighters. As Mam said, she had neither conscience nor shame.

Gladys Powell, who was in the shop with us that last time Georgie was there, told her the forecast was bad and that it was always harder up the top but of course Gladys was ignored.

I don't know where she went after the shop, but she'd gone somewhere, because it wasn't 'til we got back that we heard the car on the track. We all looked at each other but said nothing. We knew what would happen, and it wouldn't just be down to the weather.

The radio news – our telly had stopped working already – was always full of the freeze and the snow, weeks and weeks of it, and even if anyone had felt like trying to get up there it was impossible. Ordinary roads were blocked. The power lines were down, train tracks ruined, livestock dead.

Mobile fones have never worked up the top, you can't even get a TV signal, and of course the landline had gone with the gales that brought the first lot of deep snow. Georgie Zakiros had the sense not to try to get down here to the valley, and she'd got all that food, so she must have convinced herself she'd be all right. But she didn't know that place like we do and there she was, trapped and without a doubt taunted, and now forever punished because this country is hard to die in for the likes of her. The expensive food was mostly untouched and had gone rotten. She must have been frantic when she ran outside. You'll have your own sense of her when you go up there. But it says a lot that the crows didn't go near her eyes or tongue.

Anyway, there'll be nothing for you to fear. Outsiders can never learn this place like we know it because it's not in ordinary books. Even the stories we forget are in the land and sometimes, when you're older, you'll tap a rock with your toe and notice a ridge just ready for your fingers to pry apart, and when you do you'll see that's the leaves of the book.

This tale about Georgie Zakiros is one you and your friends will tell when you get to school, and you'll fashion it in your own ways for yourselves, just one chapter amongst all the others. We die comfortable here and they can't hurt you. Chew on this stone, it's from up there and it's got its own stories for you to eat, and it'll bring those teeth through, soon enough.

LIGHTENING

Rose Biggin

Weeks into high summer, we finally all went swimming. It wasn't that we didn't want to go, we were desperate – it's just tricky to get everyone together. My friend Amber was very clear about the exact spot.

"I can't quite remember where it is," she said, "but I went last year, it's lovely. I know vaguely. We should see if we can find it."

We got on our bicycles and set off in the vague direction of her memory. We had bottles of water, a towel each. The essentials. It wasn't far, she promised – just a question of specifics.

"It's one of *those* places..." she called, as we rode in a line along an empty main road, the tarmac shining in the heat like freshly quarried jet. "You know the kind. If you're not sure exactly where you're going, you can be right next to it and you'd never know."

I didn't mind how long it might take. I enjoyed creating the illusion of breeze for myself by riding through that stifling air, which on foot became immediately heavy and unmoving. There was sweat on the back of my neck, my shorts were rubbing into my thighs. The world around me seemed more open than usual, bigger somehow, the sunlight laying everything bare. We took shortcuts along narrower paths, threading through dry grasses that scratched at our legs. The sky was an endless, empty blue.

We were heading towards a forest. I knew the area: to my recollection the river was a trickle, the colour of mud. I offered this memory to Amber.

"Well in the off season maybe," she replied. "I promise it won't be like that now. Not where *we're* going."

We cycled through a field which had become parched in the constant sun. My bicycle bumped over ridges of dried mud, shaking me at the jaw. Half-naked sunbathers lay about, hats over their faces. When the trees loomed closer, we all dismounted and wheeled slowly into the shadows, going single file over dirt paths lined with papery leaves, the heat pressing down hard onto us. The trees provided some shade and made everything darker. Soon I could only see Fern's legs in front of me, her skin shiny with sweat. I could hear insects humming close to my face, and my friends slapping them off their bodies.

It happened the way it always happens, of course. Someone made a tentative comment about turning round and going back to that nice pub we passed earlier, and others began the first fatal mutterings of agreement.... and suddenly the path widened, we heard splashing and laughter, we were hit by the sparkle of sunlight on water and we'd walked into a hidden miracle.

The river flowed wide here. We leaned over to look, holding each other's shoulders to peer over the bank, pushing ourselves through the bushes to get a better view, dry twigs scratching at our faces. The water was clear enough to see silt rolling smoothly along the bed, and the shallows with golden rocks, slicked with moss green. The surface rippled steadily with the current, reflecting the sky like a flat silver mirror. The whole place looked as inviting as a lover's beckoning finger.

We freewheeled along the path and offered cries of unreserved praise to Amber for leading us here.

"Not a problem," she said. "When I promise to take you somewhere, I'm taking you there."

"Takes ages, though," I called out, from the back. My hands were slippery on the handlebars.

"It was all a hilarious stunt to make you hot and weary," said Amber.

Between us, Fern, Briony and Ash joined in with a groan.

The banks were bare of their grass, rising up sharply on both sides; but the mud was dry, and trees arched over us with silver peeling bark and leaves like new coins. Best of all, people were already in the water. The space was scattered with groups standing about chatting, drinks in hands, up to their chests in the river; or paddling casually against the current, splashing each other. On the bank, swimmers lounged about on towels, people-watching or pretending they weren't, and a group on the opposite bank had brought camping chairs. Empty bottles were steadily accumulating by their feet. The space was alive with voices. Somebody upriver was playing music, and the dulled bassline reached us where we stood. All the sound had been completely smothered by the forest until we were on top of it.

We chained the bicycles together, locked them to a thick tree trunk and huddled in an empty spot, removing our clothes as quickly as we could.

"Right," said Fern, unfastening her bra strap. "Who's getting in first? I'm kidding, it's me." She dropped her smalls to the ground, where our clothes were jumbled in a messy pile, and began a careful descent down the bank.

Everyone tiptoed after her, arms held out for balance on the slope, a troupe of naked backs and bottoms approaching the shining water. I stared up into the sky for a moment, closing my eyes and letting a breeze find its way across my newly bare neck and shoulders, and down over the rest of me. Then I came back to myself and followed everyone down the bank. It was steeper than it looked, and my feet were sensitive to every stone. I held on to overhanging branches as I lowered myself, feeling the dry bark beneath my fingers.

The bank crumbled into a muddy edge of wet mud, lined with twigs and moss, which then flattened out to become clear river. One by one, my friends took a few quick steps through the mud and into the water, standing ankle-deep and shouting about how cold it was.

People in the river waved and made sounds of encouragement. They called out things like *It's idyllic once you're in!* and *Yes, it's naked people!* – and soon everyone was in the water, wading steadily towards the centre where it was deep enough to swim. Everyone except me, who was still on the bank.

Amber, thigh deep in the water now, looked up at me and beckoned, laughing at our shared nakedness. I grinned and shook my head. She put her hands on her hips.

"You want to jump in, don't you?" she said. "I'll show you where."

"Good idea," said Ash, who was bending over slightly, his arms spread wide to keep balance against the current. The water was over his knees. "I'd flop over now and get it done with, but it's full of rocks."

Others had made it further out. Briony had put her head clean under, coming up gasping for breath, then grinning at everyone triumphantly. She made her way through the water in a crouch to keep her body under, her hair stuck to her face like thin seaweed. Everyone aimed against the current, wading slowly to the busiest part of the river.

At Amber's suggestion I followed along, halfway up the bank, wet patches of well-trodden mud squelching beneath my feet and making muddy streaks up my legs. The route took me higher until it stopped on a ledge jutting out above the water. Leaning forwards slightly, I could see the wobbly stripes of my friends' legs and backs as they carefully picked their way across the stones. My own body was reflected on the water, a dark picture stretched long and flat, as if I were lying naked on the surface. I stretched my arms above my head to enhance the effect.

"That's the spot!" cried Amber. "You can jump from there."

The humidity of the day, and the steep walk across mud and stones, made me more aware than usual of the breath in my chest. Sunlight made the mud glow on the bank and turned the grasses by my feet into thin pieces of gold. Phantom insects were landing on my legs.

"Come on! Just jump."

"Are you sure it's deep enough?" I called.

Amber nodded. "That's where I jumped in last time," she said – and at that moment Briony aimed a colossal splash in her direction. Amber screamed as a wall of clear water showered down over her head and, delighted, she turned to face her assailant, arms raised to chop down sharply onto the water. But Briony had lowered herself until she was eye-deep for protection. She stared at Amber like a crocodile.

"Do it!" shouted Ash, in the water up to his shoulders. "Can't join in much from up there."

Another insect was crawling up the inside of my arm. I ran a hand over my skin to make it go. The stones were sharp beneath my feet. The group on the other side of the bank – with the camping chairs – were all watching me.

I took several steps backwards until the ledge shielded the river from view. Casting an eye over the bank to make sure nobody was about to stroll across my path, I reached the end of the ledge, bent my legs and, to the sound of my friends crying *She's not!* and *GO ON!* – launched myself clean from the bank.

I was practically a coiled spring. I flew longer than I'd intended, and for a moment hung suspended over the water.

Through the sound of everyone's cheers, I could clearly hear Amber's approval. The surface of the river was spread out below me. Gentle ripples circled from my friends where they stood, making a loose constellation in the water. A sharp rock stuck out from the shallows, and a clump of lichen was bobbing up against it. The far bank had a dip carved into it from so many feet, and a branch close by was snapped and dangling from the main tree. The freshly revealed split flashed against the bark.

I was in the air, tucked into a ball. I had just enough time to think: *There.*

The blurry world raced past my face, and the surface of the water rose up to meet my body, and I broke through the top. All this changed, and I was acutely aware that wherever I had been was elsewhere. I closed my eyes, and everything went dark. I no longer felt wet.

My ears filled with a silent squeeze, and my eyes closed more tightly as I went down, and my body was glazed with something fresh and endless. I was an ice-cube dropped into a drink. I tipped forwards, a slow somersault, and stretched out my legs, my arms beginning a stroke, muscles working through my chest to propel myself. I didn't ascend; I kept moving further. My eyes opened.

There was no riverbed. A solid expanse of glowing white filled everything. Specks of dust hung there, completely still, winking at me.

There was nothing there, held like a multi-dimensional web in a bright frame, an empty paper shell. Dazzlingly full of emptiness.

The remaining energy from the plunge gently flipped me over and I observed this absence from the other way up. Looking down across my body below, I brought my arm to my face and wiggled my fingers. Trails of air popped into existence and quickly vanished. I laughed – the sound had its corners knocked off, and it tumbled away. The push of my voice sent me spiralling through the silence, as steady and calm as the bright expanse around me.

Within the white, a number of planes and angles seemed to vanish, in complementary shades of brightness.

I floated on through a great diamond shape. My skin had a soft glow, a dusky light like a painted reflection. I gazed into the distances: some were very far off, and some were infinite.

For a moment I let my arms drift up, my body suspended gently. Far within the nothingness, soft suggestions of walls, blocks and thin outlines of edges flashed into disappearance.

The wash blew around me. When I took a breath, I rose slightly.

I turned around to admire my powerful tail, a little longer than my legs, made of the same tough skin and bone. The tail waited. I beat it once and sent myself flying through the place I found myself to be.

I closed my eyes and kicked my new tail again, feeling the press of air on my face as I dashed on readily towards the great smooth plane of white, so far away.

THE GREEN CALLING

Storm Constantine

She feels she is losing her humanity, bleeding into the green and the damp. Her flesh is sprouting silvery, scaly fungus that has to be dabbed with ointment every night. She is never dry. And now, trapped and held by the vengeful green, the legends no longer seem implausible.

It was Canvey's notes that started it off.

At night, the man-woman looked in through the screen door. It seemed to be naked, its skin covered in a green pigment.

A man-woman? Could mean anything. An effeminate boy, a masculine girl. Some deranged dream of Canvey's. Perhaps only an illusion, kindled in the sputtering lamplight, a face beyond the screen. The green calling.

Silva wishes she'd never seen those words. It is too easy to believe in them when it's dark.

She dreamed of rain for three consecutive nights before she began the journey that led her inevitably to Canvey's Retreat, on the inner jungled slope of an extinct volcano, in the heart of the Neotropic cloud forest. Not gentle, soothing rain but furious hot downpours; unending and corroding. It was presentiment perhaps, or just an educated guess.

Now, bathed in a patina of her own sweat, she sits gazing at the gauze-covered window openings of the Retreat, wrapped in a steamy lamp-light haze, listening to the pitiless downpour beyond the mouldering walls. Dying insects convulse upon the page beneath her hands, poisoned by the odourless insecticide painted onto the inner walls. The desk she is sitting at groans as she shifts her position to glance at the place above her right wrist, where her dark-coloured shirt leaves the skin exposed. There is a strange discoloration of the flesh there, a strange consistency. Deliberately, Silva pulls down her sleeve. A rogue torturing thought meanders through her sluggish mind: *I will never go home, never. I will stay here forever until the moulds and the lichens cover me and kill me.* She stands up abruptly to stem the discouraging mantra. She opens the screen door and looks outside.

Beyond the meagre light of the lamp, the night is hot-breathed, pungent, saturated darkness. Silva feels the jungle's presence rather than sees it; she senses its voluptuous oppressiveness. She knows that somewhere out there her companion preservationist, Lal, is intruding into the brutal, deadly lushness, perhaps crouched beneath a drooping tree-fern, or squatting on the sodden walkway that cuts a perilous pathway through the foliage.

"Where are you?" Silva hisses into the night.

Lal is not human, but a multi-task biomech, laboratory bred, laboratory tested. To some degree Silva shares this heritage, even though her specialities, her genetic nudges are widely different from Lal's. In many ways, the jungle is their mother, enveloping and vast: it spawned the plants that surrendered the magical elixirs which permeated the womblike fluids in which Lal was constructed by molecular computers and Silva floated as a foetus. Silva, like Lal, is an experiment. For the experiment to be successful, she will never age. She is the daughter of Longevity Program VI. The fate of daughters/sons one to five remains unknown to her.

Silva does not want to call out into the dark. She is afraid of what she might invoke, something other than the sleek wet form of Lal, something so very *other.* Then again, she hates to be alone here at night. It's too easy to succumb to the feeling she is being watched. She has two human assistants, Luis and Jesus, who are locals, but they take one of the vehicles back down the trail to the village at the end of every afternoon. Silva is spending more and more time alone, poring over the documents and data-disks that are bursting from every damp wooden box and rusting crate in the Retreat. Most of them can be junked but there are jewels to be found; Canvey was one of Virichem's best operatives. Now that he is dead, his notes and files are treated with reverence. They are to be preserved – the paper documents laminated; the magnetic media transferred to holocrystal. Canvey supervises these procedures from the walls. There are dozens of photographs of him as a young man pinned up around the desk. He was sixty-seven when he died; alone, uncared-for, malnourished. The victim of a stroke. There are no photographs of himself as an older man. Only the memory of his youth kept him company. And who knows what wild ideas Canvey came up with, living alone up here in this wilderness? Who knows what he might have discovered?

"So much information is lost every day," Silva's mentor Alcestis had once said to her. "Every day, priceless human knowledge crumbles to dust. Data is corrupted, never to be regained."

"But surely someone else will think of it one day?' Silva had said, frowning. "There are so many of us. Someone will think the same thing again."

"That is not the point," Alcestis had replied stiffly. "Each mind colours the information it generates with its own unique tone. There is no such thing as precise reproduction."

It was Alcestis who'd encouraged Silva to specialise in information preservation. Alcestis had been a young research grad then. Now, she is a woman going grey who's discovered her metabolism is inexorably slowing down. Silva still looks like a teenager. She and Alcestis have maintained a close friendship via computer link for a long time, but never meet face to face any more. Alcestis resents growing old.

Thinking of Alcestis, Silva wonders whether she should go back indoors and call her via the laptop. The laptop will not last for much longer, she is sure. At this very moment, in this landscape of speedy adaptation, a new mould is bound to be developing that specialises in eating computers. Silva wants to tell Alcestis about the patch of strange skin on her arm; she wants reassurance. Alcestis has a medical background; she will know things the over-worked, not-too-informed local doctor will not. Silva has been putting this call off for several days.

She glances at her watch to try and work out what time it is where Alcestis lives. The watch has stopped. She notices its face is partly occluded by a yellowish stain. Tears of weary frustration gather in her eyes. A dear friend, years dead, had given her that watch. Now it is tainted, half eaten by the jungle. She removes it lovingly saying under her breath, "I hate this place."

The laptop makes a disturbingly unfamiliar noise when Silva turns it on, a tired whine deep in its micro-depths. A moment of panic, the fear of being isolated is interrupted by a more sensible thought: so, order another one! (*But what if the roof-dish falls apart? What if... What if...?*) The computer utters a musical sequence. Silva squats down in front of it and turns off the video eye. Presently Alcestis' face will appear on the screen, while all Alcestis will see on her home monitor is Virichem's logo. It is better that way. Silva is worried that if Alcestis should see her, she'll be compelled to make some kind of light-hearted sarcastic comment. Silva doesn't want to hear anything like that, because the words will drip with pained bitterness. The two women haven't seen one another for years. People like Silva never feel comfortable speaking about what makes them different. There is a kind of unity in that. At least, Silva has never heard them speak. In the centre where she grew up, there were other genetic experiments; some more obviously so than others. They never fell for the spiel that they were *special*. Some of them died too young, others simply fell apart: emotionally, psychologically and in a few sad cases, physically. Silva is one of the lucky ones. And yet, even now, at the age of 37, there is a danger Silva might begin to age dramatically, or develop a plague of cancers, become blind, lose her hair. She has seen some of those things happen to others. Bald children eaten from the inside; faulty flesh machines. The time that Silva lives through never really feels as if it belongs to her. Is that because of what she is, or simply part of feeling human, being a woman? Does Alcestis feel the same?

"Oh, you're going out." It is obvious to Silva that Alcestis has dressed up for some occasion. Gems sparkle at the corner of each eye. The woman looks good; she's lost weight, although the lines on her face seem deeper.

"Silva! How are you? How's the jungle? Oh, God it's been so long! I feel awful... I'm just..." Alcestis pulls a comical face and sits down before her video eye. "What the hell! Five minutes? He can wait!"

"You look great!"

"Nonsense! You can only see me from the waist up. Gravity is winning the battle with my willpower, my love, never mind my muscles! I've got Researcher's Arse; comes from sitting at a monitor all day!"

"No really, you look…"

Alcestis interrupts. "So, how's it going? Had Canvey discovered all the secrets of the universe as everyone thought?"

Silva shakes her head, even though Alcestis can't see her. "If he did, I've yet to come across the evidence. I think he was off his head at the end. There's some very weird stuff."

"Oh?"

"Yeah. I think he was seeing things! I've found these notes about, well, *creatures*." Silva's laugh sounds a little embarrassed even to herself.

"Creatures, eh?" Alcestis grins and wipes a lock of hair from her brow. "What kind?"

"He describes them as green men-women."

Alcestis shakes her head. "Hmm, perhaps you should lose that stuff. Sure he wasn't writing a novel?"

"Hadn't thought of that actually. He was looking into local legends, though I'm not sure whether he made them up or not. This place is a bit creepy."

"Yeah, you sound… tense."

Silva is sure that Alcestis is wondering whether she should ask her to turn on the video eye. Her concern would make her want to inspect her friend, but Silva knows Alcestis is afraid that what she would see might sicken her, anger her. She'd once said, 'the worst thing about growing old is that I can remember what it was like to be beautiful.' Silva respects that and yet she wants Alcestis to see her. She needs reassurance.

"It's bad for the health here, so damp."

"How much longer have you got to stay?"

Silva shrugs. "Until the job's done. I've got a biomech assistant, but Rodgers gave it some other task to do. It's always out collecting samples. Isn't much help. Al..."

"What?" The image suddenly shifts, blurs. Silva's heart jumps. *Don't fade, don't go...*

"I've got this patch on my arm. Think it's some kind of fungus, but it won't respond to treatment."

Alcestis frowns. "Is it spreading?"

"No... I don't think so. It doesn't hurt. I've tried a topical anti-fungal agent on it, which might be keeping it down, but it won't cure it. Everything gets eaten by mould and fungus here. I don't like it."

"Can you get to a local doctor?"

"Yeah, it was she who gave me the ointment."

"What was her prognosis?"

Silva sighs. "She sees so much, so many diverse ailments. The jungle causes them. She says she often sees cases that she knows she'll never see again. She didn't seem that worried though."

"But *you* are..."

"Well... I suppose I've got a touch of Cabin Fever." Silva laughs. "I'm scared I'll turn into a walking mushroom, like something out of an old Japanese horror movie!"

"Are there any other symptoms?" Alcestis asks, suddenly and sharply.

"What do you mean?" There is a moment of tense silence, during which Silva incubates a hot core of anger. "It's not cancer!" she says at last, "and no, there are no other symptoms."

There is another moment of silence and then Alcestis says, "Turn on the video, Silv."

"No, there's no need. I'm fine."

"We had a promise!"

"Now is not the time to honour it, Al. Really. I'm fine."

Alcestis sighs. "Look, I'm not going to mince words. Get back to that doctor and if she has the facilities in that godforsaken place, get her to check you for soft sores. You can't afford to play around, Silv."

Silva is furious. She wants to say, *you want me to die, you want me to fall apart. You're wishing it!* but it is not in her nature to confront people. "OK," she says.

"I mean it, Silv!"

"I said OK. Look, don't you have a date waiting? I'll call you back some time. Take care, Al." Abruptly, Silva breaks the connection.

For several minutes she sits stiffly, paralysed by rage. How dare Alcestis say those things. She inspects the place on her arm where the discoloration stains her skin. It is not a soft sore, she's sure. It's something else, it has to be – something jungle-born. The face of Canvey, youthfully thin, grins down from the wall. He stares beyond her.

Silva lies sleepless on her bed, the Retreat grinding and flexing around her. The forest is chastened by a hurrying wind. Before dawn, Lal comes in and stands by the window processing information. Its hum is comforting, even though it lacks the human desire or sensitivity to utter a greeting to Silva. Its shape is vaguely human so that it can give public presentations without causing distress to children. It can speak in a computerised voice that sounds vaguely West Indian. Staring at it in the dark, Silva is convinced it has a personality, a soul; Lal just keeps itself to itself. Its work fascinates it, but nothing else is of interest. It is blessed with the ability never to feel lonely. Neither, Silva is sure, can it feel afraid.

Early morning. Mist hangs down from the forest canopy in shrouds. The air is not hot, but it is very humid. Silva is standing on the damp wooden walkway that has been constructed as a precarious safe route through the forest. The planks feel spongy underfoot; already the wood is rotting. Silva is playing a game with herself. In this game, the forest is the garden of Eden, the primordial garden. In Eden, there was only one of every tree, shrub and fern. Here, it is the same – almost. Two tree ferns, remnants of a prehistoric age, grow close together in the lush foliage. Overhead, aerial gardens of orchids, ferns and mosses droop tendrils downwards. Everything is poisonous in Eden – plants, animals and insects – but Silva knows that natives to this land build up an immunity to such things. Luis and Jesus are up at the Retreat transferring some data Silva has prepared onto holo-crystals. Today, Silva is trying to feel positive, actively fighting lethargic depression. (*There is nothing wrong with me.*) Standing there, on this narrow sanctuary, she has to fight the compulsion to step off the path. Potential death lies to either side. Luis has told her to watch out for the *ajo* vine; if someone steps on one, they become irretrievably lost in the forest.

What would happen if I did that? Are there any foundations to their legends? Perhaps the vine gives off some kind of vapour if it's bruised that causes disorientation. There is an explanation for everything.

The forest canopy meets over her head and invisible animals and birds traverse the aerial pathways. Silva squints upwards, narrowing her eyes into the green.

What else lives here unseen?

The jungle is older than memory, and though partially ravished by the encroachment of humanity, still able to reserve a deep inner chastity that is both dangerous and inviolable. Silva wonders whether she can will something inexplicable to manifest before her eyes, whether she can fool the jungle into giving up one of its secrets. Green men-women? The wistful fancies of a lonely madman. No such thing. And yet, as she thinks that, the sensation of unseen eyes fixed upon her unguarded back sweeps over her like a wash of fetid, warm water. She can smell something that reminds her of vomit, or certain species of fungi, sweet carrion. Something is waiting to drop onto her from the whispering canopy; something is *thinking* of dropping down onto her. She looks over her shoulder, and there is a blur of green movement at the corner of her vision, but then there are always blurs of green movement in this place. Silva has yet to develop what Luis and Jesus call search image – a refined visual sensitivity to the teeming shadows of the jungle. There is nothing between me and the Retreat, she thinks. I can get back at any time. She can even see the walls of the place at the end of the walkway: a short run.

The noise of the forest seems to have fallen; it is like a song being sung in a lower key than usual. Silva's precise footsteps sound loud on the soaked boards. She turns her gaze back up towards the canopy overhead, strains to discern some camouflaged shape amid the green. Then, there is a sound which could have been a human laugh or the call of a bird, and a cascade of warm liquid splashes down onto Silva's upturned face. She splutters and stumbles, surrounded by a lemon ammonia reek. Urine! It has got into her eyes, her mouth. She is blind, fumbling along the handrail, retching uncontrollably. Luckily, Luis hears her curses and spittings, and comes out of the Retreat to investigate. He laughs as he hears her angry explanation, as she wrings her trembling wet hands and paws the front of her shirt.

Urine. Yes. Monkeys do that. Piss onto travellers. Monkeys.

Later, her hair and body washed in the primitive shower – lukewarm gritty water – her mouth well sluiced with mint mouthwash, Silva sits down at Canvey's desk to work. Her head is wrapped in a towel, her body in a robe. Lal lurks somewhere in the room behind her, though wrapped in its own thoughts as usual.

Earlier, Silva asked it what it thought about Canvey's notes on the subject of humanoid life-forms in the forest. Lal was philosophical.

"I would rule nothing out in this place. So much of this territory is uncatalogued, but then one would suppose the native people would know more about it, if it existed."

"Supposing they'd want to tell us," Silva added. "We are the despoilers after all."

"I doubt whether everyone holds that view," Lal said, and then utilising its intuition banks, added, "Have you discovered some more evidence to support Canvey's theory?"

Silva shrugged. "I don't think so. Perhaps I'm looking too hard for evidence, and they do say that an obsessed seeker will inevitably find what they're looking for... in one way or another."

"Whether they create it for themselves or not," Lal added. "Perhaps that explains Canvey's notes. He was searching for a dream."

Silva laughed. It amused her to hear the machine speak in that way.

"I intend to work outdoors tonight," Lal said. "Will you be all right alone?"

It was the first time it had expressed concern for Silva's welfare. She immediately became suspicious, defensive. "Of course I will! Why shouldn't I be?"

Lal was impervious to waspishness. "Well, keep the bleeper by you, anyway. I won't be too far away."

As Lal ambled, in its strange gliding gait, towards the screen door, Silva grabbed a limb that, in a human, would be an arm. "What do you know?" she asked, eyes narrowed.

"Regarding what?"

"Why are you suddenly bothered about my wellbeing?"

Lal gently pulled away from her hold. "I am merely empathising with you. You are my close colleague. It is one of my utilities."

Silva let it go.

The night presses down on Silva. She is trying to read some scrawling notes of Canvey's, which at some time must have got wet. It is a difficult, rather pointless task. She has her hands over her ears, because she keeps tuning in on strange noises outside. Of course, these noises will have been there ever since she arrived, only now her active mind insists on applying labels to them. She can hear what sounds like whispered conversation in high, clicking voices, or conversation that's coming from an old radio hidden just inside the forest. Occasionally, a howler monkey will roar like a drunken man. There are no lights outside.

Her arm is itching slightly. When she scratches the strange skin, some greasy, silver scales come off under her nails. Soft sores? No! Soft sores usually originate in the groin or armpits, moist areas. (*But everywhere is moist in this climate!*)

"Oh, stop scaring yourself!" Silva says out loud.

She turns a page. Canvey was writing in brown ink, a colour like dried blood. She realises she hasn't been reading the words for some time, only scanning the pages while paying acute attention to her own agonised thoughts. Now, a few sentences seem to leap at her from the page. Above them are some notes on forest biomass; below a list of provisions Canvey once required from the research station downtrail. But the words in between, like a bolt of inspiration, stand out alone. Curling script. A feeling of ancient times.

They come at night – though never seen. **Dawn** *– they manifest, come through to me. Green dawn – time of the undying. Like water children. Sleek as seals, or fish...*

Silva reads the words several times. She cannot help feeling that Canvey must have woken up momentarily from a lethargic state, became truly alive, to write them.

Silva can feel her heart bumping. Sitting there alone in the modest halo of the hurricane lamp, there can be no question of disbelieving what Canvey wrote. He'd meant it. He'd seen what he wrote about.

At first light, a flock of birds known as the *guardabarrancas*, the guardians of the ravine, wake Silva with their tinkling song. It sounds as if a thousand wind chimes are being subtly excited by a tantalising breeze. The light, when Silva opens her eyes, is opalescent, glowing. Gold-green radiance falls in spears across her bed, shining motes held in the beams. The air is cool, caressing, and has a sparkling taste, like fern wine. Silva is caught in a transient moment of pure Earth beauty, those times when the planet unveils itself, when it does not realise it is being observed by a member of the hungry race it spawned. Silva stretches languorously, ignorant of the moment, simply *being* it, when she becomes aware of an unfamiliar shape in the room. She realises someone is standing among the long coats – most of them Canvey's, one hers – that hang near the door.

'Lal,' Silva says, and props herself up on her elbows in the bed.

The shape moves forward a pace from the shadows. It is slim, green, alien; not Lal at all. Silva thinks: *Should I scream, jump up, find a weapon, or wake up?* These thoughts are quite lucid and calm.

Instead, she does nothing but observe.

The figure, though uncomfortably unfamiliar and impossible to categorise, has a sleek, streamlined beauty. There is a feeling about it of extreme age, yet vibrant youthfulness. It is hairless, and apparently sexless, though reminiscent of both genders. Muscular yet slight. Its eyes are a phosphorescent vivid green, like quetzal feathers. Despite its alien appearance, Silva is very much aware of its consummate Earthly origin. It is like the tinkling birdsong, the wild hazardous beauty of the forest, the magical light, made flesh. Like Silva, it is ageless.

We are kin… in a way, Silva thinks. There is no fear inside her, only a huge sense of expectancy.

Her visitor extends an arm; too long, out of proportion. It opens its mouth as if it is shaping words, but no sound comes out. It is encased by the ancient gold light of the cloud forest.

Then, the moment of pure beauty is ended, and the light changes, the birds lift from the trees in a ravening crowd, their song disordered.

Silva blinks into the shadows that are left behind. There is no-one in the room with her.

Alcestis calls midmorning.

"Can you believe it? Rod's going to be working just a hundred or so clicks away from you. Isn't that a coincidence?" Alcestis laughs. Today, she is very much 'at home', her hair tied up in a girlish knot on top of her head, peacock blue silk kimono hanging open to reveal the upper curves of a chest that is deeply tanned, but the skin is beginning to crinkle, like the most delicate tissue paper.

"Who's Rod?" Silva asks. She cannot help sounding cold because she hasn't forgiven Alcestis for the previous conversation they had.

"I've been seeing him…. Oh, he's inconsequential! The important thing is that I've invited myself out there with him! Silva, I'll be able to visit you!"

Silva is stunned by these words. Alcestis sounds like an excited teenager. She has not suggested a meeting since… since Silva hit twenty-five and Alcestis hit thirty. A parting of the ways. Tacit veil drawn over their association, the friendship mutating into whispers through the veil.

"Here?" Silva's voice sounds choked.

"There!"

"When?"

Alcestis pulls a face, shrugs. "Oh, a few days' time. Can't specify exactly when. I'll have a look around... I'm interested in Rod's field, after all. Maybe I'll play the entertaining companion for a while before scrounging some company transport and heading up to see you."

"It's not an easy journey," Silva says.

"No, it isn't," Alcestis agrees blithely.

"It's really very boring here."

"You're trying to put me off, aren't you!" Alcestis utters another laugh, almost convincingly.

"We haven't seen one another for so long."

"I *want* to see you, Sil.'

Silva is thrown into a panic by the threat of Alcestis' impending visit. She gets Luis to drive her down to the doctor's surgery in the village again. The doctor is a small Spanish woman, who, to Silva, looks as if she should be the heroine of a romantic novel.

Silva grins as she extends her arm for examination. "Can't you just scrape this stuff off?"

The doctor ignores the suggestion. "Any pain?"

"No."

"Itching?"

"A little."

"Try this ointment."

"Haven't I tried this before?"

"No."

Silva sighs. "What is it? You must have some idea."

The doctor shakes her small, perfect head. "I've seen nothing like it. At least it isn't spreading."

Silva clears her throat and utters the words she hates. "Could it be... cancerous?"

The doctor glances at her sharply. She knows nothing of Silva's background. "If it is, I've never seen cancer like it before. I'm fairly sure it's a simple fungal infection." She hesitates. "I could send a tissue sample down to the research station, if you're worried."

Silva stares at her arm for a moment, sucking her upper lip.

"Perhaps… Yes. Do." She wonders whether she should mention what she saw that morning standing in her room but decides against it. It could have been an hallucination, another terrifying symptom of an unspecified decline bubbling through, but she doesn't think it was. She doesn't *feel* it was. But then, of course, she'd make herself think that. The alternative is too horrible. She doesn't want to discuss it.

On the way back to the Retreat, partially comforted by having been touched by medical hands, Silva carefully interrogates Luis about Canvey. Luis manoeuvres the four-wheel drive vehicle with the panache of a rebellious teenager in his first car. Silva hangs on grimly to the roll bar.

"Canvey had some pretty weird ideas about what lived in the jungle," she says, as introduction. "Have you bothered to read any of his stuff while you've worked with it?"

Luis curls his lip and shakes his head. "No. He was a strange man. But these genius types often are, aren't they?"

Luis was educated in the city. Although born in a local village, his manners are very urbane, his speech barely accented. Now he works for Virichem, flitting between isolated research retreats. He has many skills in advanced technology but is essentially a handyman, doing any job that needs doing in this wild place.

"Perhaps it drove Canvey mad, living here alone," Silva says.

"He wasn't mad," Luis answers shortly. "He just didn't want to be an old man."

"Did you know him well?"

"He was a very nice person."

Silva realises this avenue of enquiry is going to be unproductive. "I wonder where he got these ideas about green-skinned people that live hidden in the forest…" There is no response. "Is that a well-known legend?"

"This land is alive with legends," Luis answers, with the pride of a man who has secrets the interloper can never penetrate. "There are whole cities buried beneath the vines. Deserted now, of course, but who knows what race once lived in them."

"Any of these ruins near here?"

"No. Not that have been uncovered anyway."

"Do you believe the green-skinned people exist, Luis?"

He grins at her as he savagely changes gear. Silva's head makes abrupt and painful contact with the roll bar. "Now what kind of question is that?" Luis says, grinning, and shakes his head.

She wonders what he'd say if she told him she thought she'd seen one of these people. She wants to believe that, because of his vague answers, Luis knows more than he lets on, but perhaps she's deluding herself, seeing evidence where there is none. Already her memory of the visitation is dimming. It's hard to believe she didn't dream it.

In the dawn, they come to her again – three of them this time. Silva slips from her bed and follows them out of the Retreat, acquiescing to, rather than obeying, their soft, insistent beckoning. Outside the air is radiant and the song of the *guardabarrancas* is a fountain of sound. Silva can see a golden walkway, a mist of gleaming rays, leading into the forest. She can walk upon it. It vanishes down through the thick foliage, down the side of the ravine. *I am dreaming*, Silva thinks, and keeps on walking. She passes the still form of a great sloth hanging from a low branch. She has never seen one this close before. Its fur is green with algae and inhabited by silver moths. A ribbon of data, remembered from Canvey's notes, which she read the day before, passes across her mind. *The majority of animals survive in this landscape by specialising... sometimes they are invisible to the casual observer...*

"I have the search image," Silva murmurs. "Now I can see."

The people of the green lead her downwards, to the heart of the dead volcano.

She stands upon a wide grey slab, gilded by lichens. A crowd of Canvey's dream people sway around her like blades of grass or stripes of viridian water; insubstantial. They reach out to touch her skin, nodding their small heads to one another, but she cannot feel their touch. One of them fingers her patch of scaly skin and recoils, as if burned. It flushes a deeper green, and communicates without speech, in an agitated way to its companions.

They believe I am the future of humankind, Silva thinks. *But I am not.* She feels they are pleased, even excited, by the phenomenon of her. How long have they been here? Are they recent blossomings of the humid, breathing green or the last remnants of an ancient breed? Silva does not know how to reach them. She feels too dazed to think rationally, too tired to lift an arm.

Alcestis takes charge as soon as she arrives, striding into the Retreat, throwing down her travelling bag, standing with hands on hips to address the two men, who look up at her with resentful suspicion.

"It stinks in here!" she announces, by way of greeting. "Where's Silva?"

Jesus resumes his work with deliberate slowness, leaving Luis, whom he knows can handle these city types, to answer the woman's question.

"She's not here."

"Then where can I find her?"

Luis shrugs. "She's probably outside."

"You're not being very helpful," Alcestis growls.

"I don't know where Ms Merin is," Luis responds politely. "She is under no obligation to report her movements to us. Can I be of assistance to you, Ms...?"

"I'm here to see Silva." Alcestis turns a complete circle on the spot, appraising the Retreat. "This place is falling apart. It smells like old mushrooms. How could anyone live here voluntarily?"

Luis is aware the question is rhetorical. "The job is nearly done," he says.

Alcestis raises her brows. "So quickly? When I spoke to Silva a week ago, she implied there was quite some ground to cover yet."

Luis clears his throat, and pointedly drops his eyes from Alcestis' stare. "It appears Ms Merin has discarded a large amount of material she felt was superfluous." He shrugs. "There was little here worth saving anyway."

Luis and Jesus do not know when Silva will be back. They say they haven't seen much of her for the past few days. Alcestis makes direct enquiries about her friend's health, but all the men will say is that Silva made two visits to the doctor downtrail. She does not, in their opinion, look ill.

When Lal makes an appearance soon afterwards, Alcestis does not find it at all helpful. The biomech is intent only on telling her about the research it has been conducting. "The evolutionary thrust in this area is towards a vast variety of species, with a wide area of dispersal. There is no spring protein pulse in the neotropics, therefore..."

"Excuse me," Alcestis interrupts. "This is no doubt very interesting, but I'm more concerned about Silva. Where is she and how is she?"

"Some varieties of species have yet to be discovered by us," Lal finishes. "Silva will be back at sunfall. She has adopted this habit recently. As to her physical condition, I would say this locality causes her stress. She is not sleeping well."

As it is early in the day, Alcestis decides to drive down to the village and speak to the doctor there. Before making this visit, before badgering her casual lover Rod into letting her come over here with him, she had wheedled her way into getting her hands on the case notes of previous longevity experiment subjects. Deterioration of their condition had begun with skin cancer; rapid aging had followed, accompanied by dementia, and paranoid hallucination. To her mind, Silva is very much in danger of going the same way. Alcestis has remained alert to the nuances of Silva's voice, even though she has refused to see her. The woman she spoke to recently was not the Silva she remembered. There had been a vagueness about her, which Alcestis felt camouflaged a kind of panic.

As she sends her vehicle screaming and bouncing down the outer skin of the volcano, she mutters to herself. "Would this be worth a few more years of youth? I don't think so! Who are they kidding! Why don't they give up!"

At the surgery, she claims to be Silva Merin's physician and friend, and demands information. The small, Spanish woman clearly objects to Alcestis' hectoring manner, and makes soft remarks about confidentiality.

"Don't you know anything about Silva Merin?" Alcestis demands, or rather accuses, and when no answer is forthcoming, replies to her question herself. "No! For your information, she is the product of genetic engineering. She is thirty-seven years old."

The doctor's eyes widen in surprise.

"Yes!" Alcestis says triumphantly. "And there is a possibility she is prone to sarcoma, oat-cell cancer in particular. I know she consulted you for a skin disorder. Didn't you bother to have samples analysed?"

"As a matter of fact, yes," the woman answers stiffly. "They are currently being processed. I only took the sample a week ago."

Alcestis rolls her eyes almost gleefully. "You should have taken a sample when you first saw her. Was there evidence of any other disorders? What about her mental state?"

"She seemed like a very self-possessed young woman. The sore she showed me did not resemble oat-cell. It was a fungal infection."

"I hope you're right!" Alcestis snaps. "Let me know the minute you get those results. I'm staying up at Canvey's Retreat."

As soon as she walks into the Retreat, Alcestis knows the men have been talking about her. The thick silence contained by the rotting walls is gravid with recently uttered criticism. Lal too has a furtive air, hovering in the background.

"You!" Alcestis says, pointing at the biomech. "Am I wrong, or is one of your functions to monitor the condition of your colleagues in remote employment locations?"

"You are not wrong," Lal answers silkily, gliding forward. "Might I be of assistance?"

"Have you monitored Silva recently?"

"I monitor her constantly, as a background utility."

"And you have computed no conclusions as to her condition."

"She is under stress. She worries."

"And the skin problem?"

"She has a fungal infection."

Alcestis makes a growling noise to signify her exasperation. "You took samples?"

"No. She has not asked me to."

Alcestis narrows her eyes and jerkily nods her head. "Well,

you're certainly fulfilling all your functions, aren't you, lovey! Have you noticed no evidence of disorientation, absent-mindedness?"

"Unfortunately, I'm not that familiar with Ms Merin's personality to ascertain whether or not she is behaving abnormally." The biomech sounds frosty. "Now, if you will excuse me…" It attempts to pass by the woman, who is blocking the door.

"Fetch her," Alcestis says firmly. "I need to see Silva now. Although none of you *appear* to have noticed, she needs attention. Urgently."

Lal answers politely. "I would comply with your request if I could but regret I don't know where Ms Merin is at this present time."

Another growl. "Don't give me that. Of course you know where she is, or else you're an inferior model in a Meg 6 skin! What are you playing at?"

The men have remained silent, almost as if they hope their lack of noise will make them invisible to this storming female. Now, Luis clears his throat and says, 'She strays off the trail. She could be anywhere. Only the walkways are monitored."

"And you haven't tried to stop her?" Alcestis explodes. "Doesn't her behaviour strike you as irrational? She is not a person to take unnecessary risks."

Luis' eyes drop back to his work.

"This is outrageous!" Alcestis shouts. She flexes her shoulders. "Well, if none of you will go out and bring Silva back, I will! Tell me where to start looking at least."

For a tense moment, there is only silence and then Jesus mumbles. "You could try the path down to the crater." He cringes beneath Luis' sudden warning glance.

"There is no path," Luis says in a low voice.

Jesus shrugs. "There is now. She's made one." He points through the window screen. "That way. Down."

Silva is lying in a pool of green radiance, surrounded by the swaying, lustrous forms of the forest-born. Their eyes glow fondly, mirroring the flashing feathers of the flock of quetzals that wheel about their heads. The rarest birds. Never more than one sighted at a time. A flock of the rarest birds. Silva sighs. She can feel her limbs melting into the green, into the moist earth. She is enveloped by the scent of unstoppable growth, enwombed by it. It all seems so clear to her now.

Canvey knew. He knew what these people were. Now, she cannot believe the emaciated husk that was found lying on the bed in the Retreat was really him. She feels he is close to her, one of them. He is watching her now, just a few feet away. She does not dispute his body died, but the spirit of him, the spirit… Another sigh escapes her like a breath of dawn mist. Canvey knew. He had the search image. He learned to see the immortals, to become part of the miracle that is unfurling here amid the green. And she is becoming part of it too. The forest spawned her; a miracle spore helped unravel the braids of her DNA and reformed them in a secret image. Sentience. Green sentience. And now she is home, unravelling once more, transforming.

The figures lean over her, spinning round in her sight, and ribbons of her essence spill out to be taken by their hands. They will dance these ribbons into a new shape. And she welcomes it.

Alcestis can see at once that degeneration is taking place. She can see Silva lying on her back in a clearing in the forest that looks as if it has been torn out by human hands. Alcestis has no doubt that, should she examine Silva's hands, they will be cut and abraded by vines and tough stems. Insects will have burrowed into her unprotected skin, laid their eggs there, liquefied her flesh to feed. Uttering a cry of heartfelt anguish, Alcestis pushes her body frantically through the resistant green. In the emerald light of the forest, Silva's damp skin looks greenish, terminally sick. There is hardly any flesh to her at all. She appears at once mummified and putrescent.

"No, no, no…" Alcestis murmurs a prayer of denial as she stumbles over the short remaining distance that separates her from her friend. She falls to her knees and scoops Silva up in her arms, horror and an unfamiliar sense of helplessness bringing equally unfamiliar tears to her eyes. She hugs the flimsy body to her. "No, no, no..." But even as she tries to deny the terror of what is happening, and fights an inevitable, desperate grief, there is a sickening part of her that thinks, *She isn't beautiful any more. She isn't young.*" The sly inner voice that utters these words is almost too soft to be heard. It can easily be silenced or ignored.

Suddenly, Silva twitches in Alcestis' arms.

"Sil! It's me," Alcestis croons. "I'm here. I'll take you back... God, why didn't any of those ass-holes do anything about this?"

Silva moans and turns her head slowly from side to side. Then she opens her eyes, and Alcestis can see that they are filmed, unfocussed, the eyes of a dead woman, or someone so old their sight is obscured by cataracts. She realises then that taking Silva anywhere would be futile. It is too late. The experiment, though undoubtedly useful, has failed.

"Al," Silva murmurs. "What are you doing?"

"Doing? Doing? I'm gonna have Virichem by the balls, that's what! That goddamned biomech must have known this was happening, must have been monitoring... God, it's sick! They knew! They did nothing!"

"No," Silva murmurs. "They don't know... They don't have..." She manages a weak smile, a grim parody that resembles the grin of a fleshless skull. "It's all right, Al, don't be scared. This is all part of it..."

"Oh, my baby!" Alcestis grips Silva's body firmly, as if trying to keep her spirit earthbound. "I'm with you. Of course it's all right."

"No." Summoning what must be the dregs of her strength, Silva tries to raise herself. "Can't you see? Can't you see *them?*"

"Who, honey?"

"The forest-born. They're all around us. Look, Al, look at them. This is why you don't have to worry. They're taking care of me, taking care of me during my change..."

Alcestis feels a finger of fear claw her spine. For a moment, she feels Silva is talking sense. But all she has to do is raise her head to see that they are alone in the forest.

'There's no-one here," she says.

Silva frowns and then stretches her papery lips back into a ghastly smile. "Oh, of course. You don't have the search image. But you will Al, if you stay here long enough. You will. And then we can be together always." She sighs weakly and her head drops back against Alcestis' arm. Her hair is coming out on the sleeve of Alcestis' jacket. Her body is a decaying husk holding the soul of a vibrant girl. So cruel.

This is what life does to us, Alcestis thinks. *This will come to me also, but in my case the stalking is slow and measured. It takes a little away, bit by bit, but at the end it will be the same.*

"Oh God!" she says aloud and throws back her head. It seems the forest, the interminable, wretched, burning green, is spinning round her head. Birds shriek and the mocking howls of monkeys fill her head. It seems they are jeering at the puny women below them. Squatting there amid the ageless green, Alcestis is painfully aware of her own mortality. It is lying in her arms. Her worst fear made manifest. Decay. Age. The bitter memory of youth. Death.

Silva's voice is little more than a grating whisper. "Don't worry," she says, as her rebellious meat corrupts. "We can be together here always, face to face. Stay awhile. Rest awhile. We can be young together always."

In the Retreat, Jesus raises his head from his work. His eyes reflect the green-glowing light as the rainclouds gather outside. "She is blessed!" he says, in his native tongue. "It doesn't matter about that other woman."

Luis is systematically destroying data, unsure of in which world his feet are rooted: the past, the present or the future. Grim-faced, he ignores his colleague's remarks. Later, he will get drunk.

Lal mutters to itself, unheard.

Somewhere, a long way away, the daughter of Longevity Program VII draws breath. Her name is Hope, the secret name of all of who came before her.

THE MYDFORD MEDUSA

Freda Warrington

Brian and Joyce had walked here since their first date at sixteen, and still walked here now on the day of their Diamond Wedding Anniversary. Mydford Ridge rose modestly above the ancient village that lay to their left. On their right, heathland rolled down into the river gorge then rose again into waves of classic English pastureland. Green and gentle, divided by lush hedgerows and oak trees that had stood since medieval times. Here on top of the ridge, the ground was eroded by walkers and pierced by slabs of volcanic rock.

Their black spaniel, Polly, was nosing through the bracken, disturbing butterflies, squirrels, and an indignant stoat.

On the village side, the ridge sloped away towards the cricket pitch and Mydford proper. Amid the grey slate roofs could be seen the church tower, the primary school and the pub, all built of granite and so old they were part of the landscape. Until five years ago, there had been nothing on the far side of Mydford except some nondescript fields and the narrow curving lane that led towards the main road. Now those fields were lost under a sea of red-brick housing. Fabulous 'Phase I' of stunningly over-priced executive homes. A certain proportion were classed as 'affordable'. Affordable in some parallel universe, maybe, thought Joyce.

No amount of petitions, campaigns or appeals to the planning officer had made a dent in the builders' plans.

"It doesn't look so bad from this distance," said Joyce. "Still gives me a start when I see all those new houses, though."

"Like a raw wound," said Brian. "Like they plonked a brand new town next to us. History means nothing to them."

"Will we ever get used to it?"

"No," said Brian. "I won't, anyway. They can use all the fine words they like: it's inappropriate development. Desecration."

"I know people need somewhere to live, but ..."

"They're obsessed with building miles from bloody anywhere,

so the new folk all have to commute," Brian said in the low, grumpy tone that had become habitual.

Joyce returned her attention to this side of the ridge, the so-far-unspoiled side: the valley with its dense greenery and the little river Myd winding along the bottom. Sorrow was a broken rock in her heart. This had been her special place, her soul-home, all her life. It was the treasure of the village, a special hidden landscape precious to the locals. Or it had been. Now it was only 'Mydford Meadows Phase II,' the site of the next development.

MYDFORD UNDER THREAT! read the huge banners that stood on every lane into the village.

The residents' campaign had delayed Phase II for three years so far, but at least half of the district council didn't care. They murmured in support of the builders, who insisted this would be a *"Sympathetic development, designed to preserve the natural features of the area."* In other words, their ridge would remain as a footpath through an ocean of brick and tarmac.

"Oh Lord, Brian, look." She pointed downhill and there, on the verdant side, was a swarm of folk in fluorescent yellow jackets and hard hats. Some walked along the valley floor in a pack; a couple of others were working with theodolites. "What're they doing? They don't have permission yet! This is outrageous."

"Oi! Hey, you!" Brian bowled his way down the steep side of the ridge, faster and faster, trampling the young bracken. Polly scampered after him. Joyce was terrified Brian would fall, the way he was brandishing his walking stick and running out of control.

"Oh," she gasped, following as fast as she could. "Oh."

"Excuse me!" said Brian, striding up to the nearest surveyor. He was a young man, pale of skin and hair. At the sight of Brian's florid face, he looked startled. "What the devil's going on here?"

"Er … surveying the site, mate."

"There is no site, *mate*," Brian retorted. "You've no planning permission. You can't start work without it."

The youth in the hard hat shrugged. "Just following the boss's instructions. We can't submit plans without surveying first."

"You're wasting your time," said Brian. "There'll be no new building here."

The surveyor shrugged and stuck his hands in his pockets. He scuffed the wiry grass with the steel toe of his boot. "I'm sorry, sir, I'm new. Just doing my job. You'll have to take it up with the council."

"Oh, we have, and we will." Brian was so red in the face, Joyce feared he might have a heart attack. "And what are *they* up to?" He pointed at the strolling group.

"That's, er, Mr Bland showing district councillors around the site. He's the boss."

"Oh, we know who Bland is. Don't forget, we're keeping an eye on you." He pointed his forefinger between the hapless young man's eyes, almost touching the bridge of his nose. "All of you. You stick *one peg* in the ground without permission, I'll have you."

"Brian," Joyce said, breathless. She clipped the lead onto Polly's collar, pulled at her husband's jacket sleeve. "Come away. Leave him alone, it's not his fault."

Brian let himself be steered away. She made him take one of his angina pills, then they trudged down towards the river. He was too breathless to head back up the slope.

After a period of silence, he spoke. "You're right, love, he's just a workman."

"With a university degree, no doubt."

"And all his fancy equipment. Hmph, still, they're only measuring. It doesn't mean anything ... yet. Doesn't mean we've lost the fight. Got five thousand signatures so far."

"That didn't stop them on Phase I." Margery rubbed her breastbone. She felt a kind of panic, like a mother whose only child was about to be snatched away. "How can anyone *not* consider this an area of outstanding natural beauty?"

"Oh, they don't care. Look at them! Council and developers, hand in glove. Families need houses, obviously they do, but why here and not in town? Because property prices are fifteen percent higher here. That's what it's about; profit." Brian stabbed at the ground with his walking stick. "We're the nimbys. We're just a bunch of old farts. We don't matter, 'cos we'll all be dead soon."

The river that looped along the valley floor was barely more than a stream, shallow and rippling over stones. Joyce had found its source once, miles away in a tangle of ancient woods and fields. She'd been six years old at the time and had never been able to find it again. One of those magical places that shows itself once, then vanishes. Springs fed the stream as it meandered all the way through the village itself, across cattle meadows and down into this small wild gorge. Deer dipped their muzzles on the far bank.

In places the flow widened into deeper ponds where wildfowl gathered: ducks and moorhens, swans and herons, even pesky seagulls miles from the coast. Each pool tipped over a small waterfall and rushed on its lively way.

The hard hat party had stopped on the riverbank. Joyce recognised the stocky figure of Gideon Archer Bland, owner of G. A. Bland Homes. He was waving his arms expansively as he explained the marvels of Phase II to his audience of councillors and other interested parties.

"There'll be no need to re-route the river," he declared. "As shown on the plans, we'll be creating cycle paths and bridges, for the enjoyment of all residents, old and new. Mature trees will be preserved, along with green spaces. The marsh area will be fenced off, so that only the authorities have access to the reservoir, for the convenience and safety of residents. We are a green company, as you know. The proposed eco-houses and increased facilities for residents will be of huge benefit for the area."

Joyce turned away in disgust. Smug little man. No doubt he was perfectly adorable at home with his family, but his public face was ruthless.

She lost herself in the green glow of sunlight through the bracken and trees. The atmosphere changed by the minute here. Her tears blurred the light, making it even more beautiful. As she and Brian walked in silence, she plucked white and pink hawthorn blossoms, some yellow kingcups, and a few bluebells, only a very few, taking care not to damage the plants.

Ultimately the stream emptied into a lake a couple of miles further on. The land became marshy, sucking at their boots, and there was the big grey lake, remote and silent. Actually, it was a reservoir, but the pump housings on the far side were discreet. On a misty day you couldn't see them at all when the lake blended with the horizon. This side was overgrown with brambles and gorse and bulrushes, quietly busy with wildlife. Willows drooped to touch their reflections. So peaceful.

"At least they can't build on water," she said.

"I wouldn't put anything past them," said Brian with a huff.

Joyce stopped at the water's edge and scattered her flowers on the surface. Brian kept walking and didn't notice.

"Annie," she whispered. "Annie."

"Si! Knocking off time!" A flock of his fellow workers waved at him from a wooden stile. The stile was set into a thick hedge that separated the gorge from the farmland beyond. A public footpath led across the meadows to the village main street. The footpath would remain, but everything around it would be bulldozed and built over. "We're off down the pub. You coming or what?"

"Yeah, er … Go on, I'll catch you up," answered Simon, graduate surveyor. The new boy.

"Suit yourself. Last one there buys an extra round!"

The truth was, Simon wasn't in the mood for a noisy pub meal with his workmates. Once they were out of sight, he walked deeper along the valley, across marshland to a fringe of bulrushes. Beyond lay the reservoir. It was small as reservoirs go, but in the gloom it looked blue-grey and endless. The world was nearly silent. Just the rustle of reeds, the occasional squawk of an owl or some unseen water bird. The lapping of water was soporific.

He sat down on the damp grass. Pulled off his hard hat and ruffled his sweaty hair; the cool breeze felt great. Off came his steel-reinforced safety boots and hi-viz jacket; that felt even better. He'd had a strange day. Ever since that crimson-faced old man and his fussing wife had come rushing at him, he'd felt off-balance.

They had been so upset. Rage and despair had flared from them like a heat haze. What was he supposed to say? He was doing his job. *Don't engage with protestors*, the site manager had warned him. But they had reminded him of his grandparents, who were old and stuck in their ways but who cared so passionately about their rescue cats and their garden and their neighbours. If he'd seen his gran in distress like that, he would have put his arms around her and done anything to make things better.

He visualised the way the sun had shone through the trees, subtly changing all day. Shadows moving, clouds fleeting. The wind in the bracken, turning the green fronds silver. Birds singing their hearts out in hedgerows that would soon be ripped up by diggers…

Most greenfield sites were plain flat acreage that earned money for the farmer only if he or she sold it off. But even the dreariest field caused passionate opposition from the locals. *We walk our dogs here*, they always said. *There will be too much traffic. It's not safe. Our children should be able to play here, like we did. There are great crested newts!*

Bats! No infrastructure. You cannot, cannot *desecrate our countryside!*

But the protestors almost never won.

Was this place any different? It was prettier than most, with its hills and volcanic bedrock close to the surface; a challenging site. The village itself was old and charming, soaked in history. No wonder the locals didn't want it hemmed in by a sea of roofs, their views ruined, masses of extra traffic roaring down the narrow roads every day.

No one owns a view, Gideon Bland was fond of saying. *Everyone has a right to a home, but no one has a right to a view.*

From a pragmatic point of view, Simon agreed. But here, today, something had changed. He wanted to side with the heartbroken locals, because there was a special atmosphere in this valley. A deep, quiet magic. To imagine all its lavish green beauty replaced by luxury homes vaunting up the hillside, and the river fenced off behind steel safety rails, tarmac cycle paths, gardens so small the families could barely squash a child's trampoline into them... it made him feel ill. Once this place was transformed, it would be lost forever.

I'm going to resign, he thought.

Then, *Don't be absurd. Put myself out of a job? No references. If I meet a girl and we want to buy a little house, no wages to pay for our dreams. No future. And me being unemployed won't stop a single brick being laid here.*

A smoke-blue haze rose from the lake, turning the world to a foggy limbo. Something moved through the water. A shadowy wave, like the wake of a huge fish, passed slowly in front of him. He couldn't make sense of it. A shape poked out of the surface, a long slim tendril that writhed as if alive. What the hell he was looking at? Cormorants stuck their heads out of the water like that, but this thing... *undulated.* A snake? More tendrils followed, rising slowly like flexible periscopes. Alive, looking around, tasting the air.

These fronds glowed with greenish dots of light, like creatures from the deep ocean.

The sight was so eerie that he froze. Blood drained from his head, leaving him in a surreal fog. He was too dizzy to move. On the edge of fainting, he felt the whole world change around him, stretching and squeezing, turning into an endless marsh: an alien, secret dimension, bluish and rippling and hallucinatory.

First the long, questing tentacles, then a shadow began to rise from the water. Must be one hell of a fish, or some big water bird – but no, it kept rising and rising, first a head, then shoulders and the dim silhouette of a body, the rough size and shape of a human. This mass was draped in pondweed and thick ropes of hair.

Simon watched, mesmerised. The creature came towards him, wading slowly through the shallows. Female in shape but barely human. A slouching creature, indigo like the dusk itself, streaming with water as if a spring emanated from the crown of her head.

Her eyes shone with their own white corpse-light. He saw her teeth gleaming, small and sharp like a shark's. And her hair was not hair but a mass of fronds, each of which moved like seaweed in a tropical ocean current, barbed with tiny spines, *sentient.*

She came to him and rested one pale, human-ish hand on his shoulder. Cables of hair caressed his cheeks, heavy and slimy. Barbs scratched his skin and left fiery pain behind, as if he'd been brushed by stinging nettles. He held his breath, expecting worse, but the spines seemed to retract, lying flat as the creepers continued their exploration. The sensation was almost silky. Sensual, in a nightmarish way, like some dream in which he felt uncontrollable desire for a monster. He felt the ropes of her hair questing beneath his shirt. Slithering, gripping.

She smelled of rank water and greenery. Lake water trickled from her and soaked into his hair and clothes. Her breath, as she leaned down to kiss him, had the scent of damp stone.

The atmosphere in the council chamber was heavy, overheated, thick with ill-feeling. Angry residents formed a glowering phalanx. A deputation from G. A. Bland Homes sat with folded arms, suited, expressionless. Thirty-one council members gave off a toxic aura of fear, irritation, restless determination. On one side, they faced pressure from Government to build, build, build or risk losing millions in revenue. On the other, furious villagers ready to lie down in front of bulldozers to save their thousand-year history. Ready to unseat every single council member at the next election.

One campaigner was allowed to speak on behalf of the protest group. Just one. And he or she was permitted to speak for precisely three minutes. Not a second longer. To preserve all that was so precious – just *three minutes.*

Greg, a retired headmaster, had been nominated to present their case. He rose and spoke with eloquent passion. He wasn't allowed to speak of views or anything emotional in nature; he must stick to planning issues. Within that framework, he spoke of historical value, sites of special scientific interest, traffic issues, pollution and lack of school places. "Natural England, the Highways Agency and the Environment Agency have raised objections to this site going ahead. The council exceeds its remit in overruling those objections. For the good of all, your decision *must* be to reject this application."

He sat down, grim-faced but composed, to a roar of applause from the residents.

A representative of the construction company droned. Council members droned. Government targets, funding, five-year regional plan. Blah blah blah.

The vote was fifteen in favour, fifteen against. The council leader, one Nick Molson, used his casting vote to grant planning consent.

"How much did they pay you?" shouted someone.

Molson turned red, muttering something about slander. He was a known crook; the type that always got away with it. Joyce despised his cruel, gaunt face and stupid beard.

The developers grabbed their briefcases and shot out of the room at speed, triumphant. Groans of despair followed them. Molson barked at the furious residents to clear the chamber before the police were called. After that, in their very British way, they left in an orderly fashion, grumbling as they went.

Annie in the well
Annie in the well
Who put her down there?
We'll never tell!

Joyce lay awake half the night, tangled in nightmares. A childhood rhyme looped round and round her mind, echoing as if it were being chanted in a school playground. That was where she remembered it from: the village school, over sixty years ago.

Annie in the well
Annie in the well
Frogs and stones and
Annie in the well

Children were snaking around one girl in the middle. Some

kind of tag game. They moved in a double spiral, a circle that wound in, then out again. The chosen child had to grab the playmate nearest to them on the last word of each verse. Then the tagged one was *It*. The spiral march would start slowly, gathering speed until they were running like mad, screaming and giggling, to avoid being caught.

Annie in the well
Annie in the well
Sleeps in the water
White as a shell
Annie in the well
Annie in the well
Eels chew her eyeballs
Annie in the well.

There were umpteen verses. Slime and pondweed and hungry fish; every imaginable horror was visited on a poor little drowned girl a hundred feet down. Joyce couldn't remember them all. Last child tagged at the end of the last verse would suffer a gruesome forfeit; a jar of tadpoles tipped over their head, a lizard stuffed down their blouse or shirt. So much fun.

Annie in the well
Annie in the well
What's that smell?
Annie in the well!

"Joyce?" Brian woke beside her. "You having bad dreams again?"

"Mmph."

"Me too. I keep going over and over it in my head. What more could we have done? This isn't the end. We can appeal."

"How? We can't afford the legal costs of a judicial review. It's over, love."

"It is not over! No good, I can't sleep." Brian sat up, pushed his feet into slippers and huffed out of the bedroom. "I'm going to make some tea. Nearly time to get up, anyway."

Joyce lay back, looking at the ceiling. A faint light flickered between the curtains: rain, catching the streetlight as it fell. She could smell marshy water, rank with algae. Hear the chanting of children playing their long-forgotten game.

"Do you remember Annie?" she said.

Joyce and Brian stood looking through the railings of the village school, a granite structure nearly two hundred years old. The well was still there in the playground, albeit protected now by a heavy wooden cover and a wire fence to keep the children at a safe distance.

"Annie who?" Brian sounded exasperated. "What's wrong with you, Joyce?"

"Nothing. Well, apart from the council meeting last night, and not sleeping. Why?"

"You've been acting peculiar, that's why. Having nightmares. Saying weird things in your sleep. Wanting to come back to the school. I try to talk to you and you just stare through me. I know you're stressed about this building business, love, but I'm worried about you."

"Do you?" she said. "Remember Annie?"

"No. What's this about?"

"There was a little girl." The railings felt damp and rusty against her palms. "I don't know where she came from; a gypsy traveller family, I think. She was small and pale, dressed in rags, with hair like long rat's-tails down to her hips. The other children bullied her horribly. You must remember her, love."

He tutted and shook his head. "Joyce –"

"They made a rhyme about her. *Annie in the well, Annie in the –*"

"Stop!" He looked red-faced, aggrieved. "Joyce, that was an old folktale. If anything happened, it was at least a hundred and fifty years ago. Some old rumour about a little girl falling in – was it an accident or murder? Just an old tale to scare the children."

"Morning, you two!" Greg came up to them with his golden retriever at his side. He too had been a pupil at the school, and later its headmaster until his retirement, ten years ago. "Ah, the old place. Happy memories?"

"Oh, yes," said Brian. "Reliving our childhood, you know."

"Mm, I loved my time teaching here." Greg grinned. "Wouldn't go back for a million pounds, though. The children were fine, but their parents tried our patience to the *limit*."

Brian chuckled. Joyce turned and said, "You remember Annie, don't you, Greg?"

He looked puzzled. "Which one?"

"The little gypsy girl who got bullied. She had strange hair."

"Joyce is confused," Brian put in. "She's talking about the old game we used to play."

"Ah yes, of course. *That* Annie. The game pretty much died out after we had the well covered over, but children love a ghoulish legend, don't they? They can be little monsters."

"We were just debating when it happened, if it was even real. 1850?" Brian wore a *please help me out* expression.

"Oh." Greg scratched his chin. "You've got me there. I always thought it was a 18th century thing."

"No, I remember it happening," Joyce said, feeling doubt as soon as she spoke.

Both men looked at her with raised eyebrows.

"She's been having nightmares," said Brian. "It's all this development business."

"*She* is standing right here," Joyce retorted. "And I'm fine. Yes, Greg, just silly dreams."

"I'm so sorry about the way vote went." Greg sighed. "I feel it was my fault."

"Of course it wasn't," said Joyce. "You spoke beautifully."

"The vote was always going to go that way," Brian added. "That bloody Nick Molson – everyone knows he's bent. He bought a listed building, intending to knock it down and build on the land. When he couldn't get permission, it mysteriously burned to the ground. Convenient, or what?"

Greg nodded. "Trouble is, they can't prove anything."

"He should be behind bars." Brian tapped the school railings with his walking stick.

"Or down the well," Joyce said with a sour grin. "With poor Annie."

"Don't we all wish! I'd better get on." Greg shortened his dog's lead and lifted his hand in a quick wave. "Good to see you both; or would be, if things had gone our way..."

Once he was out of earshot, Brian started on her again. "There. From the headmaster's mouth: Annie was just a character in a story. The children in our time used to play a daft tag game: that's where you heard the rhyme. I'm taking you to the doctor if this carries on. So please *stop*."

Joyce obeyed, but the image was clear in her mind. *No, I saw her. She was so quiet and shy, she never spoke. Her hair was long, long, like tangled ropes. When they pushed her into the well, I cried for them not to do it. I looked in afterwards. She was too far down for me to help her... but I saw her face.*

She was smiling.

Simon was climbing a steep hill, the one that rose from the far bank of the Lyd. The meadows were lost beneath the shells of half-built houses stacked up the hill. Their silhouettes stood black against the glow of the night sky.

He climbed in a panic, his feet slipping on loose hard core. He had to cling onto fences and walls to avoid tumbling down into the stream. *It's too steep,* he thought. *The ground's not stable. What made them think they could build on here? No one would even get their car up this incline. It's madness. I have to make them stop.*

"It's an industrial estate, you idiot," a voice said from nowhere.

The buildings warped, and he saw that he was walking among vast factories and warehouses. Surrounded by wire safety fences, they looked more like bombed-out buildings than new structures. The stars glowed through their empty windows. He felt nerveless with terror. So hard to keep moving, but for some reason he *must* climb the endless vertical hill between the ruins.

Annie went ahead of him. She was vast, and she glowed like a pale fish through cloudy water. As long as she went on, he had to follow her.

She turned to look at him. Her face was beautiful, astonishing, her mouth as sweet as a bud; he was enthralled. She filled the sky like a goddess. Her hair became the flowing branches of a tree, full of stars.

His heart, soul, whole body swelled with adoration and terror. His feet slipped and he lost his balance. She reached out her hand to help him, but his fingers slid though hers and he fell backwards. The ground shook. The entire hillside was collapsing, and he found himself falling, caught in the landslide.

Rocks and earth showered down around him, along with great chunks of the crumbling buildings, sections of steel fencing. He dropped too fast even to feel fear anymore. Fell until the cold water of the Lyd received him, a bowl of icy water that was also Annie's cupped palm.

Nick Molson and Gideon Bland clinked glasses. The group around the pub table was in a buoyant mood: managers, planners, architects, 'all those in favour' from the council, everyone was raucous with triumph, gulping champagne. A couple of days post-victory, after an intensive inspection of the site, Bland had treated them to dinner *al fresco*. Perhaps it would have been diplomatic to do this away from Mydford, rather than rub the locals' noses in it, but he didn't care. He winked at Mclson, who grinned.

"Job done?" said the council leader.

"Jay. Dee. Job done," Bland agreed. They shook hands and burst into laughter.

Dusk was falling over the village, a bluish cloak. Wind stirred the beech and chestnut trees that bordered the pub garden. *Shame really*, Bland thought. He could smell water and bracken and damp earth, that good smell of the English countryside. Pretty little site, but change must come. Shame for the locals, but for him – a goldmine.

"Anyone seen Simon today?" asked the site manager.

"Who's Simon?" said an architect.

"One of the surveying team. New lad. He didn't turn up at the pub, Monday evening, and I haven't seen him since."

Everyone looked blank. "Probably working from the office," concluded the manager. They shrugged and returned to their drunken chatter.

The trouble with village pubs was that they closed too early. And the other trouble was that they were full of hostile yokels. How Bland despised them, huddling in their granite cottages that were as grey as wet pavements. His buyers were sophisticated; they appreciated his bright modern homes, thought nothing of taking out a half-million pound mortgage. You couldn't put a price on lifestyle.

At half-past ten, the landlord came out and suggested they leave, as their presence was bad for business. Bland secured a deal: they'd leave in exchange for three complementary bottles of champagne.

"Midnight picnic!" he said.

Some of his employees made their excuses and called taxis. Bland, Molson and a handful of others slipped through a gate at the rear of the pub garden: a shortcut up to Mydford Gorge. A full moon shone, enough to light their way and fill it with alarming shadows. Unseen debris crunched under their feet; seeds, twigs, snails. A councillor skidded in a cowpat. An architect tripped over a rock. He cursed as the others fell about laughing.

"Shit, who thought this was a good idea?"

"The man who pays your wages," said Nick Molson.

"Your sovereign wishes to survey his kingdom," said Gideon Bland, waving a bottle in the air. A bramble tore at his arm, but he was too drunk to care. He climbed to the highest point of the ridge and stood, out of breath, on a rock under the oak-dappled moonlight. Behind him, the villagers sulked under their grey roofs. In front lay the rich estate of his land, silvered. "All this is ours. All hail Mydford Meadows, Phase II!"

"A toast to G. A. Bland Homes," called Molson. Corks flew like gunshots. "To Gideon! Hip hip *hurrah!*"

Shouts of agreement. Bland raised the bottle to his lips, nearly missed, coughed and giggled as bubbles spilled into his mouth and over his chin. At the same moment, a brutal hot pain whipped across his right calf.

He jumped, gasping. Even through his trouser leg, it felt like a whip soaked in acid. The pain took his breath away. He dropped the bottle. What the *hell—?*

"You all right, Gideon?" said Molson.

"Yes. Something stung me. Damn it."

"Maybe you stepped on a wasps' nest?"

"Or adders?" said another voice. "What the hell?"

"Could be midges off the lake …"

Then Nick Molson cried out. He grabbed at his right forearm and fell to his knees. "*Shit.*"

Bland's leg began to throb. Burning like a thousand hornets attacking him. He felt himself go hot and start to sweat. The world changed, rippling as if seen through water. He saw an odd glowing streak, like a line of fireflies. He watched Nick Molson passing out in slow motion. He saw marks on Molson's cheeks and arms, long wounds like bruises as if a dozen whips had thrashed him.

"Let's move," he said. "Down towards the river, then we'll make our way out along the footpath."

Another lash struck right across his shoulders and the bare skin of his neck. The shock sent him dizzy. He hadn't realised how steep the hill was; once you started running, you couldn't stop. Bracken and rocks tried to trip him. His companions were cursing as they spilled down the incline alongside him – with panic, or because they'd been stung too, he didn't know. There was chaos, a clamour of voices swearing and shouting. Clouds ate the moon; voices faded into the crescendo of rainfall. Then silence.

Bland found himself lying headlong on the valley floor. There was coarse wet grass beneath him and rain pouring down. No idea where he was. Somewhere near the river. Everyone else had vanished, as if the night had consumed them. There was nothing, nothing around him except the unending world of the valley, the marsh and the rain.

His vision blurred. Vicious blows kept coming, lashing across his arms, torso, face. Each one felt like white-hot iron, leaving a band of agony that fizzed as if it were eating into his flesh. Waves of heat and cold went through him like nausea.

Even the deluge failed to cool his pain. All he could hear now was the downpour blending with the rush of waterfalls. The wind rose. The world leaned sideways – so it seemed, as all the trees bent over and thrashed in the sudden brutal gale.

He saw, through sheets of rain, a shadow crawling around him. Slithering through the grass. A huge serpent-shaped thing, the same colour as the night, with scores of tentacles writhing all over its body like thrashing cables, filaments, ribbons of seaweed. An impossible shape sliding around him. A serpent with a *human face*. A dead human face with white teeth and white eyes ...

Those whips came striking at him from every part of its body. No, not like seaweed, but jellyfish tentacles. Lethal. Long, translucent stingers with their own pulsing lights. Strings of lights throbbed along each curving streamer with the luminosity of eerie sea monsters in the deep.

The serpent rose, as tall as the sky. Her snake-hair thrashed wildly like tree branches caught in the storm. She appeared both reptile and human, female in form with her endless demonic tendrils trailing down to her feet and along the ground. Surely she could attack from twenty, thirty feet away. No escape. The rain splashed off her, shining. It fell so heavily now that it seemed they were under an immense dark waterfall.

More stingers tore across his head and body, edged with venomous needles. His body was a sheet of fire. Thousands of poisonous lights danced on the wind. He felt his flesh swelling, poison filling his veins. Water choked him. He was drowning.

Eventually his hearing went. His eyesight shut down in a black storm.

Just before he lost consciousness, Gideon Bland felt her cold breath on his face. Bile and champagne came frothing out of his mouth. He saw her *smile*.

Simon came crawling out of the mud and reeds like the first fish to drag itself onto land. He lay panting, pushing slime out of his eyes. The sky was pale. Dawn touched the lake surface and gleamed off every grass stalk and leaf. The first tiny arc of the sun flooded the valley with glorious white-gold mist. He rose into an ocean of light.

He felt powerfully that he shouldn't be alive, yet he was.

"Annie?" he said, sitting up.

No one answered.

For a moment he thought he saw her — but it was only a weeping willow.

He couldn't move: he didn't know where he was or where he was supposed to be. He sat hugging his knees, crying uncontrollably. The water and the marsh and the sweet green hills with their dense hedgerows and ancient trees, all stayed motionless and silent. Holding their breath.

No one died.

At some point, Nick Molson, Gideon Bland and their colleagues woke in the wet grass, hungover and blank with horror, but unharmed. Later, whispers went around that it wasn't just Bland and Molson. Everyone, even those asleep in hotel beds in the nearest town, had had the same nightmare. A slithering, bloated water-creature, all stings and tentacles, rising up over them, smothering, *drowning* them …

A handful of them went with Bland to the nearest Accident and Emergency in town, but their visit yielded no answers. The doctors found no acid burns, no skin punctures, no signs of stings or allergic reactions. Horse flies, adders, midges? Nothing. Food poisoning, perhaps. Or some malefactor had spiked their drinks — such drugs were hard to detect, but could cause hallucinations for hours, even days, a senior medic told them. He didn't seem to be taking their plight seriously. "Take paracetamol and drink plenty of fluid," he told them with a grim smirk. "There's nothing amiss, except that the alcohol levels in your blood are *rather high*."

Bland checked his phone for reports of a hurricane in the Mydford area. Nothing. Just a touch of drizzle, according to the local weather report.

Out in the car park, Bland snarled, "That's it. The locals tried to poison us. I'll see them in court."

His threat was hollow. He knew there would be no proof. All he wanted in the cold early morning was to return to his wife and kids, a hundred miles from this accursed place. He never wanted to set foot in Mydford again, nor even to hear the name. The pain might have faded, but the memory – never. Lights chasing down the translucent, muscular lengths of a thousand tentacles. The white eyes in that hideous face. Every time he shut his eyes, her *face...*

Afterwards, those who experienced what had happened that evening never spoke of it again.

Polly trotted happily through the bracken, working in circles as Joyce sat on her favourite rock. Below her lay her beloved view, timeless. Spring was blooming towards full summer, and there was an indefinable, exciting scent of promise on the breeze.

Another dog woofed, and she saw Greg walking past with his golden retriever. He raised a hand and came over to her.

"Joyce, how are you?" he said. "I was so sorry to hear about Brian. How are you bearing up?"

"Oh, I'll be okay. It was a shock, of course, but he'd had heart trouble for years."

"A heart attack, I heard ... I'm so very sorry."

"A stroke, to be precise. I can't believe it was only three days ago. All the stress of the last few years..."

"Yes," said Greg, shaking his head. "He was a fighter, that man of yours."

"At least he lived long enough to hear the good news. I think *that* was the shock that finished him, actually."

Within a week of winning his planning consent, Bland had withdrawn the application and initiated the process of gifting Mydford Gorge in trust to the village.

"Indeed. Astonishing news. Funny old business. Perhaps the developers had an attack of conscience."

Joyce laughed. "An attack of something."

"Yes, I heard all sorts of rumours. Something very weird happened. Wasps, adders, spiked drinks – crazy tales. Never knew a few stings to stop a developer before. Nature in the raw too much for them?"

"Well, no one died," she said, smiling. "Except Brian, of course, and that *was* of natural causes."

"Did you know that one of their surveyors went missing?"

"I heard. I'm sure he'll turn up. Probably just a coincidence."

"I doubt we'll ever know."

Joyce watched her spaniel and Greg's retriever happily sniffing each other's bottoms. "Once upon a time, there was a strange little girl who came out of nowhere. But the school children were frightened of her because she had serpents for hair. So they bullied her and tormented her and threw her down the old stone well... But the well, of course, connects to every spring and stream in the area. And down there she stays, swimming through the underground waterways and lakes, thirsting for revenge..."

"Ah, the good old ghost story! The Lady of Mydford who haunts the water."

"She will come if you call her," said Joyce. "This is her land. They can go off and build wherever they like now, but I believe they got the message: not here. *Not here.*"

Once Greg had gone on his way, Joyce started walking down the hillside and along the valley until she came to the marshland near the lake. She had ruffled Polly's ears, kissed her head and asked Greg if he'd mind taking her home, as she wanted to remember Brian on her own for a while. Of course he didn't mind, he'd replied kindly, and asked her to let him know when the funeral would be.

She missed her husband desperately, but it was probably just as well that Brian had gone when he had. With her practical head on, she knew he would have been lost without her.

Her walking boots squelched. Mist came smoking off the lake, blanketing the landscape until trees and hills were just cloudy shapes. There was only the lake, bulrushes and sedges and trees standing in greyish silhouette. And a young man, sitting hunched over his knees, shivering.

"Simon?" she called softly.

He looked round. His eyes were wild, his face and clothes slimed dark green.

"It's all right, dear," Joyce said. "You were reported missing a week ago."

"A *week*? That's not... possible."

"Really. People are worried. Can you stand up and find your way back to the village on your own? You can go back now. Go to the pub, they'll look after you."

"No, I c-c-c-can't." His teeth chattered.

"Why not?"

He pointed at the lake. His arm fell and he said, "*She.*"

"Here's the good news." Joyce squatted down beside him. "*She* requires only one sacrifice in payment. She doesn't want you; she wants the one who called her. You were just a hostage. So you can leave now, I promise, because I've come to take your place."

He blinked, staring as if he had no idea what the mad old woman was talking about. But her words or her kind gaze must have reached him, because he rose and began to walk away, unsteady at first then faster and faster. He glanced back once, then broke into a run. Joyce watched until the mist veiled him.

Then she went forward and stepped into the edge of the lake. The water was cold, flowing with pondweed that caught around her legs like mermaid hair. She waded deeper, feeling the icy shock crawling up to her thighs, hips, waist, wicking into her clothes. Spreading her hands for balance, she kept on at a steady pace, deeper and deeper. There was gravel under her boots at first, then softer debris. Small fish and unknown flotsam bumped against her as she went.

Like a human statue cloaked in vegetation and flowing water, as tall as a willow, a figure stood waiting for her. Joyce looked into the luminous white fish-eyes and smiled.

"I'm here, my dear friend," she said as the water lapped over her chin. "I'm here."

SANATORIUM

Grace Alice Evans

there is nothing there, my driver repeats,
white knuckles stiff, eyebrows knotted.
his eyes are blanched marble.
i brace myself, smoothing out the skin on
my elbows – I'll pay extra, take me
home, be my deliverance. we have been
on the road for too long.
a smile, exposing the imbrued fragments
of my tongue. my driver's face as pale as
his knuckles, he asks no more – we arrive,
i descend. pearlescent milk teeth ruminate under my
bare feet as i step into the woodlands, trees
mourning in a rising crescendo, their gaunt arms
caressing my eroding shoulders. i trudge, forward, garish
birdsong from overhead filling my ears.
the light incises the veil above, making my hair
smoulder. my body is in tears by the time
i reach my haven, a rogue sanctuary, which
presents itself to me. it feeds itself off eradication,
a field of deceased flower-beds and rusted
syringes paving the way towards the entrance,
a gaunt shell white-washed by incessant sun,
arduous decades passed it's intended life-span.
a husk, weary, overtaken by invasive nature, yet
its spirits persist, having laid dormant within
the cracks in the walls, now sensing my presence.
peerless eyes appear in every
window, cavernous mouths frozen in eternal
laughter. i salute, and the eyes step back –
i can feel them lusting over my viscera.

THE LIGHTHOUSE

Emma Coleman

I walked quickly along the avenue. Smooth white buildings grew tall on either side and the streets were empty.

What time is it? I thought, and looked up; the sun was high, perhaps it was midday, *why am I in such a hurry?*

I yanked at the knot of my tie and undid the top two buttons of my shirt – the stiff collar cut into my skin – and the sweat trickling down my neck frustrated me. I wiped my hand across my throat and the coarse scraping of stubble against my palm surprised me.

I thought I'd shaved this morning?

I looked back up at the sky, and then behind me.

I didn't know why, but I had that dreadful feeling of being chased in a dream, and I couldn't help but walk faster.

The white walls and glittering windows disturbed me. They were perfect and lifeless.

"Where is everybody?" I muttered. "Where are all the people?"

The wide avenue stretched ahead. I turned, looking at the road I had just journeyed along alone; that, too, stretched away into the distance, and I couldn't remember having walked that far. But I must've done.

I had to get away, there was something unsettling about the empty avenue, made even more unnerving by my solitary pilgrimage – I could be a tiny creature scuttling through a mighty canyon – and I had no idea if anyone watched as I tried to make my escape.

There were no cars or buses. There wasn't even a sound from the nearby tramlines. I looked to the sky. Empty. No birds or clouds or planes. Hairs prickled on the back of my neck and I shivered.

I kept my head down as I walked. I only wanted to see the cracks of the pavement shooting past my feet. I didn't want to see whatever followed behind.

The cracks of the paving slabs were slow to move and so I began to run. I hadn't run for years but now I wanted to run as fast as I could, just run out of the avenue, leave those white gleaming buildings far behind and run.

But my legs...they were so heavy. I found I dragged myself onwards, the last of my strength vanishing.

"Oh, God, I'm so tired," I said, slowing down. I rested against one of the white buildings, putting my forehead on the cool wall.

I tried to catch my breath. My lungs were bursting and sweat dripped down my face and down my back.

"Hey!" a voice called. I swung around.

Leaning against the corner of a perfect white building was a man, his clothes ripped and stained.

"Hey!" he shouted again.

I stood up straight, stretching to my full height – I didn't know if I could trust this person – and I didn't know why he was the only other soul around except for me.

"What?" I said.

The man gave a sly smile.

"Hey, mate, do you want a taxi?"

"Why do you ask?"

The man sniffed a few times and then wiped his nose along his filthy sleeve.

"It'll save you all that running," he said.

"Where is this car?" I asked.

"Taxi," he said, approaching me slowly, "my taxi is just on the other side of that street." And he pointed across the wide avenue.

"Do you particularly need my business?" I asked, stepping back.

He chuckled derisively. "What do you think? Yeah of course I do, haven't had a customer for ages."

"Where is everybody?"

He sniffed again. "Dunno, but I had heard there was a big thing going on, so I suppose..." he tailed off, looking up at the building, "...so I suppose they've all gone to that."

"Why didn't *you* go?" I couldn't hide the suspicion in the tone of my voice.

"I'm not one for crowds," he replied, staring at me full in the face.

I put my hands in my pockets. They were empty.

"Thanks for the offer but I don't have any money. Looks like I'll have to keep running after all."

I went to move away when he suddenly took a step towards me.

"No matter, I'll take you anyway. Where are you going?" And he smiled, showing long, grey teeth.

I felt trapped by him, pressed up against a gleaming wall with the empty avenue on my right side; he seemed to expand and cut off any form of escape route.

"Don't worry about money," he continued, "you can pay me back some other way. You don't wanna be running about in this heat, it's far too hot for that silly behaviour. Why not let me drive you? We can have a good chat on the way, I've missed talking to people."

"No, but thanks all the same. It's a kind offer but I'd really rather go on my own."

I slid past him. His face looked crushed, trampled on, the folds of grubby skin were yellowy underneath the dirt. I chanced a quick look into his eyes. They were bloodshot but happy.

"I wouldn't think about going anywhere alone..." he said flatly, his breath as foul as the stench of sewers, "...folk have always taken a ride from me, why should you be any different?" His voice began to change, getting deeper and deeper. "Why should *you* refuse *me*? What have I done to make you insult me like that?"

I didn't know how to get out. His body twitched, and his happy eyes fixed me to the spot.

"I'm sorry," I said quickly, "I didn't mean to offend, it's just that I find it hard to accept anything for free, especially from someone I don't know."

He stepped closer, his eyes full of terrible joy, and whispered, "But you *do* know me." And he smiled again.

I tried to recall his face, but nothing came to me. He was lying. I had no idea who he could be.

He saw my confusion and his eyes narrowed as his smile grew wider.

"You know who I am."

My heart went cold. I stuttered and stumbled in my mind; *what do I do?*

"Oh yes, of course," I said, "I think I do remember now. I'm sorry, my memory isn't as good as it used to be..." And then I couldn't think of anything else to say.

The man didn't seem to believe me but through his cracked lips he said, "I'm glad to hear it. Took you a while but you got there in the end. So then, how about that lift? Seeing as how you *do* know who I am and I'm offering the ride out of the goodness of my heart, you don't really have any reason not to accept..." His voice turned aggressive, his filthy face now set for confrontation. "...do you?"

I had no choice.

"Yes, of course I accept, thank you."

"This way, then," he said, letting me by.

I moved forward and he stuck to me like a faithful, stinking dog, but this dog had no collar or lead, somehow he had persuaded me to put them on myself.

We walked into the wide road, out of the shadows of the tall buildings, and into the glare of the sun. The light hurt my eyes.

"The sun's so powerful today, I can barely see," I said, but the man had fallen silent and I felt that urge to run again.

I turned slightly to take a look at him; in bright light he seemed to wash away, his face, hair and clothes bleached to insipidity. He paid me no attention and I scanned the avenue furtively. No sign of movement, all seemed perfectly still, and I needed to spot a way out.

"Where did you say your car's parked?"

"Taxi," he said, "not car, taxi."

"Yes, sorry, where did you say your taxi is parked?"

"Not far."

"This side of the avenue?"

"Maybe."

"Please, can't you tell me? I'm tired..." But he cut me off.

He pulled me round by my elbow and we stood facing each other in the middle of the road.

"Don't you worry, we'll get there soon enough. Just keep walking and stop asking questions." His eyes were red. "Just keep up with me and be quiet, you never know who's listening."

"But there's nobody here," I said.

He still had hold of my elbow as we continued across the street.

When we reached the other side, he let go and fumbled about in his pockets. He pulled out a bent, pre-rolled cigarette and a box of matches. Putting the sorry thing to his lips, he gave me a wink and said, "My mother always told me smoking would kill me in the end. What did she know? I'm still here, aren't I?"

He laughed and struck a match along the white wall, leaving a pink, chalky curve on the pristine paintwork.

"But how long for, I don't know," he added quietly.

He lifted his hand and the flame ignited most of the cigarette, but he drew on it hard.

"I expect she's just worried for you," I said, without thinking.

"What do you know about my mother?!" the man shouted. His face became terrifying and he seemed to grow taller, towering over me and shouting into my face. "What do *you* know about my bloody mother? Nothing! You don't know a bloody thing!"

I cowered.

"I'm sorry! Please, I'm sorry. I don't know why I said it, I wasn't thinking, I'm a fool."

His face lost its ferocity and he gave me a long, slithering look, then finally he turned away and spat at the floor.

"Like I said," he muttered, "you don't know anything about my mother."

The man stepped back and took another drag on his cigarette before dropping it and stamping on the glowing stub.

"Come on, then, this way." And he shoved me along the street. "Not far now, just got to get to the end there and I'll drive you anywhere you like."

We walked side by side. I looked at his feet and saw that he wore odd shoes. One a pink, old lady's slipper but now mostly brown and torn, and the other a tired, black plimsoll.

"My driving shoes," the man said, eyeing me up.

"Of course," I retorted, and stared straight ahead.

I was getting ready to run, take him by surprise and turn back and run, but then he said, "So I suppose you'll be wanting to go to that thing as well, then? I can take you, doesn't bother me."

I waited a few seconds before answering. I felt curious and wanted to know where all the people had gone but this man terrified me, his madness brazen and aggressive.

"So...you know where it's all happening, do you?" I asked quietly.

"Most certainly do."

"But you said you can take me wherever *I* want to go? I mean, I might not want to go to that place. I don't even know where it is..."

The man stopped. He looked up to the sky. He looked behind us. And then he looked at me.

"But you *want* to go there."

I became rooted whilst gazing into those insane eyes. My mouth felt dry, the words sticking to my tongue as I asked, "Where is it that I want to go?"

He gave a wide grin exposing his sticky, grey teeth.

"The lighthouse," he sighed.

"The lighthouse?"

I didn't know what he was talking about. *There is no lighthouse*, I thought, scared.

"Why has everyone gone there, then?" I asked, gently backing away as he gazed to the sky once more. His smile faltered.

"I don't know." And he suddenly seemed confused. He frowned and pursed his lips.

I leapt at the opportunity and fled back the way we came. And I dared not look behind me.

I got back to the main avenue and was instantly blinded by the glare, but I kept running. My eyes watered as I stumbled across the glittering tarmac. When I fell, panting hard against a white wall, I finally had the courage to look back.

My chest heaved and sweat slipped down my nose. I wiped it away and rubbed my eyes.

He stood on the other side of the avenue, waving slowly.

"Oh, God..." I pulled myself up, keeping my eyes on him.

The man changed waving with his right arm to his left, but he didn't make a move.

I turned to face my escape route but all I saw was a dead end, solid white bricks with no way out.

I spun round, breathing so fast I thought I'd faint, but the man had vanished.

"Where is he?" I panted.

Shakily, I stepped forward, checking the avenue for movement, but I couldn't see him or anyone – still nothing, only roads and buildings and sky – and everything glittered so bright.

"What do I do?" I whispered. "What do I do now?"

I leaned on the wall and closed my eyes, muttering over and over again, "What now? What do I do now?"

A familiar noise in the distance roused me.

"What's that?"

I strained to listen.

"That sounds like…" I stopped, and a coldness gripped my skull. "…that's his car!"

I rushed onto the main avenue and started running along the pavement. I had no idea which way to head but I had to get away from that spot, he knew where I was, I had to run.

The growl of the engine became louder as my legs turned to jelly. I was going nowhere, and my body lurched in desperation to escape this madman.

I had to give up.

He drew up alongside me and I collapsed onto the pavement, my head ready to pop from fear and the oppressive heat.

I heard him click open his door and then slam it shut. He made no other sound, his driving shoes silent.

And then suddenly, his dirty crushed face loomed over me, shielding my eyes from the light.

"And where did you think you were going, eh?" And he leaned in a bit closer. "Eh? I thought I told you I'd take you. If you wanna go some place, I'd take you, so why did you run away from me? After all I've told you?"

He leaned back slightly, the sunlight made me wince, and I heard him strike another match along the pavement next to my head.

The smell of sulphur filled my nostrils and I tried to sit up, but the man put a hand on my chest and pushed me back.

He lit another misshapen cigarette and puffed hard. After a few seconds, he flicked it away and, with stinking breath, he put his face to mine and said, "I told you I'd take you."

He took hold of my shoulder and pulled me up.

Crouching next to me, he said, "Now, will you get into my taxi or do we have to chase each other about all day? Remember, I give mates a free ride." He smiled and patted me on the back. "Get up, then," he said as he got to his feet, "we've got a long journey ahead."

I felt crippled; all my limbs ached, and I struggled to move. The man extended an arm, stretching out his hand.

"Come on, mate," he said amiably.

I felt backed into a corner again – I didn't want to take his hand – but dared not refuse his offer of help.

With sheer force of will, I put my hand in his; it felt hot and sticky, and he pulled me up, giving me a wide grin.

"The heat of the sun," he explained through gritted teeth.

"Yes," I stammered, "the sun is very powerful today."

The man seemed pleased and led me to his car. He opened the back-passenger door and ushered me in. I sat down on a worn, leather seat – springs sticking out – and he let go of my hand.

"Right, then, all comfortable?" he asked, after strapping me in.

I nodded.

"Good," and he closed the door. He then pressed his face up against my window and said, muffled, "Let's get a move on! We're off to the lighthouse!"

He looked so excited as he jumped into the driver's seat – like an old child off to see the fair – and I felt sick. I stared hopelessly at the back of his head...and then I thought, *I could hit him, hit him really hard. Knock him unconscious...Now, do it now!* And I was just about to raise my fist when he swung round to face me.

"Don't be silly! If you strike me once..." His eyes narrowed. "...I *will* kill you." He shrugged and turned back to the steering wheel. I saw him staring at me in the rear-view mirror.

"How many punches do you think my last passenger got in before I put a stop to it? One, just the one, and he regretted it, oh how he regretted it." He paused and scratched his chin. "Now then, you be quiet like a good chap and we'll be off."

I was cold. On the hottest day I had ever known, and I felt freezing cold.

"How about some music? I like driving when I've got my tape on." And he shook a blank, grey cassette behind his head. "I made this one myself, it's the only one I've got left now and getting a bit worn."

He put the tape in the player and turned the ignition on.

"You'll enjoy this," he said, glaring at me in the mirror again. "In fact, you may even know it." He winked. "Sing along if you like, I don't mind."

He pressed play and the speakers crackled but nothing happened.

The man roughly pulled the car away from the kerb and said, "Don't worry, it takes a while to kick in."

There came some more crackling and then eventually tinny voices singing...

I knew the song. I felt sick. I stared out of the window as the perfect white buildings swam by, thinking, *I know this song...* but it was the only real thing I could grasp. I knew the song but had no idea what was happening to me, what the hell was happening? Why was I in this madman's taxi? What was the lighthouse? Have I lost my mind? I felt as though I'd woken up inside a dream inside a coffin. I had no way out, already dead but waiting for it to happen all over again.

The man started whistling merrily.

"You know it, don't you?" he asked after a while.

"Yes," I answered, not taking my gaze away from the moving scenery. The passing buildings had become an unbroken line of light. The sun reflected off the white walls and they streamed by like an endless tube train.

"What are you looking at?" he suddenly demanded.

"Nothing, just the light."

I heard him fumbling about and then a click followed by another click.

"Put these on," he said, "that light'll damage your eyes and we don't want that." He passed back a pair of sunglasses with one lens missing. I looked at him through his rear-view mirror. His eyes were on me.

"It's all about my passenger's comfort," he said lazily, "you'll learn that in time." He continued to stare at me. "Sing along, then, don't be shy. And put those on, there's a good chap."

I put the glasses on but didn't bother to sing.

"I'll start it again, shall I?" he said, laughing. "And I'll sing with you. Yeah, that sounds nice, we'll sing together. How about that?"

And still he stared at me.

Panicked, I looked back out at the scenery, the streak of light now going faster, faster, faster, but the man didn't watch the road.

"Are you alright?" he shouted back "You look a bit...not right."

I felt sick. I could barely move my head without the need to vomit.

"Oh dear, you don't look good at all. What's up? You got belly ache? No worries, just you sit tight, and I'll soon get you to the lighthouse."

"But I don't want to go to the lighthouse..." I managed to whisper as my head lolled about.

"Ho, ho! They all say that!" the madman chortled, "even me, once."

In my mind I thought we were flying; I couldn't feel the road and the pressure in my head intensified. My ears were muffled but all I could hear was his voice.

"Yep, everyone's gone to the lighthouse, except you that is. You're my last fare and after I've dropped you off, that'll be it for me. I can retire, put my feet up and it's been a long time coming, I can tell you!" He laughed and I was ready to vomit. "Eh. No, I'll have none of that. If you're going to be sick, then do it outside my taxi. Just tell me if you've got the need and I'll pull over."

The next thing I knew my door had been pulled open and I lay sprawling on the pavement. And then a foul taste in my mouth.

The man hauled me up to a sitting position and I winced; my eyes were half closed and I felt so ill.

"Better?" he asked, and he rubbed my chest. "Better now it's all out?"

As we sat there, he rubbing my chest and me staring ahead at yet another white building, I thought, *I can't escape this...I have to go to the lighthouse...I don't want to go to the lighthouse but I'm going to the lighthouse...I can't escape...*

"There, there, it's all over now." And he stroked my hair. "Do you think you're able to get up? I've got to get you to the lighthouse and, if you promise not to do that again..." His voice changed. "...I'll give you a sweet."

I got up unsteadily. Instinctively I put my hands out to him to stop myself from falling back down and he gripped my wrists tightly.

"Don't you worry, I've got you," he said.

"I know," I whispered under my breath, as he helped me back into his taxi.

While he busied himself strapping me in once more, I saw a shadow on the corner of a white building.

"The sun's setting."

"Yeah, it does that," he said aggressively, "but what it's got to do with you, I don't know."

He slammed my door shut and then threw himself into the driver's seat. He lunged round to face me.

"The sun's no business of yours, alright? You let me worry about that. All you've got to do is sit there like a good chap and let me drive you to the lighthouse, got it?"

I nodded.

"Well done." He grinned, revealing those wet, smoky teeth once again. "Righto, let's be off then but first..." and he jabbed at the tape player, "...let's have that song on from the start, eh?"

The music began to play, and the man smoothly pulled away from the kerb. While we drove along, the same white buildings passed by my window. I blocked out the song and stared at the scenery, waiting for something different but the avenue was endless. What time was it? *The sun's setting so it must be late afternoon...*

"The sun's setting," I whispered.

The man twitched.

"What did you say?" he asked sternly.

"Oh, I just wondered what the time is. You don't happen to know, do you?" I hesitantly ventured.

"What?"

"The time, do you know it? I'm sorry for being impatient...I just want to know how long it will be 'til we get to the lighthouse. I'm...excited."

"Of course you are. Now, let me see, the time..."

He abruptly slammed on the brakes. I lurched forward but instantly got thrown back, my skull smacking into the headrest.

"The time is..." And I watched the man roll up his tatty sleeve. "...the time by my reckoning is just coming up to six forty-eight."

"Should we get to the lighthouse before dark?"

The man chuckled as he started to drive off.

"I should hope so, we've got all day to get there."

"But," I said, "it's getting on for evening, we haven't got all day."

He swung round in his seat, still driving on.

"What are you talking about? It's six forty-eight in the morning, the sun's rising!" He laughed. "Are you mad? It's the bloody morning!"

"It can't be," I whispered. I *knew* the sun was setting, I knew that I'd started running from him when the sun was high. He was lying again, trying to confuse me even more, make me give up all hope.

"The sun IS rising!" he bellowed and began driving like a

complete maniac. Faster and faster we went, swerving all over the road, speeding past road signs and traffic lights. He was possessed.

"You think you can tell me what I already know?!" he screamed.

I knew that at any moment we would crash.

He turned the music up, the speakers crackled and hissed under the strain, and he started singing loudly. Between shrieking the lyrics, he shouted out as though he couldn't control himself.

"...he wouldn't stop crying, you know? And I'd say, what are you crying about now?" Followed by more bursts of song. "...it's crazy, I know, but what can you do? I hadn't hurt him, I'd not *touched* him at that point, but the tears...the tears!" he screamed.

My whole body clenched like a fist, waiting for the smash and the agony.

"I ask you! What can anyone do? When you get a reaction like that! Jesus Christ, just STOP crying! Stop it!"

Suddenly, the man switched the music off and calmly said, "I get more and more confused the more I talk."

He had forgotten I was there. The car slowed down but still I braced myself. I had no idea what he would do next.

"So time goes on, I told him, six forty-eight becomes six forty-nine then six fifty etc etc etc, little movements, bits of time being sucked into a bigger bit of time until it stops. That's right, stops. It does stop, it does...but he didn't believe me." There came a pause. "And all he did was cry. If only he'd got it."

He was driving carefully now. The explosion of rage and madness had vanished leaving only a calmness I found even more sinister. The way he had said, "If only he'd got it," was almost as though he talked of a lost love; it felt tender.

"He shouldn't cry. I told him, time and again I told him, but he must've been deaf...or he just didn't want to listen to me."

The car stopped.

"You'd listen to me, wouldn't you?" he asked gently.

What had happened? What had he done?

A long silence reigned. The light was getting brighter and I looked outside; there were no shadows on the white buildings, the sun now high. It was midday again.

"Are you listening to me? You *are* listening to me, aren't you?"

"Yes, yes I'm listening to you it's just that..." And I shut my mouth.

"Just that what?" he asked calmly. "You weren't thinking about the sun, were you?"

I panicked.

"No! I was listening to you! Of course I'm listening to you! I heard everything you said, about how the man cried and how time stops but starts and that the man wouldn't stop crying but you didn't know why, and six forty-eight becomes six forty-nine, bits of time being sucked into bigger bits of time, but the man wouldn't stop, he just wouldn't stop crying and you were so sad! I was listening! I was listening to you!"

"Then what are you crying for?"

"I'm not!"

"Yes, you are."

I was shaking in my seat, tears pouring down my face; I was a wreck and I hadn't noticed.

"I'm sorry," I whimpered, bursting into fresh tears. I couldn't help myself.

"Stop it," he said, "please stop it."

His words made me cry harder.

"I can't!" I whispered. I was utterly gripped with shame – the embarrassment of crying in front of this man – and I couldn't stop.

"I thought you said you were listening to me."

"I am listening!" I wailed, desperately trying to stop the tears.

"Then please, stop crying."

He seemed so serene, so gentle, and I wanted to do what he said but couldn't.

And so I took one deep breath after another, all the while muttering, "Calm down, calm down, don't cry..."

The man sat perfectly still in his driving seat. He didn't turn to talk to me, nor did he look at me through the rear-view mirror. He simply stared straight ahead through the windscreen while all I could do was sniff and wipe my face with my sleeve.

Suddenly he said, "It's twelve noon again, see how high the sun has got?"

I wound down my window and looked up at the sun.

"Get out," he said coldly.

"What?"

"GET OUT! GET OUT!" he screamed. He jumped out of the

car and yanked open my door. With one powerful move, he managed to pull me out and dump me on the pavement.

My heart froze. He towered over me. His head – a shaded smudge – blocked out most of the strong sunlight.

"Ride's over," and he got back into his taxi.

I was confused and in pain.

"But I thought we were going to the lighthouse? To see everybody else?" I called after him.

The man leaned out of his window. Lighting another cigarette and, without looking at me, he said, "There isn't anyone else and the lighthouse...what lighthouse?" He started coughing and then laughing. "There is no lighthouse!"

"What do you mean there's no lighthouse? And where are all the people?" I got to my feet and the heat of the sun pounded my brain. "What do you mean there isn't anyone else? What have you done to them?"

He continued to laugh; phlegm clogged his lungs and I could hear it.

"What's up with you? You're acting all twitchy and paranoid!"

"Of course I'm paranoid!" I screamed, his laughter making me angry, and I tried to steady myself. "You chase me and drag me into your car..."

"Taxi," the man said, "my taxi, not my car"

"Whatever!" I shouted. I was panting hard and shaking all over. "You tell me you're taking me to the lighthouse..."

"But there isn't a lighthouse," he uttered quietly.

"You TOLD me that's where all the people are and that you were taking me to them..."

"What people? What the bloody hell are you talking about?" He laughed again, wheezing and gasping for breath.

I saw red.

I put my hands through the open window and grabbed hold of his neck. I held on hard. I dug my fingers into his skin and pressed my thumbs against his windpipe. He choked. He spluttered into my face, the scrawny butt of his cigarette popped out of his mouth and stuck to his chin. He cried through bulging eyes, now sobbing for breath as I squeezed tighter.

"Stop it!" I shouted, "stop crying and take me to all the people! I want to go to the lighthouse!"

But still he managed to shed tears.

"Stop crying! Stop crying! You've got to take me to the lighthouse!"

My desperation intensified.

"You told me you were taking me to the lighthouse," I said through gritted teeth. I throttled him. His head flopped forward and I let go.

"Take me to the lighthouse!" I shouted. He didn't move. "You said you were taking me to the lighthouse, so take me!"

I pushed his head back away from the steering wheel and I heard a crack. He didn't move.

"What?" I asked sternly. "What are you doing?" I poked his face and he fell sideways. I looked around and the bright sunlight reflecting off the white buildings hurt my eyes.

"Take me to the lighthouse," I panted, looking back at the still figure lying on the passenger seat. "Where did you take all the people?"

The sun was terrible, the penetrating heat now boiling my brain.

"What have you done to all the others?" I screamed. His lack of movement incensed me, so I opened the door and took hold of his legs. He weighed hardly anything as I dragged him out of the taxi, but his head broke on the pavement when I pulled him off the seat. Slowly, a puddle of blood emerged.

I crouched beside him, inspecting the bright red of his blood.

"You're not going to take me anywhere, are you?" I asked and pushed his face away. I saw the oozing crack in the back of his skull and let go. "No, you're in no fit state to do anything right now."

I looked about the avenue, the light now turning to a warm glow and the shadows were long.

"I told you the sun was setting," I said to the dead man on the pavement, "now, let me see…what time is it?"

I grabbed the man's arm and pushed up his shirt sleeve. Six forty-eight.

"It must be evening…"

I was confused. I unstrapped the watch and put it on my own arm.

"It must be evening." And I stood up. I stared at the wide road stretching ahead. "I'll wait, I'll just stand here and wait for something to change, however long it takes…"

I didn't know how much time passed, but eventually I rubbed my face roughly, and gazed at the sky.

"It *is* the evening, it just has to be, it *is* the evening…" And yet the warm glow had gone. The sun was high again and there were no shadows.

"Already?" I asked the sky and glanced at my watch. "Oh, so it is. Midday again." And I watched the second-hand tick forward from twelve.

I blinked in the glaring light and the avenue glittered.

"So it is, midday…"

I turned to the dead man lying on the pavement.

"You were right." And I carefully stepped over him and got into the taxi, "you were right…about time." I slammed the door shut.

I turned the ignition on and looked in the rear-view mirror, expecting to see myself, sitting in the backseat.

"Why didn't he stop crying and tell the truth about the lighthouse?" I sighed. "Well, I'll just have to drive around and find it for myself, won't I?" And I pulled away from the pavement.

I pressed play on the cassette player and turned up the volume.

"I remember this song!"

I sang along with the tinny voices as the same white buildings passed by.

After listening to the tape several times, I stopped the taxi and rolled up my sleeve. It was exactly twelve o'clock.

I started to drive again.

I lost count of how many times I listened to that tape. But I drove through the streets for what felt like days.

I couldn't find the lighthouse. Instead, I became more and more entangled in the avenue, but I couldn't stop driving.

"It's got to be here," I muttered, as I saw the shadows on the very tops of the buildings.

I drove into a side street and turned the engine off. I got out, needing to stretch my legs.

As I walked about I listened to the silence – trying to pick up the slightest sound – but there was nothing.

"They've got to be here somewhere, but where are they?"

And then I saw him. He peered around the corner of the building opposite me.

"Who's that?"

I stepped out of the side street and into the avenue.

The man looked straight at me and quickly retreated.

"Hey!" I called, "hey, wait up!" And I ran across the road.

By the time I reached the spot where he had stood, he was a small figure at the other end of the long, narrow street.

"Hey! I've got a taxi, we can drive together!" I called, still running. I felt so excited to see another human and didn't want to let him escape me. "Wait!"

The man stopped, and I stopped about thirty feet from him. The light was dingy; the tightly-packed buildings blocked out the blinding glare, and all I could see of him was his long, brown overcoat, his back facing me.

I tentatively approached.

"Do you want a ride? I've got a taxi parked just across the avenue."

"Why do you want to take me for a ride?" the man asked, muffled. He still didn't turn around.

"Because you're the only other person I've seen, and it'd be nice to have someone to talk to. I tell you, this place could drive you mad when you've only got yourself for company." I laughed, remembering the dead taxi driver.

"But you have no idea who I am, do you?"

"That doesn't matter, I can get to know you. We can go and look for the lighthouse together, that's where everyone else is, you see."

"Where?"

"The lighthouse." I halted about four feet from him. His hair was thinning and his coat filthy with stains. An intensely sour smell struck me, and I gagged but couldn't tell if it was my own stench or if it came from the man with his back to me. I quickly looked down at myself. My clothes were in as rotten a state as his.

"Heh, looks like we've both had a rough time of it today. So, where have you been? Seen anyone else on your way here?"

He turned his head slightly but, for such a brief moment, I only caught an impression of his profile; it was flat, his nose beaten down against his face.

"No," he said, "no one at all."

"Well, it's a good job you appeared when you did, I'd just about given up hope on finding anybody in this avenue."

When he didn't respond, I laughed nervously but silence had descended. He said nothing, and he didn't move.

I anxiously turned to see the long, narrow street stretching further into the distance. The bright light of the avenue seemed so far away and, for the first time, I wanted to be in its dazzling glare.

"So, how about it?" he suddenly asked, very quietly.

I swung back round only to see his shoulders hunched and his head bent so far down it looked as though his neck had broken.

"How about what?" I asked, reeling back in disgust.

"That drive? I can take you anywhere you want to go."

"What?"

"Aren't you going to accept my offer of a drive? I don't charge and besides, we know each other already, don't we?" His voice had choked with phlegm – I could hear the bubbles in his throat – and I coughed involuntarily.

"What?" I asked again.

"Yeah, I've got a taxi too, see. It's parked a little way away, on the other side of the avenue. Maybe you saw it?"

I stared at his back, puzzled.

"No," I said to myself, "no, I didn't see any other car..."

"Taxi."

"Taxi? Yes, yes, I meant taxi, but no, I didn't see one."

He laughed, "Funny that."

"Yes," I said, looking back along the never ending, narrow side street. I was thinking but I didn't know what about.

"Haven't you decided yet? Come on, mate, seeing as how we both want company, seems silly not going together, doesn't it?"

I turned back to him, his great, dirty coat appeared black and the smell of rotten meat hit me so hard I nearly vomited.

"You are listening to me, aren't you?" the man asked threateningly.

"Yes...yes...but I'm not sure if..." And I tailed off, confused and scared. I didn't know what I was going to say and my heart beat fast.

"And besides," he continued, "I'm pretty certain there isn't a lighthouse, or anyone else for that matter. There's only me. Surely you must know that by now?"

"But what about me?" I asked, taking a step back, "I'm here too."

The man said nothing but began to stretch; I could hear bones crunching as he lifted his head up slowly and his long neck – covered in patches of coarse, black hair – seemed to keep growing and I stumbled backwards.

I turned sharply when I felt myself fall against something solid.

"What the...?" I muttered in terror.

A white, brick wall – as tall as the buildings themselves – blocked my path.

"No, no..." I uttered and tried to push the wall down, "this can't be real..."

A small patch of white light highlighted my feet. One brick was missing, and I threw myself to the ground and gazed through the gap with desperation and joy. On the other side I saw the busy sunny avenue. People walked – I saw their shoes, men and women's – I could smell the fumes of cars as they drove up and down the street, and the sound of a city full of life made me want to cry.

"Have you got the time?" the man spoke softly.

I looked up, startled.

"What?" I asked, my heart thumping hard.

"The time, do you have it?"

I ignored him and, when I turned to look at the avenue once more, it had gone, the wall complete.

"No...no, no, no! Where's it gone? They were there! They were all there!" I screamed.

I got up shakily and hit the bricks with my fists wanting to smash them down. But my knuckles were shattering, and I screamed with pain.

The man chuckled and I felt warm, moist breath on the back of my neck. He stood right behind me.

I felt too frightened to move, rooted to the spot, and all the while I could hear his   heavy breathing and feel his rotten odour seeping over me.

"It's time to take a ride in my taxi," he whispered, and spittle sprayed my neck.

"Who are you?" I stuttered, pressing my bloodied hands on the cold brickwork to steady myself.

But I didn't want to know. My palms were damp, the blood mixing with the sweat, and my body shook uncontrollably and the silence...he let the silence go on and on and then, faintly, I heard him say as if inside my head, "Who are you, then? *Who are you?*

Who *are* you?"

He placed a large, powerful hand on my trembling shoulder and pulled me round gently. Too numb to resist, my burning eyes wide open, I stared in amazement at his face.

"There is nobody else. Like I said, there's only me."

THE WINTER WIFE

Kari Sperring

The sound of wings woke the king's third son early that morning. It was the last day of summer, the day on which night and day hung in perfect balance, and the white storks had risen to begin their long migration. The third son rose from his plank bed, wrapping a blanket about himself, and stepped out on the wooden balcony. Outside, the first fingers of the sun pulled their way up behind the wooded headland. The storks circled their untidy nest on the top of the new tower, and turned south, the parent birds leading their brood to their other home. The third son watched them fly, away along the course of the estuary, with the salt wind at their backs and the peaks of the mountains a distant lure. They shrank in size, the sound of their wings fading, yet he continued to watch until they were no more than an uncertain blur over the distant shimmer of the river. The mountains beyond them smudged the skyline, purple and grey. Soon they too would become hard to see, as the clouds closed in with the start of the autumn rains. But, as he watched, a single point of white light danced for a moment over the topmost peak, a breath of chill air caressed his cheek, and from the waters of the estuary came a sound that was almost the ringing of a bell. It spoke for but a moment and then was forever gone, yet that moment was enough. The third son ducked back into his chamber. He dressed with speed, pulling on the stoutest garments he owned. From a corner, he took his spear and his long knife, but left his shield behind. From the next room, he took a leather bottle and a half-loaf of bread, which he stuffed into a leather satchel. And then, as the sun rose and the village began to awaken, he walked away down the track, through the wicket in the great gates, past the high banks and away. A single dog noted him pass and raised its head to sniff his footsteps. His own dog still slept, curled on the straw next to his red mare. His brothers, his father, were yet to stir from their own chambers. In the great central hall, a single servant woke and began to rebuild the hearth fire. The third son did not look back as he made his way down to the estuary.

Behind him, the sea whispered and rolled. The tide was in: the waters turned this way and that as salt met sweet. Birds hunted through the mud for food: the light dawn wind made patterns in the reeds. A long wooden jetty reached out, small boats bobbing on their tethers. The third son walked past its end, sparing it no glances. The mountains had called him, and the river was to be his guide. Underfoot, the path was packed earth and stone: his stride along it was long and easy. These first few miles were as familiar to him as his own skin, travelled over and over with his father's household on their travels. The fish in the waters, the goats and sheep on the hillside, the nuts and fruits of the woods all wove threads in the tapestry of his life. The dogs that guarded the flocks did not bark as he passed, his scent being known to them. The rare shepherd or gleaner nodded and smiled. His people, his home, his family.

And at the heart of it, the river. It had measured out every stage of his life. His mother's attendants had washed him, new-born, in its water. Its shallows and banks had formed both places to learn and places to play for him and his brothers. Here, his father's priest had taught him his letters, tracing them out with a stick in the mud. Here, he had in turn taught his youngest brother to fish. When, four years since, fever had carried off a third of the household, including his mother, the river waters had closed over their trinkets, sealing them away in memory for ever. Its voice woke him in the mornings and sang him to sleep at night. It was his oldest friend, companion, mentor, and more. The river was the lifeblood of his family's fields and flocks, the vital conduit between them and the markets to the south and east. The river had nurtured his father, his grandfather, and all his forefathers beyond them back into the darkness before family memory began. The river ran in their veins.

All his life, it had been a fixture, always there, always whispering and moving and dancing. He had ventured in small boats from the shelter of its mouth along the coast to the next settlement; had rowed across it to collect wood and nuts and mushrooms. He had poled his way upstream with his father, to make alliances with neighbouring lords. He had ridden, a time or two, along its banks almost into the lee of the mountains, to trade with the herdsmen who kept their cattle and sheep on their flanks.

He had never thought to follow it further: always, it had come to him.

Until today. Today, the river had called to him in turn, and his heart had answered. The sun rose over the far bank, its pale autumn rays striking red and orange from his hair, but he did not turn to greet it. Ducks dabbled in the shallows; in the branches of the willows, small birds told each other of his passage. Small animals rustled in the undergrowth. Each sound wove itself around the melody of the river. Each sound became some small part of its promise. Now, here, upwards and inwards: always changing, always, somehow, the same.

Once, his ancestors had called this river a god. She had been mother and bride, protector and destroyer, life and breath and death. They had given over tithes of all that they held most precious to her arms. Once, perhaps, the third son himself might have been made sacrifice to her moods. Now, her rituals were kinder; the memorials for the dead, the garlands to mark spring and harvest. His father would never ask him to shed his blood for the waters (though he had already shed it more than once in war). The pact of lord and waters was changed, through long years of new masters, new notions, new gods. And now, it had summoned him.

The first day's walking was easy: the banks were wide and the paths well-known to him. As the day progressed, others came to share his route, to fish in the salt marshes or to labour in fields nearby. They called greetings to him and he responded in kind, stopping to talk and exchange news. Around noon, a group of women washing clothes hailed him, bidding him share their meal of bread and cheese and apples. They admired him as he sat amongst them and he smiled and blushed (a little) and took it as his due. When the sun sank and the sky began to darken, he halted again and sought lodgings with a friend of his father's, a lesser lord whose compact hall lay a mile or so from the line of the river. He was well-fed and hosted, plied with cider and meat, and slept late on a pile of blankets near the fire. He left mid-morning with a pouch of food and a flask of cider-brandy to ease his way. The river made no comment on his lateness, only shimmered and murmured over its muddy bed. The next day passed much like the first. The path was perhaps less well-known to him: he was nearing the edge of his father's home domains. But still the people knew him and sounded like home. That night, he slept at a farm, whose owner did not know his face. Still, she was kind enough, once she recognised the quality of his garments and fed him well, even if his bed was further from the fire.

On the third day, the river led him out of the lands he knew. Those he met watched in in cautious silence as he passed, though the fields themselves were little different. The river began to narrow, its banks growing steeper. Its waters were brown-green now, where they had been flecked with aquamarine and blue; sand giving way to mud and rock underfoot. Where his father ruled, the banks were open, gentle, interspersed with sandy strands, and edged with meadowlands. Now, trees closed about him, their roots a trap for unwary feet. A little before noon, the path forked. The main route turned west, away from the river, towards a hamlet curving about a low hillside. Beside the river, there was no more than a rough track, muddy and uneven. For a moment, the third son hesitated. It had started to rain about an hour before and he was chilly and damp. His host of the night before had not offered him any food for the day ahead. In the hamlet, there would be warm fires, fresh bread, perhaps even a pottage of peas and grains. A stranger he might be, but he had coins of copper and silver to offer. His stomach rumbled, and he took one slow step towards the west.

The river sighed. The third son stopped and turned. Wavelets tugged at the edge of the bank beside his feet. Pale light flashed as the water moved. The third son looked back once more at the hamlet and strode forward onto the narrower track. If his pace had been slow on the first two days, delayed by friends and neighbours, now the terrain slowed him further. The path stuttered and struggled underfoot: here, it thinned to a plank's width between a tree and the crumbling edge of the riverbank; there it failed entirely, washed away by the spring floods, and he must scramble through dense undergrowth or climb round misshapen trees. Ash and willow and elm: their sweeping branches caught at his cloak or pulled his hair loose from its braid. Their leaves were all the colours of fire; they shivered free as he passed to squelch underfoot, or to rest on the surface of the river and be carried away to bring tidings of change downstream. The light came and went, filtering down through the trees. Leaning on his spear, he picked his way on and on, following the slow curves of the river. It was harder, now, to judge the passage of time: the sun hid away behind the clouds, above the trees. The ground began to slope upwards. Despite the rain, he was hot and thirsty. His breath sounded loud in his ears, blanking out the rush of water, the soft murmuring of the trees. On and on: head down, he concentrated only on the ground underfoot. The light shaded from dove grey to charcoal, and all of a sudden the bank gave way beneath him.

For a moment he seemed to hang there, suspended. And then he was falling, sliding down slick mud, with no chance of a foothold. The spear slithered away from him. His cloak caught on a low branch and tore. And then he was in the water. It swallowed him whole, filled ears and eyes and mouth, and for long moments he floundered, limbs flailing. Nothing to grasp, nothing stable on which to stand... The water had him and would carry him away as easily as it carried the leaves, back down through the woods to the wider lands and the sea beyond. The river had called him – and betrayed him.

The river was his friend, his sister, his beloved companion. Even as its waters reached for his lungs, his head cleared, and his feet found purchase on the rocky bed. The waters steadied him, held him in place, and, at last, he stood once more, safe in its clasp. He shook his head, blinking moisture away from his eyes. The river had brought him almost to the opposite bank: to his left, it sloped gently up to a cluster of hazel trees. To the right... Just beyond where the ground had given way, a deep channel cut its way through the woods, where a tributary rushed down to join its bigger sibling. Its sides were treacherous with broken branches and great chunks of rock. Had he fallen there, rather than a few feet sooner...

The river had saved him. He cupped a hand, raised a palmful of water to his lips and breathed into it his thanks. Around him the waters shivered, then pushed him gently towards the shore. The pebbles did not shift under his feet as he moved; the current did not tug at him. He stepped out onto the shallow grassy bank and found it firm and dry. The trees here still retained most of their leaves. There was space to build a small fire, and enough deadwood to feed it. There were nuts on the trees, and fish swam lazily in the shallows, easy to catch. The third son had never taken strongly to any faith, whether that of his forebears or that of the new priests, but that night, making camp, he whispered words of praise to the river.

Days turned into a week, and still the third son walked. The woods deepened, thickened about him, and the river valley grew narrower. A stout fallen branch replaced his spear as a walking aid. His belt knife grew blunt from hacking at the undergrowth. A day passed, then two, and he saw no-one. The third night, he came on a tumbledown shelter, perhaps once a herdsman's hut, and curled up inside to sleep. He lived now on what the river provided: the small fish he could tickle, where the banks allowed, and the nuts of neighbouring trees. The river was slimmer, now, and faster over its bed, which was studded with boulders. More and more, he must climb, as the banks deepened. On the fourth day, the trees began to change, hazel and willow giving way to mountain oak and thorn and beech. The third son went hungry that day, though the beech trees did at least thin out the undergrowth and make the going easier. But the bank grew ever steeper and just after noon he was forced away from the river's edge by an outcrop of slick, treacherous rocks. This was not the river he knew, not anymore. This river, this new mountain traveller, was a thing of noise and tumult, cutting its way through the bones of the earth. The banks were becoming cliffs, and he must climb ever higher. Grey rocks, these, and grooved and scored by years of water and wind. He climbed as best he could, feet slipping on the stone, fingers growing numb with cold and strain. Here and there a ledge provided respite; stubborn trees found purchase in crevices. Droppings showed where mountain goats had made a path. Where he could, he followed them. They would know where was safe and where not. They would know how to find shelter.

Finally, he reached the top. He hauled himself over the edge and lay a while to catch his breath. It was not the top of the hill, not quite: rather, it was a broad spur that carried on round to the east and south. He looked down at the river again, seeking to be sure of its course. The light was fading: he could make out little detail in the gloom. He hesitated. He could rest here until dawn then climb back down to try and make a way along the side of the cliff. They had come this far together. He struggled to his feet, uncertain, and, away to the south, on the very edge of the horizon, white light flashed. He turned, and it flashed again. He took a step towards it, and from below, from beside him, the river once more spoke with the note of a bell. The third son lifted his chin and began to walk along the spur. As he turned round the first bend, a path came winding up from the other side, and beyond, further into the mountains along the line of the gorge. He joined it, his pace picking up for the first time in days. The wiry grass was a comfort to his feet: he was above the trees, here. Up ahead, along the skyline, marched the line of the mountains. They were purple and grey against the clouds, but the sharp peak of the very highest was wreathed in a scarf of brilliant white. Ice, preserved in the crevasses and folds of rock. Ice, that fed the mountain streams that, in turn fed the river he had known all his life.

Winter never truly left the heart of the mountains. A travelling poet had told him that, once, but he had not understood what it meant until now. Winter birthed the water that fed all the lower lands. His gaze traced the line of the river gorge, winding away towards those peaks. Perhaps his river also took its birth up there. Almost, it seemed to him, he could feel the touch of that ice against his skin, as the wind blew along the ridge. If the river was the limbs of that distant shard of winter, this was its breath.

He rounded the corner of the spur, and the ground widened out in front of him. An apron of land curved gently around the hillside, following the trail of the river below. Goats browsed the grass: a great brindled dog set up an alarm as he neared. The third son stopped. The mountain dogs were bred to guard their flocks from wolves. It would take care to convince it he meant the goats no harm. And the truth was, he was hungry. His hand went to the hilt of his knife. He'd need speed and accuracy to avoid the dog, and he was tired. He began to circle towards the edge of the gorge, as far as he could from the flock. The dog growled, and he came once again to a halt. Several of the goats raised their heads to stare at him from yellow eyes. The dog began to creep towards him, stiff legged.

The light flashed again. The dog looked round, startled. Then, away across the pasture, something – someone – whistled. The dog's head came up, and it turned, trotted away towards the sound. The third son stared. For a moment, it seemed, a pale female shape glimmered, and was gone. He hurried on down the path, towards the next bend, and what safety he might find beyond it.

He slept cold that night, and poorly, huddled against a scrub oak. But the river pulled him onwards. He lost track of the days: now, it was light, and he was scrambling down through rock-tumble and low bushes towards the river. Now, it was dark, and he snatched moments of sleep curled in the lee of boulders. Sometimes, the sides of the river were steep, and he must pick his way, sometimes they softened again, and broadened, and the walking grew easier. Water, he always had, but food was scarce: a few late berries here, a handful of beechnuts there. His clothing grew ragged and his beard filled out.

At last, there came a day when the trees failed and the sides of the valley closed in around him, and there was only him and the river. It was narrow, now, and noisy, and its waters were ice cold. Several times already he had had to scramble across tributary streams and claw his way under small cascades. Now, he staggered through the edge waters, feet slipping and scrabbling on the rocky bed, hands aching with cold. He was high up in the mountains, now. He could no longer remember the last time he had seen another human face. Here, even the birds were few. Often, it seemed he climbed more than walked, and the river wrapped her chilly arms about him. She tugged and dragged, pulling him back, and still he forged ahead, feeling through her touch the lure of the ice that crowned the mountain. He moved without thinking, almost without awareness at all. He was the water and the stone, he was the leaves that the river carried and the trees it felled. He was the grey mountain light and the thick mountain darkness. He was the land as it turned towards winter and the memory of the summer that was gone. The river encompassed him and filled every sense.

Close in the water's embrace, his climb brought him deeper into darkness. The mountain had closed over him: here, within its bones, there was neither day nor night. He moved as in a dream, as the water grew ever more shallow.

And then there was light. He came to a halt, blinking, eyes streaming, as it fell around him, blue and pale green and violet. Under his hands, the walls of the gorge shimmered. Flecks of crystal glinted, set reflections dancing. His breath steamed. Under his feet, the river was wholly ice, forming uneven stairs, carrying him upwards into the heart of the ice. He stepped lightly, now, hunger forgotten. From time to time, he glimpsed himself, mirrored in the walls of the glacier. Now and then, another figure formed, shaded in all the subtle shades the ice knew, long limbed and sinuous. Her eyes met his, and they were the dark grey-brown of the river at the estuary. He reached the top of the stair, and the ice opened out around him, a great hall of frozen pillars and frescoes of silica and quartz. And, at its centre, a woman of water and earth and light. Water ran from the ends of her long hair and meandered in small rivulets towards the passage back down towards the river. Her hands were filled with light. The third son staggered the last few paces towards her. Her shining arms reached out for him and her breath, cold as winter, caressed his cheek. She drew him closer, and her ice crowned him in brilliance.

Outside, on the peak of the mountain, the first snows began to fall.

THE ROAD TO TEMPOL

Wendy Darling

As an archaeologist in the employ of the state government, David Dobson was often called in to inspect and, if necessary, investigate what appeared to be ancient dwellings, ash pits, or other traces of long-ago inhabitants. And so it was he found himself driving west to a dreary town along the state's northern border at 4 o'clock on a Friday afternoon.

David had never actually visited Tempol before, but he had driven through it on numerous occasions. Based on other towns in the area, he had a good idea what it was like. Too large to be a village, it met the definition of a town, and yet driving through on the narrow state highway, it seemed that just as you'd expect to arrive at the center, it was disappearing in your rearview mirror.

It often seemed as though such towns were almost randomly placed upon the road, with no real purpose. Intellectually, of course, David understood. Tempol, like most of the towns along the northern border, actually sat beside a small river, which at one time had powered a mill. That mill, along with farming and a couple of small factories, had been enough to grow and nurture a community. But the mill had shut down at least a century ago and farming was long gone as well. The town was fading, had been fading for decades, but it hadn't quite disappeared.

He was about 25 minutes out now, already in the familiar landscape. To his left snaked a narrow river strewn with rocks and the occasional fallen tree. To his right loomed a pine forest climbing a steep hill, so that from his perspective it looked like a dark wall. The road itself was only two lanes, the sort of thing that locals still referred to as "the highway," even though it had been replaced by a modern highway three decades earlier and a dozen miles to the south. He had passed through a couple of towns similar to Tempol on the way, and in between those he'd driven past the occasional isolated house fitted into dips in the hill. Sometimes there was no house to be seen, but just an old driveway or a road, neither of which he could see the end of.

Where they led, he couldn't say.

David was circumspect about his job. Most of the time calls like this were false alarms. A construction crew digging a road, or a kid walking in the woods, would turn up something they thought might be a Native American burial ground or a treasure trove of old silverware. But then David would arrive and determine it was a couple of dogs or even a deer that had been buried, and the silverware was more or less junk, put in a box in the ground a century ago and forgotten. Treasure once, but in the present, worth little. There were positive aspects to his job, however. First, he actually *had* a job in his chosen area of study that was out of academia — something many people with an archaeology degree or two could not claim. Second, on occasion he actually *did* arrive at a scene and discover that there was real work for him to do, something that would keep him occupied for a day or week or even longer.

At the moment, ten minutes away, he didn't know which way this job would go. A call had been taken from a local man regarding a "secret sanctuary" he'd come upon below ground level on state land in town. David would have dismissed this call entirely — mostly likely what they had was an ordinary old cellar, standing where the house had once stood — except for the fact the man reported elaborate paintings, carvings, and a secret door leading into what was described as an 'undisturbed passageway'. That did sound unusual. Then again, perhaps local teens had at one time discovered the same space and used it as a secret 'club'. He could imagine the drinking and sexual liaisons. That did leave the matter of the secret door and passageway, however. There was only one way to find out: question the man and visit the site.

At length he arrived in Tempol, and when alerted by his phone GPS, slowed even below the 25 miles per hour speed limit to read the street numbers on the houses. The red clapboard house was just off the highway, on a street sloping upwards into the ever-present forest. He parallel-parked out in front – the driveway only accommodated one vehicle – and after placing his things on the ground, climbed out and took a moment to examine his surroundings.

The house, unlike its neighbors, had been recently painted. Flowers were planted out front. Light green velvet drapes hung in windows facing the street; they looked expensive. Altogether it was not quite what he'd expected. He'd imagined a bedraggled house with a rusted vehicle or two in the front yard, along with an assortment of cheap children's toys, strewn about and worse for wear. This home looked far more respectable. He was curious what sort of people lived inside.

Attaché case in hand, he approached the front door up a brick path, also newly resurfaced, and pressed the doorbell. After a few seconds he heard the sound of brisk footsteps, and moments later the front door swung inward, revealing a tall woman in a business suit.

"Good afternoon," she said, extending her hand. "You must be Mr. Dobson."

David shook the woman's hand and when she subtly motioned for him to step inside, he did so. As with the house, she was not what he expected. A business suit? Perhaps it was time to let go of his assumptions.

"I'm Leslie. My husband is out back, refinishing an old picnic table... I think." She walked them into dining room just off the front hall. Have a seat here at the table and I'll go get him."

While he waited, he drew out the contents of his case and arranged them on the table: notepad, pen, iPad, area map, and a printed copy of the report, taken from his office's electronic system. Satisfied with this, he glanced about the room, finding it full of unpretentious antiques and family pictures, with an arrangement of dried lilacs on the sideboard.

There was a quiet knock. When David looked over, he saw an extremely tall man standing in the doorway – his head nearly touching the top of the frame

"Hi, I'm Quinn," the man said. "Sorry I wasn't right here to get the door."

David started to rise to shake the man's hand but was waved back down. "I hope to keep things casual, Mr. Dobson. This is our home and you're welcome to just relax." Quinn certainly did seem like a man who liked to keep things casual. He was wearing a faded T-shirt and pair of black cargo shorts. A few bits of sawdust were caught in his short brown hair.

"Sounds good," David acquiesced. "You can call me David, if you like."

"Cool." Quinn sat down opposite and gestured to the papers and the iPad. "I guess this is when you interview me to get the facts?"

David nodded "I have the basics you called in, but I'd like to hear a more complete version. And then if we could go over to the site, that would be great."

"Awesome." Quinn, who had his elbows down on the table, now clasped his hands together. "I guess you have flashlights and all that? Cameras?" When David nodded, the man resumed. "Great. So should I just tell you what happened?"

"Yes. But let me turn on voice recording," David said, turning on the iPad and clicking on the app icon. "It helps me to get every detail down. I also take notes on paper." He looked up at Quinn. "Ready?" The man nodded and he pressed *Record.*

"We've only been out here a couple years," Quinn began. "It'll be two years in July. My wife and I moved out with our kids here to the country, some call it the sticks, where it's quiet. She's a marketing consultant and works mostly remotely, on her own, teleconferencing. I'm a writer and also watch the kids when they're not in school."

That explained a few things. The couple had likely bought the home as a 'fixer-upper'. The mortgage on it had to be nothing, compared to Boston area. Tempol was well out of the range of extended suburbs and their inflated real estate prices. Leslie's job also explained the business suit.

"Go on," David prompted. "It's mentioned on the intake sheet that you made your discovery while out with your kids. What were you doing out in the woods?"

"Maya and James go to public school here, but I do some homeschooling as well, as a supplement. Some of that involves doing things in the outdoors – identifying birds, ecology lessons, that kind of thing. So a couple of weeks ago it was a pretty nice day – for April – and I decided we'd go out and follow some unmarked road around here to, ah… see what we could see."

David was taking down notes, despite the fact there'd be a digital recording. *Newcomer to the area and curious,* he wrote.

"Wasn't the road marked as state property?" he asked

"As a matter of fact, it wasn't," Quinn replied. "I had no idea we weren't supposed to be there, as state land, although logically, yeah, it had to belong to someone. But it definitely didn't seem occupied and there weren't any 'No Trespassing' signs anywhere."

"OK. Describe what you found," David encouraged.

"We parked at the start of the road, right by the highway. I didn't know how long of a walk it'd be or if there was even anything interesting in there, but I figured it could at least be a nature hike. No benches or paths like a state park, but at least a road.

"So we start on in and just like most places here, it's a hill, though this one isn't too steep. The road's old gravel, covered in pine needles – the trees are mostly pines, hemlocks, but a few oaks."

David could picture the scene in his mind's eye.

"We went along for over a mile and it was nothing interesting. The kids ran ahead for a while, but it was just like a tunnel of pine trees. We heard crows but didn't see any.

"Anyway, I was about to turn back when I saw the track opening up in front of us. The kids saw it too and jogged on ahead. A couple minutes later I get there and the kids are looking around. The clearing's not huge, not football-field size. More like the size of a kids' baseball field, including outfield. It's got high, wild grass, low bushes scattered around, scraggly trees and some small rocky outcroppings, like you always see in the woods out here. Not huge boulders, but rock."

The woods throughout the state were indeed dotted with rocky ridges and boulders, left over from the last ice age. Walking through woodland, it was quite usual to come across formations of boulders that, apart from being impressive in their own right, might even form a shape like say a turtle, if you used your imagination. Some people even imagined these boulder groups were ancient ruins of some kind; in his career with the state, David had received numerous reports of that nature. He almost never went out to investigate these in person, as a simple call or a request for a photo sent by email usually confirmed it was an entirely natural formation.

"The road kept going around the side of the clearing, and we stopped to explore. I thought at first the spot might have been the site of a house, but when I walked around, I didn't see anything like a foundation. The land looked to me like it might've been cleared maybe a hundred years ago? There was land like that where I grew up in New Hampshire – old farm, closed up in the '20s.

"Anyway, James saw a hawk flying overhead and I was helping

him to identify it when Maya called over, saying she'd found a door. I assumed she meant some random door, like someone had dumped an old door there, but when I went over to the middle of the clearing, she was pointing down to an actual door set in the ground."

"How is it you didn't see this door yourself when you were walking around before?"

"There were bushes and high grass growing around it. And it's rusted metal, so it doesn't really stand out." Quinn drew up his shoulders, taking a deep breath, then exhaled. "This door was set in some old concrete and had a handle on it like you have on a bulkhead door into a cellar.

"Naturally I was curious about it, but not as curious as the kids were. They immediately started telling me to open it. Common sense told me I probably shouldn't – maybe it was some kind of contaminated waste site: who knows? But there weren't any signs around, and normally that kind of stuff has warnings all over it. I grabbed the handle and after some yanking and pulling, I discovered it wasn't locked, although the hinges were rusted, and the door was heavy. And I pulled it all the way open."

Quinn was a good storyteller. His report was considerably more interesting than what David usually got to hear. "But you didn't find contaminated waste or ammo or anything like that, did you?"

"No. There was set of stone steps. I was surprised it was stone, I figured it would be concrete. But it was stone and it was pretty long, turned out to be twenty steps – I counted on the way out. We flipped the door backwards away from the opening and started going down.

"The only light I had on me was my phone flashlight, but it was still light out, so the stairs were OK. It was darker in the room at the bottom. It was stone like the stairs, with a stone floor and stone walls and a kind of reinforced stone ceiling. It looked old, though I couldn't tell you how old. It kind of reminded me of a dungeon, or you know, a cliché of a dungeon."

"Like there should be manacles and torches in it?" David supplied, half-joking.

"There *were* torches! Or actually there were holders on the walls where you would put torches. For the rest of the room, there was a whole set up of a couple card tables and a dozen folding chairs. These were all old and dusty, not anything anyone had used recently. There were daddy-long-legs spiders down there."

David nodded, noting it all down. "OK. Now you reported there were paintings on the wall?"

"Yeah." Quinn looked over to the dining room wall as if he might be able to picture them there. "It wasn't like the walls were entirely painted, but there were light-colored paintings on them. I couldn't see very well because I only had the phone flashlight, but I know I saw an eagle – or maybe a phoenix? And a moon, what looked like maybe people flying. It was weird.

"But it's the back wall that's really cool. The kids thought it was a big fireplace, because the stones were shaped and carved and there was an indentation, a stone rectangular frame, and something like a mantel piece. But I don't think it was a fireplace; it's an altar. The mantel piece bit has residue on it like many, many candles have burned down."

This was getting stranger by the minute. The report David had received hadn't provided this level of detail and he frankly hadn't expected it. "What does this 'altar' look like, besides the mantel?"

"Well, the main thing is a central panel. It's flat and in the middle is a symbolic depiction of some kind of... *person*. I would guess some kind of god, but not like anything I've ever seen at a church – not a crucifix or Jesus or Mary or something like that. It seemed to be wearing some kind of headdress. But remember, I couldn't see it very well and there were all these shadows."

This sounded quite bizarre.

"And is this the panel that opened up?"

"Yeah. Around the figure, in the background, there were carvings of a moon and the sun and all these holes that I guess were supposed to be stars. And for some reason, going up to look with my flashlight, I stuck my fingers" – he held up his index, middle and ring-finger – "to see how deep they were, I guess.

"The kids were still over by the stairs where it was light, because I'd told them to stay there. I was just worried about them – which was lucky because right after I put my fingers in there, a door opened up on the right. It had just looked like the rest of the walls. I jumped back and kind of screamed "Holy shit!" or something. It was like that bookcase scene in *Young Frankenstein*, except totally not funny. The kids screamed too and then went to run over. I shouted at them to go back where they were."

David was having trouble believing such a thing existed in Tempol. "So now there was a doorway leading to an older – you reported – 'untouched' chamber?"

"Right. It was much darker in there than it was in the first chamber, so I couldn't see far in and I wasn't going to go in either. No thanks! But from the smell and the dust, I had this definite sense that it hadn't been opened in a very long time, like centuries. I can't even tell you why I knew that, but I just did. It felt like something out of a, you know... I really hate to say this to you, but an Indiana Jones movie."

David raised an eyebrow. This case did seem interesting, but he really doubted this back chamber was hundreds of years old. And spare him any more Indiana Jones references. He'd had enough to last him a lifetime

"After that, I tried to take a few pictures with flash, but they came out so bad, they're not even worth sharing. You'll just see for yourself.

"We wrapped it up after that. I left the stone door open because, honestly, I was just kind of scared of it. And then we just went back to the car and went home. But later I asked a couple people in town about the land, if they knew anything. Of the three people I asked, none of them had actually been in there, but one said he knew a couple people who used it for hunting. And then the same guy told me that the state actually owns the land."

"Did you mention the underground chamber to any of them?" David asked

"No." Quinn looked sheepish. "I guess I kind of wanted to keep the secret to myself."

"Only for a little while, though," David observed. "Then you must've decided that since the state owned the land, you might be able to reach out and let us know."

"Yup. And now you're here." Quinn set his hands flat on the table. "Ready to see it?"

"I think so. Just let me gather up my things and, if you don't mind, use the bathroom."

Quinn got up from his chair and move towards the door. "Would you like some coffee? I can make us each a little thermos and we can take it with us."

"Sure," David agreed, picking up his case. "Just point me to the bathroom and we can be off when you're ready."

"It was a challenge at first getting our foot in the door here," Quinn was saying, as they drove over to the site. "This isn't a tourist town, or a business town either, so the attitude is sort of 'Why are you here and what do you want?'"

David nodded, glancing down at the GPS app, which showed two miles to their destination. "I understand. My job involves showing up in a lot of small New England towns."

"Right. And I'm from small-town New Hampshire, so I get it. But it's a little frustrating when you say you've bought a house in town and people are suspicious." Quinn sipped coffee from his thermos. "I guess we'll always be 'the new people.' Twenty years from now, we'll still be 'the new people.'"

"That's true," David agreed. "When you live in an apartment block, people come and go, so even if you just stay as couple years, you're an 'old timer.'"

"Yeah. We had an apartment in Boston when we were first married." Quinn peered up ahead. "Hey, this is it, coming up on the left. Slow down a little or you might miss it."

The track wasn't that easy to see, just a narrow cut in the trees and, as Quinn had noted, there wasn't any sign. Once they made the turn, the car rumbled up the gravel road.

"I'm driving all the way up," David said.

Quinn was sipping on his coffee. "Saves time."

"There's also some equipment I'm bringing down there."

Quinn's description of a 'tunnel of pine trees' had been apt. There was enough light to drive on without headlights, but the forest dropped off into darkness quickly. There seemed to be a lot of undergrowth.

After a couple of minutes, the trees opened up into the clearing. It wasn't an empty field, but rather an area of high grass, stunted bushes, and a few sickly saplings.

"You're right," David said, stopping the car and putting it in Park. "It does look like the land was abandoned a hundred years ago or so."

Quinn got out of the car while David pulled the trunk release.

"Yeah. And it looks natural, as far as I can tell," Quinn said, stepping around to the back of the car. "No stumps like if someone had cleared it out, although I guess they could've pulled them. But I don't see any evidence that it was a farm, and like I said there aren't any remains of a foundation – no wood, no stone, no brick. That thing isn't a foundation."

David agreed with Quinn. But looking around the clearing, feeling it, it seemed to him that something else was off, though he couldn't put a name to it. Something that made it seem as if they were on a hill, a place of importance, above all others.

He wheeled over a hand truck from the back seat and opened the trunk. "Since you're here, Quinn, help me load up equipment."

"Sure. Just tell me what to put on first." There was a case with lighting equipment, another that was a video camera set-up, and a tub full of archaeology sample containers, solutions, tools and the like. They all stacked pretty neatly on the cart and held together with three long bungee cords.

David pulled out his sturdy courier bag, where he kept his most frequently used tools and essentials like pen and paper, then closed the trunk. "Ready to lead on?"

Without a word, Quinn took the cart and wheeled it into the field, navigating around the biggest bumps. David shouldered his bag and followed behind.

Taking in the pine circle around them, it felt right to be moving into the center of the clearing, as if a localized gravitational field was drawing them in. Or the trees were pushing them away. David's scientific mind told him there had to be a commonplace reason the land had been cleared out.

"Well, here it is," Quinn announced, parking the cart and gesturing to the door set close to the ground. "Want me to open it, or would you like to have a look for yourself?"

David walked over. "From here on out, I'd like to go first on everything, if you don't mind," he explained. "Feel free to speak up and explain, of course."

He pulled out his phone and went to the notes app. "I'm going to take my notes in this," he explained. "Most of it in voice notes, some in dictation. Just easier and quicker then stopping and writing everything down as I go. And I'm doing it right as I see it."

Quinn nodded. "Go ahead."

"Door is approximately four by three feet," he dictated. "Steel, deteriorated, with a layer of gray paint, which has mostly flaked off. From the state of deterioration, and judging from the door handle, I would date it to the early 20th century. Door is set into concrete, which appears consistent in age with the door. Opening is located in approximately the center of the field although I have not taken precise measurements."

Next he pulled open the door, which as Quinn had said now swung much more easily on the hinge. With the man's help, David set it so it was lying back on the grass.

David had assumed, after looking at the door, that the steps and the chamber below would be consistent with either early 20th century construction or old New England building forms. It was not.

"This stone..." he said to Quinn. "When you described it, I didn't picture it looking this way. The style of the cuts, the whole way it's laid... it's not something I'd expect to be here."

He dictated his findings. He was very familiar with how New England farmers and Colonial settlers had built their homes, including stairs and walls, and these stairs didn't match that. He'd expected the stairs to be fairly rough, the stones probably not all that finished. But these blocks were all evenly cut, rectangular. Perpendicular. And set with such precision, no mortar had been used. He climbed down as he made his notes. Looking more closely at the surface of the blocks, he was amazed to see the workmanship. He was going to need to take a lot of pictures.

At that point he stopped to bring all the equipment down. Quinn was helpful in this endeavor, as it was a long staircase and the fewer times David had to run up and down, the better. Soon all the items were at the bottom of the stairs and David set down his bag on one of the old tables. The chamber was as Quinn had described, although the details did not match up with what David expected. Yes, the floor, walls, and ceiling were stone, but it wasn't the sort of stonework he'd expected. And the paintings on the walls were peculiar. He moved closer to see them, but his shadow fell over them, and he realized they really were going to have to set up lights. Sunlight from outside did not reach the far end of the room.

With Quinn's assistance, David had two lamps set up in about fifteen minutes. The lights employed powerful rechargeable batteries designed to last for hours. He placed one in the front corner shining backwards, diagonally, and asked Quinn to set the other at on the far end, diagonal.

Once the room was fully lit, both men stood staring.

Quinn had vaguely described some paintings, and the altar, but seeing it fully illuminated brought clarity to both of them.

"This is weird," said Quinn. "I mean... what was this, a clubhouse for a cult?"

As Quinn had said, the room was set up as a meeting place, with chairs facing forward and a few tables. But it didn't look like any kind of Christian church.

The line-paintings on the walls, laid down over the same precisely cut, unmortared stone, glowed white, dusky blue and ochre. While the actual images had the appearance of petroglyphs – eagles, buzzards, men with wings, and inexplicably a peacock – when David stepped closer, he concluded they'd been made with store-bought paint, sometime in the past hundred years. The colors were even, strong, and did not match paints employed by Native Americans. Had a group of locals attempted to emulate natives, or create paintings in what they thought was a native style? If so, they had failed, because the style the paintings most closely resembled was Babylonian or Assyrian. David was puzzled.

The 'altar' was another matter altogether. He couldn't imagine it had been created by any local 'club', although whatever masons had laid down the stones of the vault possibly could have – if they'd studied ancient Near East civilizations. Quinn had been able to make out a figure standing at the center, possibly wearing a headdress, surrounded by an array of stars, a moon and a sun. But it was all in the details. The figure's face, robes, jewelry, the curls of his hair, all matched ancient Babylonian styles. The headdress he wore was made of peacock feathers, with the stylized head of the bird as the crown. The man's wings, which draped down to meet the top of the mantle, were that of a vulture. All the other carving details were the same: not contemporary, not North American, but harkening back to designs he'd studied at university and seen with his own eyes in collections of archaeological relics – at the British Museum in London, the Pergamom Museum in Berlin, and other establishments that preserved faces of the ancient past. These images did not belong buried in a field in Tempol, Massachusetts.

"I'll be honest with you," he said. "This is not quite what I had pictured in my head when you were describing it. I mean, everything you said was accurate, but…"

Quinn was examining the peacock drawing, head cocked at an angle, hands thrust into his pockets. "It's not just me, then?"

"Oh, no. This is definitely an interesting discovery, *very* interesting. And you did absolutely the right thing calling us." David pulled up his voice recorder app again and turned the screen towards the other man. "Do you mind if I start dictating again?"

"What? Oh, yeah, go ahead." Quinn walked over to the stairs and sat on one of the lower steps. "You said you were going to do that and I'm sure there's a lot to record here."

And there was. For the next twenty-five minutes David poured forth descriptions of all he saw there, even the old tables and chairs. Later he'd be taking photographs, measurements, various types of samples, but his immediate priority was getting down his first impressions.

There was one thing he did leave out of his dictation, however: neither the paintings nor the carvings seemed North American in origin. If David had been alone, he would have speculated aloud his theories on what the paintings were based on, or which era of Babylonian art the carvings most closely resembled, but with Quinn present, a member of the public, he had to keep that knowledge close to his chest. Quinn was obviously an intelligent man and perhaps had already made some suppositions himself, but it would be careless indeed to confirm such suspicions and risk exposing the site. The man might tell someone, who might tell someone, and soon it could end up on a blog and from there… No, it couldn't be risked, and so David described everything in as much detail as possible, knowing he'd revise the notes later to add in whatever he couldn't say out loud.

It took more than an hour to obtain all the pictures he needed. As with bringing down the equipment, Quinn was again quite helpful, moving chairs as needed, making adjustments to lights, and a few times noticing small details that might require a close-up. David didn't need all the advice on the photography, but he appreciated it.

"Well, that leaves the mysterious back room," he announced, shutting off his camera for the moment. "Shall we?"

They moved to the back, where the opening gaped like the maw of a cave. Once he found himself standing at the threshold and peering in, David couldn't believe what he was seeing, even with his own shadow blocking some of the light.

While the first room featured fine-cut, immaculately set stone, it was somewhat dusty. This room gleamed. The walls of the entrance chamber were predominantly flat stone and painted, with only one wall of carved rock, while all the walls in this smaller room were worked from floor to ceiling, in the same ancient Babylonian style. And while the room they'd left had old wooden chairs for seating, a large stone throne stood at rear wall of this one. It was carved in the shape of a peacock.

One thing at least was familiar, and fairly modern: An old oil hurricane lamp, set on the floor just behind the throne. But whoever had left it was long, long gone.

David began dictating more notes, a reassuring ritual, which postponed having to consider the implications of what he was seeing. This had to be an elaborate hoax, a nineteenth century folly, a fake. "But what if it isn't?" a tiny contrary inner voice asked. At any rate, as he made his notes, David didn't voice these suspicions out loud. And once again, he left out any direct mention of similarities to ancient Babylonian art, to keep it from Quinn's ears.

It was while he was taking photos that David realized what he would have to do: return to the site the next day. True, the photos would be complete, and he had most of his notes, but there was more to be done. He could complete his notes, adding in everything he'd left out. He could look for clues in the field above. And above all, he had a sense, a gut feeling more than a professional assessment, that he would get something out of a second visit, by himself, that wasn't to be had now.

"I have what I need for the time being," he announced, packing away his camera and heading towards the door. "I'll come back tomorrow to get the rest."

"Oh, you're coming back?" Quinn gathered up a couple other packs of supplies and brought them into the main room. "Do you need me to come out again?"

"No, I think I'll be fine alone. I won't bring down nearly as much equipment and if I do, I'll just make a second trip. It was nice to have your help today, though." He'd pulled up a photo of the altar in an editing program. "Speaking of which, if you show me what you pressed to open that door, I'll mark it on here so I get it right."

After that, David carefully made sure all the equipment and supplies made it to the foot of the stairs, and together the men carried it up to the field. Predictably, it was considerably more difficult to get out than it had been to get in. Both of them were slightly winded by the time they stood next to the cart strapping everything back in place. The temperature had dropped, and twilight was descending. As he drove back to Quinn's house, David asked about local hotels.

"There isn't anything in Tempol," Quinn replied. "Which isn't a surprise. But there's one in Selbridge I've driven past, about seven miles away. Old motor lodge."

"Sounds like what I'm looking for. If there's a clean bed and bathroom, great. If there's Wi-Fi, I'll be grateful for the bonus."

He dropped Quinn off with a promise to keep him updated on the case and perhaps even call the next day if he made any significant discoveries. They parted with a handshake.

Less than a half hour later, David was walking toward his room for the night. The hotel was clean but dated, harkening back to the late 1950s, early '60s, when families would actually vacation in the area. Fishing in local streams, visiting small state parks, and breathing clean air away from the city were all quite enough for a luxury getaway in those days – no theme resort or massive amusement park needed.

The hotel had changed very little since those times. The office David checked into was simple. A gray-haired woman worked the desk with half her attention on a program streaming on an old laptop. The place did have Internet, to his satisfaction. The keychain was a plastic triangle, stamped 'Selbridge Lodge', and the number on the door shared the same quaint font.

Once inside, David placed his small travel bag on the carpet, did a quick survey, and was satisfied all was in order: average, if slightly sagging, double bed, clean comforter, desk, chair, lights that worked, and yes, a properly scrubbed bathroom with towels. After locking the door, he moved the bag to sit atop the desk. A horrible little coffee maker stood there, with two measly packets of coffee, non-dairy creamer and sugar substitute. He fixed himself a cup, knowing he'd be going out to dinner later. But first, he had work to do.

After dragging the chair over to the bed and setting down his laptop bag and attaché case, he powered up and verified that yes, there was working Wi-Fi. Then he dug in: area maps, town history, local geology. Time to dig deeper, into some different corners of the Internet, into other databases, back through newspaper archives, searches of libraries and literature. There were the usual ghost stories and "unsolved mysteries" of the land, which one found all over but particularly so in the more rural areas of New England. With so few people around, who could refute the stories?

It was in the newspaper archive that he came upon a couple of tantalizing leads. There wasn't much in the way of crime in Tempol, and the only violent deaths were car crashes from folks gunning it down the same road he'd driven down himself that afternoon. They'd met with trees, skid on ice, swerved into the river. The biggest crime news in the area wasn't even really a crime, but a disappearance, which back in the 1930s had been the fodder of numerous headlines, not only in small local papers but in the Worcester paper and the Boston papers. A long-time resident, a farmer, had disappeared one night in 1937. One Raymond Dyer had been home, had breakfast, and at some point, left the house. But he didn't use the family's single car, so his wife didn't realize he'd gone for hours. She contacted Dyer's friends and, alarmed, they launched a search of the area – his usual haunts, including some land he owned outside of town… located on the very same road he and Quinn had driven down that day. Yes, the man had owned the land which was now state property. But of him not trace was ever found, or at least nothing had ever been reported to the police, who never found any clues.

The next step was delving into archaeology and architecture, checking for sites similar to this chamber in Tempol. His fingers flew across the keyboard as he ran searches of journal archives, databases, an online book library, a couple of excellent image galleries. As he'd expected, he found nothing on similar underground chambers, certainly not in North America. However, as soon as he switched to looking at *Mesopotamian* sites, stones, statues, he knew he was on track.

The styles matched, as did numerous symbols. The central figure of the Tempol site, with its glorious wings, was not unlike Marduk, the patron deity of Babylon, or Ashur. But it was clearly neither of these. The peacock feathers in the crown? The fact the wings were vulture wings? They didn't match. Neither did the figure's clothing, which although of a similar style, appeared to include some kind of cape, perhaps also made of feathers. Who was this figure? And the larger question: What was this Babylonian temple doing here in New England?

It had to be a fake, but that in itself had to be an interesting story. Who could've built it? Or… wait, maybe it was all stolen at some point from an actual ancient site? The idea seemed preposterous. Why Tempol?

David's growling stomach eventually brought him back to the hotel room, where his disgusting coffee sat on the end table, virtually untouched. Three hours had gone by without him noticing. Time to find dinner and some kind of a drink before everything closed up for the night. He couldn't imagine either Selbridge or Tempol having a lot of night life.

The bar was about a two-star, but since it was the only bar in Tempol or Selbridge, locally it rated four stars. The wood veneer walls were slightly water-damaged, the carpet a dusty color that couldn't be determined in the low light. The stamped tin beer ads on the wall were rusted around the edges and, David noted, represented several brands that hadn't been produced in years.

The establishment was all of a piece with the locals at the bar and tables, David reflected, as he sat on a stool waiting on a BLT and fries. Not all the patrons were old – some were in their twenties, he judged – but all of them had an out-of-time, out-of-sync air to them. The old men in their khakis and work coats, plaid shirts and faded baseball caps inhabited their own universe. They knew nothing of hipsters, chic bars that sold high ABV craft beers at $10 a pint. He guessed if he tried to check into the place on Facebook, it wouldn't come up. Not that David was judging the place; it was what it was. And he'd been able to order a beer that wasn't one of the big three or four sold everywhere, though it certainly wasn't local.

He was eyeing the old beer ads again, glancing over to the kitchen door for signs of his meal, when a man approached the bar and sat down next to him. David tipped his glass in greeting and started to read the labels on some of the liquor bottles on the shelves against the wall.

"You're not from here, are you?" the man said.

David glanced over and saw the man had turned in his seat slightly and was giving him the once-over. He wanted to make a joke about the line being a cliché, but instead set down his beer and nodded. "No, just visiting. Business."

The man, who looked to be in his 70s and wore the khakis and plaid of the other patrons, nodded and grinned in victory. "I knew it. I always know."

Just then the bartender reappeared, a friendly smile on his face for the newcomer but no food. "What's it tonight, Jack?"

He took Jack's beer order and shifted over to the tap to fill it. "Your order's coming. Sorry, only one cook. And yeah, it's not like there's much cooking on a BLT and fries, but you know how it is."

David nodded vaguely. He pictured a grizzled old 'chef' in back, wearing a greasy apron and muttering as he slowly filled out orders.

Once Jack had his drink, he resumed talking. "Yeah, so you're visiting. On business. What kind of business are you here on that makes you stay overnight?"

Was the man a detective, or just nosy? Either way, David didn't mind offering at least some details. He explained that he worked for the state as an archaeologist – and, to his gratitude, the man knew what that was – and had come around to examine a local site.

"Like a ruin?" Jack asked.

"Yes, actually," he confirmed. "I was there earlier with the man who called it in. I did a decent initial investigation but decided to stay the night so I can go back in the morning."

Jack nodded and took a sip of his beer. "Uh huh. Well, I'm sure I know exactly where it is you're looking."

"You do? I mean… you know of a ruin in town?"

Jack took a deep breath and exhaled. "Sure do. You're investigating the underground… ah, 'meeting place,' I'd guess you'd call it."

David nodded, all the prompting the man needed. "Some of us old-timers know about it, though we don't go near it." He took another sip. "Or at least we haven't since we were kids, out there on a dare because our daddies told us never, ever to go up there."

What the old man was saying was really too good to be true,

thought David, but despite the cliché factor of the "knowledgeable local," he found himself intrigued. He *had* to ask questions!

At this point, the bartender reappeared with David's dinner and set it down on the bar with a packet of ketchup and a paper napkin. The man was headed over to take another order when David had an idea.

"Hey, wait up." He turned to Jack. "Do you want something to eat? Sandwich? Dessert? Another beer?" Both Jack and the barman looked up. He leaned in towards Jack and spoke quietly: "If you tell me more about the meeting place." Jack nodded and put in an order, the same as David was having, plus apple pie.

As David started in on his BLT, the old man began to talk. It seemed that back when he was a kid, in the 1930s, a group of local men formed a kind of club. Only it wasn't a typical club, like a card group or hunting, but something that sprung out of a discovery in the woods.

According to his father, one day a man from Tempol was up on some land he owned, scouting it really. The land had a strange reputation, even at that time, with hunters saying they never had good hunting there, little game, and their dogs would be spooked off. However, on this visit he came to a clearing in the forest, weirdly devoid of trees or large bushes. It appeared to be natural. Walking around, he discovered a large, flat slab of rock, covered in lichen. It looked like a gravestone.

"Long story short, he discovered he could slide the stone aside, then found a set of steps and down underground, some kind of... little room, kind of like a chapel, as I understand it." He squirted out some ketchup. "Not that I was ever down there – barely went down the stairs, on a dare – but my daddy said it was just one room, where they met up. And there's a long staircase. They put a metal door at the top because the stone there was inconvenient to move every time."

David ate slowly, then ordered a second beer.

It seemed that Raymond – yes, the very same Raymond Dyer, who'd later disappeared – decided it should be the site of a men's club. Or a 'society', as he put it. (Jack's father had always called it 'The Society'.) There were about twelve of them, all local. Together, they created what to David sounded a lot like an improvised, vernacular-style Masonic Lodge.

Quite peculiar given that these men were hardly the sort of elite that formed secret societies, or even knew of them. But when David asked Jack about it, he said he had the same reaction. He asked his father about it and he just said it seemed normal at the time, something they *had* to do.

They created their own rituals, stories, added in things they got from the library, and ran meetings around them. The actual talk was usually town gossip, some business, and drinking too.

"That went on for, I dunno, five years? And everything was good, nice diversion, Dad said," Jack went on. "Helped to get out of the house. Anyway, things were good until Ray got weird."

"What do you mean, 'weird'?"

"Well, according to Dad, Ray started spending more and more time down there. His wife and all started to wonder where he was off to. The minister noticed, which I'll bet was awkward. The other members started to get worried they'd all be found out, 'The Society' exposed." Jack signaled the bartender and asked for a cup of coffee. "And he started pushing them harder into ritual – getting quite complicated. My dad said it seemed like spending all that time alone started to make him peculiar.

"This went on for a while until one day Ray announced he'd found something at the edge of the field, after having a hunch he should go dig. He invited the men out there and showed them this… stone slab. Like a gravestone, with carvings on it and some language nobody could read. It looked like the stuff on the walls of the temple. That was mysterious in itself, but then Ray said he'd been getting 'visions' from the thing. You know, sitting there meditating or something, and getting flashes of stuff in his head. They all thought he was nuts.

"Looking back, I realize my dad was acting strange at that time, too. Not crazy, but worried. Quiet. My mother would ask him what was wrong, and he'd say nothing… and then they'd have a fight about it. They hardly ever fought, even about money. But if Ray was saying stuff like that, my dad had to either think his friend was bound for the loony bin or that he shouldn't have touched that stone."

"Did your father mention what Raymond said he saw?" David was both delighted and spooked by what he was hearing. He told himself he shouldn't be feeling either emotion, but the story had drawn him in.

"No. My dad and everyone kind of said 'Sure, Ray,' but were worried. He was obsessed to the point it was making him act cuckoo. But they all left it at that – agreed to just watch him and be sure it didn't get worse."

David had reached the bottom of his glass but was too absorbed to ask for another. Plus, he knew he'd have to drive back to the hotel. "So this is the part where you tell me why your fathers forbade you to go there?"

"Right." The bartender laid down a mug of coffee and gestured at David's mug. He shook his head. "A few days later, Ray went missing. I mean, flat out missing. His wife didn't see him at all. The car was at the house, so he hadn't run off that way. Dad and a few other 'Society' guys decided he had to be in the 'clubhouse,' so one day after dinner they snuck out to go see. Said they were going to the bar, of course.

"So they get down there and Ray isn't there. Instead they find a lot of burned-out candles, an empty beer bottle, and some spent cigarettes. Ray had banned cigarettes from the place himself, but they were his brand, what he smoked outside of there. He had been there. But they never found him, you know? He just disappeared off the face of the earth. No letter to his wife, no body. State police ended up coming in but nothing came out."

Naturally none of the men had spoken to the police about the meeting place or any of the clues they'd discovered. They reported that they'd looked for him but hadn't found him. That much was true, but they didn't want to give away the existence of "The Society."

"Did the club keep on meeting?" David asked, already guessing at the answer.

"Nope." Jack set down his mug. "Not only that, but one night they all went up there and smashed that damn stone tablet with sledgehammers. Then they loaded the pieces onto a pickup truck and buried them in the town cemetery."

"Why the cemetery?"

"I guess because it might've been some kind of gravestone, plus if anyone saw it there, they'd think it was just a really old grave that'd been smashed or crumbled to rubble. It was hidden behind a big tree. Fact, it's still there. Guessing the only people who look at it are guys like me who know the secret from their dads. There are only a few of us left."

"That's some story," David admitted.

"Local legend," Jack confirmed, sounding satisfied with his tale-telling. "Though I swear it's all true. My dad told me never to tell anyone, but... it can't hurt anyone now. Wherever Ray is, he's certainly dead."

The bartender delivered a beer to a man at the other end of the bar and David signaled for a check. "Well, I'd agree it could be true, in some way." He glanced down at the check. The price for two people would barely have covered two high-end craft beers in Boston. "From digging in the records, I found out that his family gave the land to the state in the early '40s."

"Right. The wife – I don't know if she knew anything about 'The Society,' but she knew her husband had spent five years being away a lot of the time and acting more and more peculiar. She decided it was one less thing to worry about."

David pulled out his wallet and counted out bills, tucking them under his beer glass. "And that's where I come in. Going back there tomorrow."

"Wish you luck," Jack said, raising his mug. "Although personally I think you ought to stay out of it. Just go home."

"Thanks for the story," David said, as if he hadn't heard the warning. "I may or may not put it down in my investigation notes."

"Don't." Jack's eyes were serious, his expression stern.

"OK," agreed David, not knowing if that would be the case.

He was supposed to be a serious professional, not a ghost hunter or lore collector, but nevertheless David found himself on the way to the local cemetery. It was close to midnight and there was no moon, but Google Maps led him there unerringly, and he parked on the dirt shoulder of the road.

Taking out one of the flashlights he had in the trunk, David followed a rusting iron fence until he found the gate. There wasn't a sign or even a warning about entering after dark. Locals didn't need such a thing, he supposed.

Where was the tree Jack had mentioned? He was halfway across the field of memorials – some obviously new, others the sort of classic New England, Halloween cliché stones one would expect – when the flashlight beam hit on the bottom of a thick tree trunk.

He immediately knew he'd found the right spot. Though covered with brown oak and maple leaves, the hump of the pile stood out. Down on his knees, he brushed the leaves aside. Chunks of stone, none larger than the size of a brick, glowed white under the artificial light.

Jack's description had been accurate: the carvings, from what he could piece together, matched the style of those in the temple. And there was writing that certainly wasn't English. Some form of cuneiform, actually. What *was* it doing there?

David slid down and arranged his legs Indian style to examine the stones further. He took one in his hands and turned it over. The carving looked to be part of a wing – quite weathered but still discernible. He put the stone on the ground by his crossed feet.

Crickets chirped as he sat and pondered. What was this stone? Was it actually an ancient relic? It certainly looked it. But such fakes weren't at all unprecedented. The famous 'Piltdown Man' of the early twentieth century was only one such example. But if someone had made a fake, why leave it in a field in Tempol?

As his mind contemplated the possibilities, his thoughts began to drift. The stone had been a marker, a guidepost key explaining how to enter the temple and what to do there.

Wait, where had *that* thought come from?

David nonetheless felt certain of this.

Damn, he was tired. And still a bit buzzed.

With some reluctance, he set the stone back on the pile and obscured the hump with leaves.

Time to head back to the motel.

After adding an addendum to his investigation notes, David got ready for bed. It was after 1 am and he wanted to get an early start on the second site visit. The earlier he started, the sooner he could finish up and head east. And then move on to researching in earnest.

The hotel bed was adequately comfortable. He drew the blinds, set a wake-up on his phone, and shut off the lights. For a few minutes he ruminated on the stones in the cemetery and Jack's story, but after not too long, he dropped off.

Sometime later, he woke up to thoughts of huge birds soaring over a valley. He'd been dreaming something of the sort. Something about talking to the birds... or had he actually dreamt he was a bird? The wisps of dream started to dissolve.

Turning on his side, he glanced at the alarm clock. 4 am. He'd get up at 8.

But why not go right then and sit on the throne?

That impulse was illogical. And not like him at all. He was going to visit the throne room again, of course, but why did he feel he had to do it immediately?

He got out of bed and used the bathroom. "I am not going out there," he told himself. "Not now."

Though it would be pretty thrilling to go there in the middle of the night. David liked to think he wasn't afraid of anything, and this would be a story to tell: the time he sat in an underground chamber in the dead of night.

He decided not to do it. *You need sleep.* He talked himself back under the blankets and dreamt of vultures.

There were no wisps of dreams when David woke up at 8. Despite this, he flicked off the alarm, deciding to enjoy a couple of hours' sleep. He felt exhausted. At 10 o'clock, he awoke feeling much better.

After enjoying a surprisingly generous 'Continental breakfast' in the motel, he went back to his room to pack up. But before he'd even taken his key out, he decided he'd go straight to the site. He probably didn't have to check out by 11, so why not just come back? Just then he spied the manager about to enter a unit, a cart of cleaning supplies in tow. He asked him if he could do a late check out. Sure thing!

It was about a twenty-minute drive to the site. David went over his plans for investigation. He could be more thorough this time and wouldn't have to worry about Quinn noticing his intense interest.

He could go sit on the throne as long as he wanted, and it wouldn't be weird.

Curious. He was thinking about the throne room again. He vaguely recalled such thoughts from the middle of the night. Some subconscious desire there, he supposed.

"Keep it professional," he told himself.

"Get a hold of yourself," David muttered, as he examined the large carving on the altar. The attenuated central figure looked down on him, his head ensconced in a crown of peacock feathers, his wings draped down like a cloak. David had dreamt of wings like that.

He'd managed to get in a good hour and a half's work. Before descending the steps, he'd pushed aside a bush and found the great old stone that had once covered the entrance. Underground he'd taken more pictures, close-ups from which he or some other expert might be able to deduce the method of carving He was nearly done sketching the winged figure, scribbling down notes and ideas attached to the various parts.

All along, however, he'd felt that urge, as before, to enter the throne room.

Eventually, he gave in.

Despite all the photos and notes he'd taken the previous day, David felt himself marveling at the beauty of the room's carvings. Quinn's presence had distracted him. This was spectacular. Even if it was all a forgery, it was a *magnificent* forgery.

But it didn't feel anything other than ancient at the moment. He could be somewhere underground in Iraq, in an undiscovered tomb or temple.

David stepped toward the throne and pulled out his notepad. He may as well sit down while he examined the carvings, right? The back of the chair was carved into the spread tail of a peacock and each slender arm took the form of an elongated peacock neck, with a small head at the front where one's hands would rest.

Settling into the seat, David began by combining sketches and notes, just has he had for the altar.

He was absorbed in this task for ten minutes or so before a thought occurred to him: *Had Raymond sat in this chair? All those times he came to the temple alone, is* this *where he went?* And as soon as those questions occurred to him, he knew the answer was yes. Raymond had been where he was now. And Raymond had disappeared. Like a coin falling into a slot, another question occurred to him: *Will I disappear, too?*

For some time, David sat completely still, staring into space when he heard a noise. Looking through the door, he saw feet descending the staircase in the outer room, and then Quinn appeared.

"You *are* here!" he exclaimed. "I was out on a grocery run when I decided I might just say hi."

179

How irritating. Quinn was likable enough, but David at that moment wanted to be alone and able to contemplate his thoughts.

He gripped the arm of the throne, grasping the peacock heads. The fingers of his right hand passed over a slight depression with what felt like a coin-sized bump rising up in the middle. He leaned over and checked the left arm; it too had a depression and at the center was a button. He sat back and on impulse, pressed his two middle fingers down simultaneously.

The door began to grind shut.

"David! What are you doing?" He could see Quinn rushing to the threshold. "And how the hell did you do that? I didn't know..."

But it was too late. The door was shut.

He'd set up lights in the room, of course, so it wasn't dark. It was, however, absolutely quiet. He couldn't hear Quinn, who he presumed must now be yelling.

"So what do I do now?" he wondered aloud. His fingers stroked the buttons he'd just pressed but he refrained from testing whether or not they would re-open the door. Let Quinn tire of waiting and leave.

He stood up and turned off a light, then went to the other and turned that off too. He felt like he had to. The chamber was now pitch black.

Once more seated on the hard stone, David listened to the silence. He still couldn't hear Quinn, nor had the door ground open, which surely it would have done if Quinn had entered the 'combination' on the other side. *He must've*, thought David.

"I've locked it from the inside," he whispered into the darkness.

"Who am I but a mind floating in space?"

He couldn't see his body or anything else. He existed in a void.

David closed his eyes and the view did not change.

A small voice inside him wondered what in the world he was doing. He ignored it in favor of experiencing the void.

He was dreaming of the field above. Only it was no clearing, but instead a thick forest, much denser than it must have been in the last few centuries. He was looking into the past.

Millennia ago the trees had grown unencumbered by humankind and their drive to destroy, to conquer the land. They had grown huge, reaching the sky. The moss had grown thick.

Large animals had prowled in the woods and exotic birds had perched in the trees.

David knew all this instinctively. Now, his consciousness hovering amid the trees, he saw a group of men and women weaving single file through the deep green shadows. Presently, they stopped, and two men slid a great stone aside, uncovering the entrance to the underground chambers. The group disappeared down the stairs.

The image changed, and now David was below the ground. He saw the figure on the altar and, before it, a splendid, living man with the same long face and great height. He wore the wings. His headdress was made of quail feathers, with a quail head, but the style was the same. Incongruous, but still beautiful.

The man was speaking to those assembled, emphasizing his points with long, slender fingers. Fingers that were now pressing the nearest three stars on the altar.

The stone door opened. Four women and four men entered the throne room.

And then it was dark. Just *dark*. David was in the void. These people were in the void.

Now the room was light. And empty. They had all gone home, David knew.

A shorter figure entered through the throne room door. He was wearing a hunting jacket and wool pants. *Raymond.*

The man, with almost a drugged look on his face, sat down on the throne and pressed the buttons in the arms. The room went black.

Suddenly David awoke. He was sitting where Raymond had sat and where those strange people had sat. They had disappeared. He could disappear as well.

Before his eyes a spectral figure appeared. Like the man who had worn the wings, he was tall, with a long face. From his shoulders hung the ghost of wings. In the darkness he appeared to be made of moonlight.

"You wish to travel?" he asked. The man's lips said something else, another language, but David understood. It was an offer.

"Yes," he found himself saying. It seemed the only answer.

"Then it shall be so."

David found himself in a dark place, but there was some sense of light penetrating the darkness. He was sitting in another chair, perhaps another throne. He stood up and stumbled towards the light. The floor was rough, and reaching out, he felt walls of raw stone.

He followed the stone passage, which grew brighter and brighter. He was in a cave.

As he approached the entrance, the cool of the cave transformed to warmth. He saw blue sky. He stepped out onto a ledge of orange rock. The sun was strong and hot.

The ledge jutted out of a cliff. He was a few hundred feet up from the floor of a valley. An unfamiliar valley. Not a valley in Massachusetts.

He gaped.

And then he saw a carving, small but instantly recognisable, on the rock face to the right of the cave entrance. The man with the wings. And next to him, three stars.

He pressed the stars and after a moment, heard the sound of grinding stones. A set of stone steps slid out from the side of the clip, leading from the ledge.

What choice did he have but to follow them down?

CRABTREE FIELD

Jessica Gilling

Nell sat in the long grass, just outside the back garden gate; the view filled her with awe, as it had always done. As a child she'd always thought this must have been the top of the world; from here, she could see as far as Hulme Quarry nature reserve, seven and a half miles away. From north to south, the city scarred the earth for thirteen miles, as it sprawled awkwardly between the undulating foothills of the Pennines to the east, and sloped easily into the Cheshire Plains, of the west. Nell had the perfect view of around ten square miles of it and had watched it grow and change over the years.

The slag heaps from the collieries of a time almost forgotten had been transformed by local green initiatives. They were no longer dark masses that rose from the earth to puncture the skyline, which had once glowed red with pollution emitted from the pottery works of the surrounding five towns. Much to Nell's surprise they looked like any other unassuming geological feature; they seemed more like dense green scabs, over deep wounds. She imagined they were vast ant hills with networks of tunnels, hollowing out the earth deep beneath the city. The ants had taken what they could, and abandoned them when they'd had their fill, before turning their attention to new endeavours.

She surveyed the fields immediately below her. Nell was used to hearing the childish squeals of joy, and shouts of *bang bang, you're dead!* as they echoed around the valley slopes. She listened, intently. Nothing but the far off call of a jack daw, and the wind as it quietly whispered through the grass. Steadily, over the course of five weeks, the sun had baked the earth dry. The grass in the garden, and the fields and the golf course in the valley below, was parched and had yellowed under a blanket of oppressive heat that seemed to have no end in sight.

Brambles had started to snake their way through the field and were inching ever closer to the foot of the hill. As a child, she'd been able to navigate down, and back up, the steep hillside with little difficulty. Now she wasn't sure if she would make it three feet, without falling. It felt strange, as if the longer she had been away, the more alien the landscape became.

Nell leant back on her elbows and breathed a deep and heavy sigh; the air was thick, almost suffocating. She closed her eyes, tilted her head slightly, and quietly remembered what it had been like growing up here. She relished the memories she'd gathered like wildflowers as she'd run, skipped, and danced through the fields as a child. Fighting for territory, building primitive settlements in the bushes along the foot of the hill, and forging friendships that would never be forgotten easily. She couldn't remember the bullshit. She could only remember the happiness, and she was thankful for that at least. For Nell, the memories seemed to be mashed together, as if all she could ever remember happened over one long, hot, summer.

For a fleeting moment, her mouth curled, and she smiled her first genuine smile in weeks. The sun was warm on her skin, as she stretched her legs out in front of her, and Nell felt at peace for the briefest of seconds, because she was home. But, as quickly as it had appeared, it was gone. An emptiness had replaced happiness, and Nell felt as hollow as the earth beneath the ant hills. She was tired. It was the type of fatigue that made her feel as if she were about to be swallowed whole by something unknown. The type that made movement cumbersome, almost as if she were wading through treacle. The type that was in her mind, as well as her bones. The events of the last few weeks had drained the life out of her and left an ache in her belly. A nostalgic sickness; a longing to be home.

A shadow was cast over her, she frowned and opened one eye.

"D'ya mind? I'm trying catch the sun 'ere," Nell said, grinning.

"By the looks of it, yer dunna need any more. Yer'll be crispin' soon. Git tha' dine thee neck, duck," Micky said as she sat up, and passed her a glass. He sat down beside her, Nell rested her head on his shoulder. Clouds frothed in the distant sky, they had slowly begun to replace the deep azure, with an ominous grey.

"Didn't think I'd be back 'ere, Micky. Thanks again for letting me stay," she said.

"Dunna werrit thee sen. It's times like this yer'll be needin' someone." Micky smiled and slipped his arm around her shoulder.

"It didn't have to be you, though, did it?" she sighed.

"Yer wanted come 'ome, dint yer? Ah get it, ah'm glad yer called me. Yer still me little buddy, dunna want see yer come to any 'arm." Micky smiled at her and squeezed her gently.

"Out of everyone in my life, you're the only one that wouldn't, I truly believe that." Nell lifted her head and took a long sip from her glass.

"Yer want tell me what's goin' on, or do ah 'ave to guess? Ah can 'ear it in yer voice, Nell, ah can see it in yer face, somethin's different." Micky looked away. After a moment he continued, "Duck, yer 'ere for a reason, and ah never wanted the reason yer back 'ere t'be pain..." His voice trailed off, as he fought to find the right words.

"I know, mate. If I could explain it, then I would, but I can't. It's like I've been thunder punched in the throat. Every time I try, the words just fall away from me, and I've just..." Nell looked down at her feet. She didn't know how to explain to her oldest friend that she felt lifeless.

Micky shook his head. "Well, yer back now, duck. Ah'm goin' look after yer, like ah used to. Ah dunno, yer go away for fifteen years, an' come back talkin' all weird and cravin' oatcakes. Kinda life is that? 'Onestly duck." Micky laughed playfully.

"Easy for you to say. Sometimes I swear I can see people mentally crawling up their own arse, when I open me mouth,"

"Nah, they just feel sorry fer yer, on the account of Stoke being a shit team, dunna tek it personally." Micky laughed again, his eyes bright. He searched her face as if seeking for the faintest hint of what it was that really caused Nell's reappearance after so many years.

They sat in silence, and thirstily drank in the view. Nell felt their collective memories provided their souls with nourishment; it was as if the second helping of their childhood was tastier than the first, even if somewhat bittersweet.

"So, what's yer fella like then?" Micky asked. Nell suspected he was trying to make small talk more than anything else. Obviously, he'd sensed something was not quite right with his old friend when she called and asked to stay. Nell had skirted around the issue, when he brought it up in the conversations that followed, she said she'd be fine, that it was nothing to worry about. She said that she just needed a bit of time. But even so, she could tell

Micky wasn't buying that. She knew he thought her to be the type of woman to carry the weight of the world on her shoulders with ease. She would let that weight crush her before she'd hand it off to anybody else. He believed her strength knew no bounds. He couldn't stand the thought of something breaking her.

"I ain't got one."

"What d'yer mean?"

"Things kinda got a bit weird for 'im when I started struggling. Came 'ome from work the other day, and everything of 'is was gone. Things hadn't been right for a while but, if that's 'is reaction to it then fuck 'im. I ain't got time for that kind of cunt-ery. Fuck 'im." Nell drained what was left in her glass and placed it between her feet.

"That's a bit shit. Ah'm sorry, duck."

"It is what it is. No use crying over spilt milk, is there?"

"Either way, yer learn to understand and 'elp if yer love someone. Mate, 'e's a prick, seriously. If 'e felt anythin' for yer, 'e would 'ave understood. Wished ah never asked now, duck, ah truly am sorry.' Micky kissed Nell's forehead and stroked her hair, just like he used to.

The pair had known each other since they were practically brand new, and untainted by the world. Their whole group of friends had been close, Micky and Nell especially. Micky was just four days older than her; they had both known that their mothers had secretly hoped for a wedding. Out of everyone in their motley crew, it had been Micky and Nell they'd held out for. Unfortunately for their mothers, being so close from the beginning, saw to it that they only ever regarded each other as like siblings, and nothing more.

Nell could still remember the shock on her mother's face when she'd gone home one evening and had told her about her relationship with her friend, Dean. Her mother hadn't been ready, and neither had Nell. The only reason she had told her, was because Mr Bibby had caught them kissing in the shade of the oak tree, at the top of Crabtree Field. The last thing her mother needed was to be told by Mrs Patel, from Harry's shop while she was buying her weekly grocery's on tick, because she'd been told by Mrs Tarpsey, who'd been told by Mr Hughes, who'd been told by Sheila Wainwright, because she was a nosey old cow who loved to watch people squirm. No, she definitely hadn't been ready to tell her mother that she liked girls as well as boys.

It happened late one July afternoon, much like this one. The sun had hot, and everything that had once been green had all but given up hope for rain; not even the shade had offered relief. The air had been suffocating, and it had been quiet. No bird had sung. There had not even been the gentle hum of insects; only the sound of a dog barking in the distance and a house alarm could be heard. They'd been sheltering from the sun in Crabtree Field, watching the clouds slip glacially slow across the sky, through the boughs of the tree. Their hands had inched closer at a similar pace, until their fingers had become entwined. Dean had moved closer. Before they knew it their lips had met. A few weeks after that, Nell had moved away to university. After a few months, her and Dean had ceased to be, and she'd filled her time with her dreams and thoughts of the future.

A few years into her adventures, Nell had noticed something about herself that she couldn't understand. She had been sitting on the ledge of her window, watching people walk down Edgecumbe Avenue, a busy street in Newquay; some walking from the beach, some to. As she'd watched every passer-by, she'd imagined the complexity of every person's life. Their hopes, their dreams, their fears, how many other people were they connected to? How many other rabbit warrens? How many ghosts? How many footprints had they left in their wake? Did they tread lightly? Could these footprints take her to the moon? Then, suddenly, she'd felt an overwhelming fear, as if the icy claw of panic had reached down her throat, draining her of hope as it nestled comfortably and safe in her belly.

Nell had felt small and lost, almost childlike. Suddenly, the vastness of the universe had humbled her. It had made her aware of how small and insignificant she really was. How heavy had her footprints been? How many ripples in time had she made that had affected others? Affected the earth? Was everything she was doing even worth it? She'd proceeded to spend the next four days in her bedroom but had emerged victorious. Albeit, unwashed and ravenous, she had still seen it as a victory. She'd launched herself into her work; it had seemed that the sucker-punch from the universe had renewed her lust for life. The vigour in which she threw herself head long into every second of her waking minutes had made her glow and had given others wings.

Periodically over the next decade, the feeling had come back to haunt her. That familiar panic would engulf her, crush her, and would turn her to jelly in its grip. With each new wave of depression, the chasm had got wider, and deeper; and, subsequently, harder and harder to fill. Her glow had gradually weakened, until, eventually, it had died out altogether. All the people she had ever given wings to had flown onto a brighter future, leaving her alone once more.

A few weeks ago, when the pain had become too much, she'd understood what she needed to do. Home was where she needed to be. Home would make her whole, would make her new. As her Nan would always say *"never be afraid to return to the beginning, if you're lost and need to find a way"*.

Now, she sat drinking with her best friend, in the fields behind her childhood home, (that was now owned by Micky, in a bizarre twist of fate), and craved only one thing… To lie upon the earth of Crabtree Field.

Nell cleared her throat. "Micky, I think I'm going to 'ave a walk down to Crabtree Field."

"Why would yer want t'be doin' tha'?" Micky looked at her, puzzled.

"I think I just need to, clear my 'ead a bit, walk up an appetite."

"Fair enough, duck. Want me come with yer?"

"Nah, I'll be awright me owd," She knew she was unconvincing.

"Yer sure? Yer might need someone carry yer back, in this 'eat."

"I'll be fine, 'onestly. I'll give you a ring if I start struggling, you can give me a piggy-back."

Micky wrapped his arms around her once again, and the pain radiated from Nell in waves. She may have been able to convince others that she was fine, but she knew he could see the shadow. They sat for a little while longer in silence, entwined in each other's arms, both drowning in an ocean of thought.

A warm wind rushed up the hillside.

Nell stirred, and then slowly got to her feet. "I suppose I'll be seeing you in a bit?" she said and helped Micky to his feet.

"Yer best watch yersel' down there. It ain't like it used ter be."

"I'll be fine, stop yer werriting!" Nell laughed, as she set off at a steady pace down the hill.

As she neared the foot of the hill, Nell appreciated Micky's warning. The grass was thick and came up to her chest. What had once been an open field of wild grasses, was now fast becoming a thicket. It really wasn't how she remembered it.

Nell stopped for a moment. All the paths that she could easily follow through the fields and down to the brook were overgrown. Nothing remained of their childhood footprints. As comforting as that thought was, it was still an ache in the tits. She looked around in the hope of finding a better footing before she continued on. She saw a small cluster of oak saplings poking through the grass and was warmed by the thought of nature slowly starting to reclaim what had once been rightfully hers. Nell looked out further and noticed that, here and there, groups of saplings had pushed their way through the earth, and up and out of the top of the long grass. What she thought were brambles were in fact small clutches of young oak trees. She shuddered, the icy fingers of unease slowly awoke in her belly. Nell didn't like the thought of the destructive effect that her friends and she had had on this small section of earth. But more recently, she had tried to be a glass half full type of person, so, she took comfort in the fact that she gained pleasure from her and her friend's destruction. They had spent countless hours tearing up grass and pulling limbs from trees, so they could fashion tepees from the materials, in order for them to camp out. Nell had a memory of stealing tools from her dad's shed, so they could make an underground base. It had taken them an entire day to dig a hole big enough for her friends to sit in, simply for them to give it up as a bad job and fill the hole back in. No, it wasn't anything on the scale that humans had destroyed the landscape around here over the years.

Chell Heath hadn't even been a place until after the war. Miners had come, the council had built homes for their families, and it hadn't been long before it was paradise for the hard-working man. Everyone had even had a garden to cultivate and make their own. Worlds apart from the two-up-two-down terrace streets, where everyone lived on top of everyone else. Between Chatterley Whitfield and Hanley Deep Pit similar communities had sprung up, and the land in between had been used as marl holes, and rubbish tips. This particular one was a favourite of the pottery works of Wades. During the 70s, when Nell's mother and her friends had played here, the earth had spat back countless animal whimsies made of porcelain that had been sent to the spoil tip in previous decades. Both generations had amassed collections of hundreds, over the years. Sometimes they would be lying on the ground, other times they dug for them, in the hopes that one day they would complete a set. At least Nell's destruction was childish play, and nowhere near as traumatic for Mother Earth as being ripped open for precious coal, and filled back up with useless shit, anything to fill the void.

Nell started off in the direction of her own paradise, moving slowly through the grass. Eventually she found an easier route through the valley, one that was possibly walked by dog owners, or people thinking it would be a good short cut from Chell Heath Road to High Lane. Not knowing how arduous the trek really was, even in Nell's younger days she would rather walk around than walk through. She supposed it was her lazy streak; playing here was one thing, but to walk through it? That was a different matter entirely. Unless, that is, she was paying a visit to Crabtree Field.

It was a strange place. It wasn't a field at all anymore. It had once been a walled clearing, hidden by a line of trees running perpendicular to the hill. It stood to reason that it was a remnant of when the landscape had been farmed years before coal had been found, a small walled field that remained so, even after all the other walls had been taken down. It couldn't be seen from anywhere in the valley, or on the slopes, you only knew it was there if you knew it was there. The seasons came and went, and over the course of centuries trees had begun to grow here and there within the field. Nature had taken hold once more and had concealed it, offered it protection, wrapped it in its own kind of love, and had hidden it from the world, so that this place may always know peace. Nell had always felt comforted there; it refilled her in times of need and acted as the backdrop to a thousand mental battles. All of which were easily won; it was simple, it was intoxicating, a different sort of magic.

Nell reached the edge of the field. The trees stood like silent sentinels that guarded this tiny green oasis, as time on the outside slipped slowly on towards its inevitable chaotic end. She ducked beneath the low hanging branches and through the opening in the low stone wall.

Nell was taken by the sweet subtle scent of the wild dog-rose, growing on the edge of the field. She looked around and inhaled deeply, wanting nothing more than this place to fill her soul. From tip-to-toe she ached for its serenity. Dappled sunlight hit the ground and created soft shadows beneath the canopy of green. She followed the stream that ran down the centre of the field, up to its source, listening intently as a trickle of water tumbled over the stones on its bed. It ran adjacent to the tall oak tree she'd once spent many a happy hour climbing. Her fingers danced over its bark. She felt its age, and its strength. The centuries it had stood were etched into its skin. The touch was almost electric. She felt the aged oak breathe a lifetime beneath her fingertips.

Nell lay down at the base of the trunk and looked up through the branches. The sky was turning dark as clouds drew up from the south. Wind started to move through the trees, disrupting the blanket of heat and cooling her skin. She watched as it made the branches sway, and what was left of the sunlight seemed to dance delicately to the ground. It caught the leaves in different ways, making the field glow with an ethereal beauty that forced her to see each colour with a new appreciation. The effect was heady, almost dizzying, overwhelming every cell in her body. Goosebumps rose and fell in waves across her skin. Nell inhaled deeply again and closed her eyes, determined to savour this moment of peace.

She spread her arms out wide. The ground was warm beneath her, and she ran her fingers through the soil and woodland litter. The wind pressed through the trees again, more forceful this time, bringing with it the sound of thunder as it tumbled through the atmosphere. Nell concentrated on the earth where she lay. She could feel it breathing, as if it were breathing with her and for her.

Then came the rain. It whispered softly through the air. A tinkling sound surrounded Nell, as raindrops hit the leaves and fell to the ground. It gradually became a steady drumming on the canopy, and Nell started slowly to get soaked. Her skin ran with beads of rainwater. As the sky wept heavily, Nell wept with it, more freely than she had ever done before. She didn't hold back the torrents of pain. Her walls tumbled around her under the force of the deluge. The life-giving rains that had been absent for the last five weeks washed over her. The earth opened up and drew Nell's poison from her, into it. Nell sobbed, her tears flowing freely, and reached for the soil, melting beneath it on contact. The leaden weight of her sorrow was carried away with every raindrop.

In that moment she was reborn. She let go of everything that she'd ever been and replaced it with the notion of all that she was now. Made of star-dust. Energy, present at the Big Bang danced in the blue of her eyes. Her bones, composed of the elements that came from the cataclysmic death of a star, and a wish whispered centuries ago, ebbed and flowed in her veins. Her mind that was frayed at the edges like worn cloth, and damaged by years of abuse, was beautiful once more. Nell didn't move. She let the rain pummel her through the canopy, ensuring every last slither of miasma was washed away.

The molten disc of the sun hung low in the sky, when the rain eventually abated, and clouds cleared as quickly as they came. The familiar smell of the baked earth was carried on the breeze and welcomed Nell when she re-emerged from Crabtree Field. Her step was light, and her skin shone as she made her way silently and slowly homeward. Everything about her radiated stillness, a pure sort of energy that this time gave *her* wings. Steam rose from the grass as she let it play through her fingers; it rose up in wisps, back skyward, towards nothingness. Only to come back down again in time to come, to meet her once more.

ON VENUS STREET

Liz Williams

We came to live near St Dunstan's after my father's death in the war. My mother could no longer afford the big house and so we moved to a small one, in a dingy side street not far from the churchyard, in the outskirts of London. I found those days very hard, not only because of the loss of my father, but because of the loss of the world I had known which was, I suppose, just a pause, a filling of years in the sandwich of the wars. I missed the spreading chestnut tree, filled with candles when we left Highnam, and the cow parsley which laced the hedges, and the weed-filled pond with its freight of tadpoles. I could have talked forever of the things I missed but no-one wanted to listen, or perhaps could not bear it. So, already a silent child, I became even more silent, and held in the things I remembered. Perhaps if I had been a boy, this might have been noticed more, but a quiet girl is held to be a good thing, and the only remarks I had upon it were approving. So my silence fed upon itself and would have become all-consuming had I not had to attend the local school, full of children who stared at us and laughed at our country ways. I had my little sisters to defend, and I did, with a tongue that grew sharper through the end of spring and the beginning of summer.

And we went to church, of course, because that was what you did in those days, even if your faith had been eroded by loss, not strengthened as it was supposed to be. I didn't mind. I liked the church, though I did not like the Sunday school that followed, and I was told off, for drifting off, daydreaming. I sat in my stiff, starchy Sunday best, wishing the elastic on my hat was not so tight, and watched the light. For St Dunstan's was filled with light: even on cloudy days it poured through the windows, as if the sanctity of the place drew it in, rejoicing. The church was ancient, a Norman relic, and although the stained glass of its windows was of course more recent, it was still old. Some of it looked very thick and bubbled, as if it had come from a different place. In the curtained-off area where the Sunday school was held, the windows depicted Christ holding a lamb. Christ's face was gentle and downcast, and he looked young. The lamb lay in his arms, not on his shoulder, but across his chest. They were looking into one another's eyes, and Christ always struck me as a bit sad, as if he knew that the lamb might grow up to become a sheep, and Sunday dinner.

It was explained to me that the lamb represented the sinner, in this case myself and the other children of the Sunday school. Perhaps we were all intended for mint sauce in the end, I thought, but it was a thought I kept to myself, having learned the hard way that contentious opinions were rarely popular. I liked looking at Jesus and the lamb, but I didn't like listening to the Sunday school teacher. I thought I might learn more from Jesus directly, and so I sat staring up at the window, watching how the clouds behind the coloured glass moved and shifted, depending on the time of year (the time of the day, of course, was always the same). In winter the light was hard and grey, but the glass changed it into something softer, something that was often so clear and bright as it fell across the stonework and the boards of the floor that it almost hurt to look at it. In summer it was always soft and flashed as the sun lit the glass. If I was lucky, and sat in the seat closest to the window, I could turn my hand a deep and secret green, or blood red.

We were all in together, regardless of age, although I suppose the oldest of us was about twelve. Older than that and you were expected to join the congregation proper. The youngest was three, and I and my two sisters were somewhere in the middle. They enjoyed the class even less than I did and fidgeted throughout.

One Sunday night, my sister Clodie sat up in bed and told me she didn't want to go to Sunday school any more.

"No-one likes it much, Clodie."

She pulled a horrible face. She was about seven then. "I hate it, hate it, hate it. And I won't go again."

"Oh, come on. Miss Danes is not that bad."

"I don't like her. She smells." She did, a bit. It probably wasn't her fault. "But it's not Miss Danes," Clodie went on. "I don't like that *room*."

"It's not very nice." Apart from the window, it was cramped and stuffy, and smelled as well, which was mainly the fault of the ancient furnace which bellowed and roared throughout the winter. When the thick curtain was pulled across the annexe, the place grew unpleasantly fusty. So I could see why Clodie didn't like it. She plucked at the sleeve of my nightie. "Annie, make Mummy not make me go again."

"I'll try."

"I don't want to go back."

Our mother, however, was having none of it. Exhausted, grieving and anxious, her time in church was probably the only peace she was getting at that point. As kids, we couldn't see it. There was an argument, which Clodie and I lost. Our third sister, Maggie, who was the youngest at six, sat on the sofa wide-eyed, with her thumb hovering near her mouth. My mother turned on her with a kind of contained ferocity.

"*You* like Sunday school, don't you, Mags? *You* want to go back, don't you?"

Not unnaturally, Maggie nodded.

"There you are!" my mother said to us, as though this actually proved something. "Maggie likes it."

But in the end, none of us went back to Sunday school.

The bomb fell midweek, halfway between Sundays. A Wednesday evening, I recall, just as it was growing dark. This must have been quite late, as it was July, and the dusty London nights were short. We had the windows closed and blacked out, and the house was warm, smelling of cabbage. I can't remember if my mother had the wireless on or not, but I do remember looking up from my homework when the siren started. On and on like a hypnotic wasp, rising and falling, a familiar sound that drove us all under the kitchen table. We did not have an air raid shelter and the nearest was a street away. Besides, we felt safer in the kitchen, which I later realised was ridiculous. The siren continued and then there was a huge soft noise as though a pillow had fallen over everything. There was a crash from above. My ears rang. Everything went dark but I don't know if that was because the lights went off or because I actually blacked out. Eventually we realised that we were still alive. Nothing else happened. My mother clutched my sisters and I clutched her leg, clad in its scratchy woollen stocking, until the all-clear. Then we crept out from under the table, like mice, and my mother lit a candle. Everything looked exactly as it had done, except that the big jam pan had fallen off its hook on the wall and bounced across the kitchen: that was the source of the earlier crash.

Slowly, slowly, we took stock. My mother looked out of the front door and reported that Venus Street was still standing. The bomb had been close but, it seemed, not that close. It was only on the following day that we discovered that the bomb had struck the vacant building on the other side of St Dunstan's and thus part of the church itself. The steeple was intact, remarkably. But the roof was not. Hand in hand with my mother, I stared at the smoking remains. The place stank in the summer rain; it felt like swallowing soot.

Clodie burst into tears when told and said, "I didn't do it! I didn't!"

"I know," I said. "It was the Germans."

"But I didn't say anything!" She seemed to think that she was, nonetheless, ultimately responsible. Needless to say, we were banned from going anywhere near the ruined church and, needless to say, we ignored this. We were allowed to play in the street in the summer, and I think my mother took advantage of the relatively good weather to, once again, yes, have some peace and quiet. We were under strict instructions to run straight home if the air raid siren went off.

The first thing that Clodie and I did was to go to the churchyard. The air still smelled, but the rain had conquered the worst of it. And the first thing I found, there among the still-intact gravestones, was Jesus' sad face. It completely took me aback. It was staring up at me from the wet grass.

"No wonder he's sad," Clodie said.

"I'm taking him home," I told her.

Her eyes grew wide. "Are you allowed?"

"They'll never know."

I stashed Jesus' face in the folds of my cardigan and we took him back, along with the lamb – also partial, but recognisable with its bleating face and one white foot. There were big chunks of the old thick glass, green and scarlet and amethyst, jewels scattered throughout the churchyard.

It was not looting, I told myself, which was a dirty word in our household. It was *rescuing*. Over the next week, we rescued more glass, which I hid wrapped in newspaper in the bottom of the toy box. It became my secret, and Clodie's. Sometimes, we would take the glass out and hold it up to the sun: our favourite was the big piece of emerald glass which had formed one of the diamond panes at the bottom of the window. Looking through it was to look into a green world, and the sun cast our faces and hands into greenness, too.

Once, when I was sick in bed, and Clodie was downstairs with our mother, I took the green glass out of the box and held it up. Time seemed to slow down, the sunlight falling treacle-thick through the glass, and I stared and stared. I think I had a fever, because the room seemed suddenly very hot. I looked down at my hand, cast in its green glow, and it was an adult's hand. The fingers were long and slender, like my mother's, and the nails were short. It wore no rings. But on the middle finger, up near the first joint, there was a faint white scar – made by falling against a rusty drainpipe when I was three, and at nursery. It had bled a lot and on my own hand it was still pink. I stared at the hand until holding the glass became too much and I let it fall against the covers.

After that, I left the glass in its box for a long time, so long that when I next took it out, we had moved from the house on Venus Street to a village in Devon, nearer to my grandmother. But by then the war was over, and Clodie was gone.

I have said that I did not take the glass from the box until later. Clodie, however, did not want to give up her favourite game and even though I said I didn't want to, I sometimes woke up to see her sitting up in bed with the green diamond in her lap. We were allowed a nightlight, as long as the blackout curtains were in place, and once I saw the light on her face. She looked like Clodie, and yet not. I squeezed my eyes shut and when I opened them again it was morning.

Then, one night, I woke and Clodie was holding up the glass. The light flickered and for a second, a grown woman looked back at me. The air raid siren shrieked into life.

"Come on!" I shouted.

Doors banged. My mother, holding Maggie, grabbed me by the arm.

"Clodie!"

"I'm behind you!" Clodie said.

I did not think to look back. We pelted down the stairs to the kitchen, but when we reached the illusory sanctuary of the kitchen table, Clodie wasn't there.

It was the only time I heard my mother swear. "Hell!" she said, and I was so shocked that I shut my eyes. I heard the whine of a doodlebug overhead; hear it and you're safe. It exploded some distance away and the house shook. Maggie and I grabbed each other.

My mother reappeared. "I can't find her! Stay here."

The siren was still going but I could hear my mother's footsteps echoing throughout the house and her voice, calling, calling. Then the all-clear.

We never found my sister. The bomb had fallen on the next street, flattening it. She must have run out of the house, everyone said, panicked, opened the front door, fled. No-one blamed my mother directly, but there were looks. Two months later, we moved: a cottage had become available, on a farm. My grandmother's neighbour, an old lady, had died.

I need hardly say that my mother was never the same. We all retreated, into our different shells. Maggie was perhaps the least changed, because she was so little. But I felt that I held a secret, encased in me like the seed of some poisonous flower, and it was this: that Clodie had not left the house that night, had not been killed by the bomb, had not been killed at all. I found the green glass lying on her bed that night, when we finally went to sleep, and I put it back in the toy box, but when we reached Devon, and the softer nights, I gathered the courage to look into it once more, hoping to see my sister.

I did not. But I did see, very small, the image of an adult woman, turning to look back at me. Her expression was measured, grave. We looked at one another for a long time; I tried to memorise her face, because I knew it would be my own. Her dark hair was worn up and she wore long earrings. She was all in green. She stood among ferns and far over her shoulder there was a castle on a hill. It did not look like Devon. It did not look like anywhere I knew.

I put the glass away and tried to put my sister's disappearance into the toy box, too, but it didn't work as well.

When I was seventeen, I went to college in Plymouth, to learn how to type. The war had been over for a number of years and we were all getting back on our feet: I had a young man in the village, and we were talking about marriage. Then, in the spring of that year, two things happened: my young man joined the Navy and broke off our engagement, and my mother quite suddenly and quietly died. She was not old, but I think my father's death and Clodie's disappearance had broken her. Maggie was still in school and I moved back in with my grandmother, travelling to Larkdore, the nearest small town, every day for work. I had a job in a local solicitors' office.

On my first morning, I looked in the gilt-framed long mirror in the hallway of my grandmother's house and recognised the woman I had seen in the glass. I had become her now, all grown up and dressed in my work clothes, with my grandmother's pearl earrings in my ears. That evening, I took the glass out of the toy box and peered into it once more.

The woman was no longer there. I could see the castle on the hill, though, and a little figure toiling up the path towards it. Everything moved slowly, from the figure to the clouds in the sky.

"Clodie," I whispered, but the figure, whoever it was, did not turn its head.

My grandmother died too and left us the cottage. By this time, I was in my mid-twenties and married; I'd moved out and was living with my husband, a trainee solicitor, in Larkdore. The toy box came with me and by this time was used as a blanket box. The glass, still wrapped in its wartime headlines, was relegated to the attic. I did not tell my husband what it was. I told him Clodie had been killed in the Blitz, the story to which we had stuck when coming to live in the West Country. But I did not forget the green glass, or my sister, or the castle on the hill.

Life takes you in its current and whisks you downstream, so fast that there's little time to think of anything else. But when my two girls were grown and out of the house, and my husband was spending his pleasant life at his office and in the garden, I finally found myself with that thing called spare time. I used it to clear out the attic and at the back of the room, I found the toy box.

All the glass was still intact. I thought of the bomb, blasting it out of the leaded frame and into the churchyard, the window's petals shattering and falling in a blossom of fire. Christ's face gazed up at me from its newspaper wrappings, and now, so many years later, it no longer seemed sad, but tranquil. I picked up the shard and looked through it: there was nothing, except that Christ's pale face bleached the attic view. The crimson glass, though, was different. When I looked through that, I could see a desert place, red sand in endless undulation, and an army with spears. They marched swiftly: the red glass speeded time up. Through the green glass, I now saw a garden, a fountain falling softly. As I watched, a child walked through the garden and my heart lurched. *Clodie,* I thought. But it was not Clodie; it was myself, perhaps aged about ten. I turned, looked back into my own eyes. There was no recognition. The child ran towards the fountain and disappeared into green shifting light.

St Dunstan, I now know, is the patron saint of goldsmithing, but also of alchemy, the art of transformation. He is early – ninth century, earlier than the Norman church which bore his name. Stained glass dates from the 7th century but reached its height in the late Medieval period. I do not know where the church windows dated from. Emerald glass is iron oxide, chromium, tin oxide and arsenic: a potent combination of chemical elements. Is it possible that the windows were an accidental alchemical work? I have no idea, and no way of checking. But I do believe that the self is a thing that strives to be golden, free of dross, the Stone and the subject of transformation. I cannot tell you, now, that I passed through the green diamond, into that world of the castle and the garden where the light is the colour of grass. I cannot tell you that I found Clodie there, that she had been there all along, that she had no need, perhaps, to be perfected and thus could take the shorter road. I cannot tell you any of these things, only that in the green world I am a child again, perfect at last, beneath the emerald sun.

WORK – DIE, HEH HEH

Paul Houghton

So, to take Sue's mind off her 'episode', we talk about something else: the best way to die.

"Oh… that's got to be drowning – Ophelia style," says Sue. "I'd just like to drift – further and further out, then down, down, down in the cold numbing sea. I'd be happy to go that way. That sense of abandonment… I wouldn't even miss you lot. Really, I just wouldn't."

"Except it's not like that at all," says Al. "Drowning's painful. Excruciating, even. When you get a lungful of water it burns like acid, then you get the convulsions as the body reacts. So it's not so much a watery death as the flames of hell. Agony."

"Oh, but I wouldn't know that unless you'd told me." Sue crosses her arms in pique; she'd momentarily forgotten that her husband knows these things. After all, he works for the emergency services.

"Well I'd jump off the top of a tower block – massive heart attack before you reach the ground," says Vick.

How we laugh, here, in the rumbling pub, where we get down to the nub of things. No doubt we're talking about this because of our life-affirming and death-defying afternoon. We walked up the mountain, right to the top where there was nothing but sky and rock and none of this man-made world existed at all.

"But it's the guillotine that's the clear-cut immediate death," says Rob.

"Nope, 'fraid not!" I'm pleased to be the bearer of these bad tidings. "Heads can live on for up to six minutes, blinking, etc. The brain's still oxygenated."

"Oh, but at least you'd be in shock," says Sue, hand to throat.

"Yeah. But you couldn't scream. Maybe though – you could gurgle or stick your tongue out at the executioner? Joseph Guillotine thought he was a humanist, you know."

"Ding, Ding," says Vick, and Sue gets up.

"Whoah! Mustn't forget to keep drinking too much." She points to our glasses and we all nod for Round Four.

It's New Year's Day and we've not long come down from the mountain where mist poured from the top like Vesuvius. That vast green and grey mass of landscape, towering above and falling below: its epic scale and vertiginous view was mind-blowing. We saw fantastic sights up there; buzzards and other great birds of prey swooping in circles amid rays of silvery gold beaming through charcoal clouds. There were two rainbows. Sublime and impossible, it was enough to make you believe in heaven. After nearly four hours, we were at the top, almost in the clouds. In the far distance, we saw a great grey rock suspended in the sky; we couldn't decide whether it was an illusion or some kind of projection. The fact we'd been drinking champagne up there didn't help – celebrating our escape from the mithering banality of suburban life below. It had long become obvious that the 21st was going to be the worst century, all of us subject to its corporate control, digital enslavement, lies as truth and economic implosion. Down there, we were just inputting data menials but up here none of that mattered. You couldn't even get a signal up here. Our everyday world had fallen away, and we were free and grateful, walking in the heavens where it was cold but beautiful. We were well insulated in walking gear and, thanks to global warming, there was no snow. We sat on the rocks and drank in the sublime. Sunlight slanted through the clouds and we could have been standing in a huge mountain landscape by Caspar David Friedrich. We were on the edge of the world: the heavenly abyss.

This was just before Sue's episode. It had been totally silent up there and even birdsong had long been left behind. While we'd started off amid the dark and goitred trees in the valley, we'd climbed way, way up until there was nothing more than rock and sky, mist and light. We'd escaped from everything down there: our responsibilities and the confines of our trapped narrow lives. All that had fallen away on the ascent. The air was pure, and we could breathe. We'd escaped that man-made world, and no-one could reach us here, where there was only us, the mountain, the sky. We were laid bare before the Almighty.

Sue's episode occurred on the descent. A thick screen of mist in front of us had slid right to left; it exposed a colossal wall of sheer rock on the opposite mountainside, silver and gold. Sue's scream was blood-curdling and there could be no doubt that it was genuine; it was so shrill and loud that it echoed across the valley. It was unprecedented too: Sue was not the kind of woman who screamed. She'd seen something across the valley, and even though the mist had moved off, she couldn't or wouldn't tell us what it was. She was staring at the great rockface opposite and she was speechless, in shock.

Vick plants the new pints in front of us and more bubbles rise. Beer hits you in a particular way when you've been up the mountain. It numbs the back of your knees and the front of your brain. A natural high. We're tired but relaxed now and somehow invincible. If only the effect could last. I think we all knew that if we kept drinking it would.

"Ah, it was so great up there. Like a dream." Al twirls the base of his empty glass before moving on to his full one. "Sublime," he says, "that's the word isn't it?"

"Yep, enough to make you believe in something other than this. Even Heaven," I say and notice that Sue is still quite pale. It'll take a few more drinks for her to normalise. If the rest of us are still quite flushed from the wind and sun up there, as well as our exertions, it's strange that Sue is still this paler shade. It's worrying but Al acts as if he's seen it all before and of course, he has.

"So much of life is deadening," says Rob, who's come out from behind his desk for the day. You can see that he sits at a desk all day because of his posture: his neck subsiding, shoulders hunched, his stomach a little heavier than the rest of him. Still, we're all a bit hunched right now. Well, apart from Sue that is. She's sitting bolt upright, drinking quickly in long, deep swallows.

"Oh, shoot me in the head, then," she says, and I wonder if she's on the turn. If she's going to have one, it's usually about this time in the evening. Either this will happen, or she'll drink herself sober. For now, as if attempting to delay it, she lights her cigarette with a dangerous precision.

"Not today, though," Al says to Rob. "Today was really different."

We nod, sage and replenished. We've walked miles over those silver rocks, way up into the pale blue sky. Up into the heavens where the billowing and luminous clouds had soft grey underbellies that might have been rendered by Michelangelo or Poussin.

Once the fronds of ferns had subsided, there was only scrabbly bracken with the occasional twisted tree, dark and clawed against the sky. The gales had made them cower. Not even the sheep came this high, where the air was as sweet as violets and soft as velvet. Here the buffeting wind betrayed the whispering voice inside it, in a world quite separate to our own. We were miles away from the murk of humanity. The only sound was the tread of our feet, our breathing and that buffeting wind. The rest of the world did not exist and never had.

"Alright, then," says Sue. "I'm ready to share and if you don't believe me, you can fuck right off. I mean it, you really can."

Silent and ready, we lean forward, cautiously, as if we're inspecting a wasp's nest.

"It happened when that great cloud of mist slid by. And I saw the rock on the other side. It was only a flicker at first, but then... I saw it as clearly as you or me."

"Yes, yes, go on. Tell us what you saw." If Al is more impatient to know than any of us, perhaps it's because there's more at stake for him. Sue's scream had been as startling as it was genuine. It echoed across the valley, primal and spine-chilling. I remember my face running cold.

"At first I only saw a flicker," says Sue. "And put it down to the light, the mist, the wind, the altitude. But that flicker was the eyes... the eyes opening."

Everyone who has been leaning forward now leans back.

"The *eyes?*" says Al at last. "What d'you mean? The eyes? A sheep? A stag?"

"No, no – think bigger, much bigger," says Sue. "It was in the rock. Two eyes opened and stared at us."

There is a stunned silence. We all look at each other and then at Sue, fearing the worst.

"When the lips began to move," she continues, "I could sort of make out the rest of the face. I mean, it was all rock, but the face was sort of... embedded in it and... lit by the sun. Apart from the eyes and mouth it was faint and shadowy, but it was there, and it was talking to us. Mumbling at first but talking to us... This face, this huge face."

A shiver sweeps around our circle, just as it had up there during the event – except that then, we didn't know what the event was – we'd only heard Sue's scream and its echo across the valley. The scream was genuine, there was absolutely no doubt about that.

"I saw it as clear as any of you lot," says Sue. "The face was at least fifty feet tall and sort of inside the rock or part of it. I'd say it was the face of an old man. He was staring at us, mumbling."

"What... what is it you're trying to say?" says Al and he gets a Sue look.

"There were no distinct words, it was just a kind of rumbling grumble. But he was... definitely angry."

"*Wow*," says Al. He's perhaps shaking his head in disbelief because his wife has said this now as well as allegedly seen it. "D'you like, think it was, I don't know...*God?*"

Sue stares at her husband without blinking. "*Fuck you.* And you, and you, and you," she says, looking at each of us in turn. "You can all just fuck right off. I saw what I saw and if you didn't there's something wrong with your perception."

"Or prescription," says Vick, trying to make light of it.

A sudden shriek of scraping wood as Sue shoves back her chair. She marches out of the bar in a straight line and slams the door.

The pub falls silent for the longest time. It's obvious that everyone in it has heard something of our last bit of conversation. Now there is only the sound of the crackling log fire and Al swallowing – not his drink so much as his words. Nobody dares speak.

We stare into the fire, at our hands, at the table, anywhere, for a very long time. It's impossible to say anything just now. What can we possibly say? Without a doubt, Sue saw what she saw and found us deficient in not seeing it. But now something needs to be done and no-one knows what that might be. It's pretty damn tricky when someone claims they've just seen something like God – whether it's up a mountain or anywhere else. But there really was something more than soft cold air up there. Its voice was in the trickle of the stream and the echo of the valley. Those great birds of prey knew all about it and so did the cowering trees.

"Al," I say, "d'you think you should go after her?"

"Not right now. She'll be locked in the ladies and she'll need time."

"What if she buggers off into the wilderness again?" says Vick. "Look, I said the wrong thing. I'll go and see where she is. And if you don't see us, it's because we've both got a taxi back to the B&B."

"Okay." Al shrugs.

Vicky leaves us and we sit silently for the longest time.

"This isn't how I thought today would end," says Rob.

"No," says Al. "But then it hasn't ended yet."

"I believe Sue," I say at last. "I didn't see what she saw but I definitely felt it." It's getting easier to talk now because the eyes of the pub are not on us and the hubbub has come back.

Al gets up and offers more drinks as well as crisps and nuts. When he's at the bar, something surprising happens. Vick and Sue come back and they both look kind of okay with it all. They take their seats.

"I hope the Great Disbeliever is getting me one in," says Sue. "Otherwise..."

"I believe you," I say. "And it really was... the most amazing presence. You could feel it in the light and the air. It was all so vivid. And there was that flickering. So if you saw more than that, that's because you're more tuned in than the rest of us. I think we could all agree there was a real presence, couldn't we? I became aware of it soon after the earth beneath our feet was all rock – that's when everything changed. Everything was steeper, sharper, more extreme. That landscape's so abstract and fantastic. It's another world inside of this one... or outside of it. There was that strange gold light too, like candlelight, that velvet air and distances that appeared far away and near at the same time."

"Well, thank you, Matthew. Some people I could mention are not at all tuned in to the landscape let alone the cosmos. The type who aren't interested in art or music or God forbid – perception."

Al's clocked that Vick has come back with Sue, so he's managed to acquire a tray to get all the drinks on it.

"Cheers," we say, as if the last half hour hasn't happened.

Tomorrow we will all return to work. One civil servant, one systems operator, one fireman, one sculptor, one man on a sofa.

Our own time, our own thoughts, will be stripped away as if we don't own them or deserve them.

"D'you know, last year I saw a man drop dead in the street? He was waiting for the traffic lights and then he turned purple," I say.

"What did you do?" asks Vick.

"There wasn't much I could do. I did a little shopping. But it was weird because no-one in the shops knew someone had died right outside."

"I never go shopping." Sue lights one cigarette off another.

"Well, except to the off-license," says Rob.

"*Fuck you*," says Sue but then she smiles sweetly.

Some of us are married but you'd never know it – the drink's the thing. Our pact.

Our bond. Take Sue, charming until her fifth. Then she gets personal. She'll say to a woman: "Where did you get a crap haircut like that?" or "God, look at the mouth on you – like a bottle opener." We all wonder about her. How she does it. How she keeps her hand steady on the sheet metal cutter or the lathe, let alone drawing. But while she's mostly in pubs around town, her work is in galleries around the country. Al gets phone calls at work to rescue his own wife. He'll prise her off some pub floor or street corner where she's been causing a disturbance.

"She's B.H.," Vick once told me.

"What's that?"

"Beyond Hangover."

"Whew. Sounds good. It's only the hangovers that stop me from drinking like a cunt every day."

Blue wreathes of smoke drift around the ceiling. Billiard balls chink from next door's pool hall and, through a window in the door, I see a blaze of green surrounded by two figures, headless above the bright light. "It was great to see those buzzards," I say.

"Hovering."

"There'll be plenty of those tomorrow. When the world's back to normal," says Rob. His office overlooks the High Street.

"All those motherfuckers shopping and breeding," I say.

"I'd rather hollow out my own leg and sail down the river in it," says Vick.

"Rather than what?" asks Al.

"Breed. Imagine! We wouldn't be able to do this." Vick takes a good glug to demonstrate.

"Just not being able to leave the house would drive me bonkers," says Sue.

"We'd drink less," I say.

"Or more?" says Vick.

The stodgy dread of tomorrow is rising, and I know someone's going to say something.

"I get paid to do what I'm told." Al yawns. "I turn up and get paid to do what I'm told." He nods. "But what else could I do? Where else could I live?"

"Oh, *shut up*," says Sue. "Everyone feels like that. At some point."

"You could always have multiple lives," says Rob. "Tell one person one thing and one person another."

"Is that what you do?" I ask.

"No. But I know of people who do. D'you know there was this woman on TV who was a compulsive liar and she was splitting her time between her two families – her two husbands and kids. It didn't make sense how she went from one family to the next but somehow she did it. You can never be sure people are who they say they are, anyway."

"Like us?"

"Like us."

"I love life," says Rob quite drunkenly. "But I can't say I'm in love with my life. That's all."

"It's your choice," says Sue.

"One choice cancels out a hundred others. Like having a kid. It limits what you can do," says Rob.

"I'm liking this. Most people are in a state of closedown. They might think about this stuff, but they sure don't talk about it," I say.

"*Pff!* Nobody's thought or said anything worthwhile since 1999," says Sue and we all know what she means.

"I like to be provoked," says Sue. "It makes me feel *alive.* "

A gust of new people come into the pub, media types out in the country. A houndstooth jacket, even. Young Toffs with quiffs.

"*Ugh*," Vick shudders.

"Doesn't Rob have a nice smile?" says Sue. "And twinkly eyes?"

Al sits Cheshire cat smiling, so used to it, not a flicker of discomfiture. All those nights he's had to scrape Sue off the floor. This is nothing.

"Oh, you're so fickle," says Vick.

"Fickle! I am not fickle. How can you say that? Am I fickle?" Sue asks the rest of us and all she gets is a "*Well...*" from Rob. Rob gets a Sue look.

"Uh-oh, you just got a Sue look," I say, leaning in quietly. Sue shouldn't hear this because she's leaning back, polishing off her pint. She slams her glass on the table.

"Whaddaya mean, a Sue look?" She leans forward, staring. Her irises are flecked like those of a wild animal and she's waiting for an answer.

"It's nothing," I say. "Just a look. A humorous look, eyebrows up." I demonstrate.

"Well I'm getting another drink," she says, stabbing out her cigarette. She stands up and walks over to the bar. She's going to think about this.

"Ding Ding," says Vick.

We don't know whether Sue's getting a round in or preparing for war. Sue talks to someone at the bar and nods towards our table.

"It's expected." Vick nudges me.

I shrug.

"We were almost in Heaven this afternoon," I say. Nods and a "Hmmm" from all, who are really watching Sue. The barman is handing her a tray for all the beers again. He takes forever to pour them. Sue walks back across the floor slowly and slopping the pints. I hear her mutter: "*Shit, double-fuck.*"

"These are all for me," she says when she arrives at the table. "Because I think you're all a bunch of bastards I really do. You are. *Really.*"

"Thanks Sue," say Vick and I, taking the beers and handing them around.

"You're welcome." Sue lights a cigarette.

"I like it here," I say. "It's like we're always here."

"Some of us are," says Rob.

"Yeah. But I mean always. Like there's nothing else. No other place. No other time."

"Just wait till tomorrow," says Al.

Vick's got this look in her eye and I know what she's going to say. "Eh, feeling cunted yet?"

"I'm getting there," I say. "I'm almost there."

"Then keep drinking," says Vick.

BORDERLINE

J.E. Bryant

The Gog Magog Down was alive with dog owners that chilly November morning. Cars were bunched around the entrances to the walks, and the usual, relaxed spacing of vehicles had vanished, replaced with something less provincial, more inner city. None of which soothed the annoyance Gordon Harrison was experiencing as he nudged his battered, but now considered 'classic', Ford Capri into a space way down on the lower car park. He was already on a tight schedule.

His assignment, as allotted by his irksome editor, was to travel down to London and dig up something for the 'Mysteries of History' section of the magazine and website.

"Get me something on subterranean tours of the capital," his editor had whined while still trying to sound authoritative. "It won't be the bloody Parisian catacombs, I realise, but there must be a tomb, or nuclear bunker, or whatever in London that'll fit the bill, right?"

Gordon had only just landed this job on the well-established history magazine published out of Cambridge, and yet here he was on the cusp of missing one of his opening assignments. He could, of course, slum it in some pseudo historic attraction, but he'd already set his heart on a disused underground station called Down Street that had recently opened its doors to tourists.

Time was against him, he realised, but there was no way he could leave the girls without their morning walk. Plus, if he could just shake the nagging belief that everything was conspiring against him, he was certain he would get ahead of schedule somehow.

He drew the car to a halt and stretched his neck to examine the rear-view mirror, partially to ensure his beard wasn't too unruly and partially to make eye contact with his passengers. Gordon's two spaniels sat primed with anticipation on the slim back seat of the car.

"Sorry to say, short walk this morning ladies. Back late

afternoon, so we can head out for a longer stroll then."

With a well-executed series of grabs, shuffles, clunks and lassos all three stood outside the vehicle surveying a grey sky. A light breeze occasionally stirred the air, which excited the spaniels' twitching noses as they drank in a wealth of information that Gordon could only imagine. Their owner looked at the relatively high cloud cover behind the hill and imagined the decent views of south Cambridgeshire that awaited the trio. No time to daydream though, he thought, rousing himself from the moment and looping a hand through both leashes before clomping up across the weather-worn parking bays towards the waiting grassland.

"To the Gog Magogs, my dogs, my dogs." Gordon's ritualistic chant was acknowledged only by himself.

There was light rain down in London which had been forecast to persist throughout the rest of Saturday and into Sunday. Here in Cambridge, though, a typical breeze off the North Sea was shrugging the rain off south and further inland. The chill of the night lingered, making the terrain under Gordon's walking boots frosty and firm – a good omen for the planned pace he was already working up to.

Navigating a five-bar gate he strode down the north side of the hill, the noise from the main road more intrusive as a result of the intervening trees having shed their leaves.

The spaniels did their best to ruffle every motley pile of dead foliage they encountered, their inbred incentive to flush whatever they could into the path of their surrogate leader dictating their behaviour. Previous passers-by that morning had spooked all but a few hardy squirrels who hopped about the branches overhead, eliciting an occasional sense of longing rather than a drive to action from the two dogs below.

The group met a few other walkers and runners on this opening stretch, and the meetings, while not openly rude, were cursory – such was Gordon's desire to get the dogs home and himself to the railway station in the quickest possible time.

Away in the distance, the Victorian water tower at Linton acted as his first navigation beacon. He squinted at its sentinel presence and wondered, not for the first time, about its construction and the fact that any elevation in this flat, thirsty, windswept land was essential for agriculture.

He and the spaniels had discovered a lot about the area in their years of wandering, and he'd proven time and again that he had a keen mind for historic detail – something that had led directly to his articles finding recognition with a growing audience of mainstream historians. Yet there were always fresh details coming to light in this seemingly uncharacteristic landscape, a stack of budding facts pushing their way up through the old. Fascinating in their own right, but Gordon's skill was his ability to strike an essential balance between turning a good tale while still enthusing his readership.

Turning eastwards through another lichen dusted, latched gate he skirted Magog itself, one of three hills that formed the only notable features in the otherwise flat swathe of arable Cambridgeshire.

He knew it was ill-advised to let his mind wander when in such a rush, but the hill always seemed to call out to the historical sleuth in him, its contradictions driving speculation on an almost daily basis.

His musings were of particular relevance today as his plan was to head to the Lord Mayor's Show immediately after his subterranean tour. Two wicker effigies were to be part of the parade, misappropriated by ancient London as the giants 'Gog' and 'Magog', and Gordon wanted to at least get a few pictures of their apocryphal procession through the capital.

He trudged on, the hump of the hill sliding past to his left. As he stared at the cordoned-off copse near its summit, his thoughts drew back to Geoffrey of Monmouth and how the ancient cleric had sown, or maybe popularised, the story of Gogmagog. It was said he was a Welsh giant, the last of his kind, who was defeated and cast into the sea by the Trojan hero Corineus. The invader and coloniser earned principality over a part of Albion as a result and so Cornwall was brought into existence.

Monmouth, as unreliable author, was an interesting topic in his own right but how a hill so far from Wales and Cornwall should earn such a name was a compelling mystery. It was expanding this, though, out to a Cambridge and London connection that really fascinated Gordon. The historical road that lay down the timeline between these two cities tugged at his imagination as he pushed toward the corner of an open field, the spaniels turning wide loops every twenty steps or so.

He glanced over his shoulder and saw the white clock tower at

Wandlebury Ring, the second of a series of hills that made up the Gogs. Evergreens hid the clock face, making it impossible for Gordon to get a time-check. He glanced down at his watch and felt confident he could still fit the walk in and make the station in good time.

Satisfied with his pace, he allowed himself the luxury of letting his thoughts wander once more. Why, he puzzled, should a giant who had been cast into the sea now be sleeping beneath the hill he currently circumnavigated? And yet, the bastardised story of the titan merely resting, ready to return at a minute's notice to defend an Albion in dire need, was seductive. Apparently two World Wars weren't enough to animate this spiritual defender, leading Gordon to speculate on just how terrible things needed to be to rouse the leviathan from his slumber.

The lower, southern stretch of pathways offered the best view of the hill in its entirety and, as his pace slowed, Gordon could easily project an image of a giant man curled, foetus-like beneath. Not laid out like a nobleman in a stone sarcophagus, but bunched and crammed into the restrictive space, the hunch of his back pushing up against the summit. Although the morning air was crisp and clear, Gordon felt a tightening in his chest at the image, almost experiencing the hot, fetid atmosphere that a sleeping giant would generate in such confines. Earth warmed by millennia of gentle respiration, he mused, would be sodden to the touch, muddy and cloying. He inhaled and tried to shake memories of being wedged into tight spaces playing hide and seek as a child. The condensation, the headache inducing carbon dioxide rich atmosphere, the unfolding joy at being discovered... It was odd that all of this should crowd in now, distracting him from his immediate goal, but there it was. A single, sleeping giant, divided by myth and now two wicker effigies featuring in today's Lord Mayor's Show. So very strange.

Shaking the sense of oddity, he lengthened his stride, and let the hill fall away until it became a peripheral presence on his right. From there he rounded another corner on the trail and scaled the gentle incline that led to the back of an old chalk quarry. The vista from this stretch of pathway always left him in awe. There was something timeless about it, a huge spreading sky that acted as a constant backdrop for the vintage aircraft that flew in and out of Duxford. Odd that his anticipated tour of Down Street had the opposite effect on him as it began to become an impending reality. Laden with history, as he was sure it was, the station seemed scrappy and trite compared to the horizon in front of him.

Gordon moved away from the view, deeper into the shedding trees, and popped the two spaniels back onto leads fished from a deep pocket. The final part of the walk led through an enclosed picnic area that had been commandeered by dog walkers as a free play zone. Hounds, breeds and mongrels of all shapes and sizes belted about, tongue-filled grins plastered on grubby faces. But the usual play wasn't an option for Gordon's dogs that morning. A series of anticipatory and pleading looks were shot up at him from below, but he did his best to ignore them, apologising under his breath as he took a more determined line through the supervised chaos. A slew of nods, the occasional tactful "morning" and he was beyond the final latch gate and heading back towards the car park.

The Capri sat like a trials bike at a gymkhana, its low brown form an interloper among all the high-sided and fat wheeled off-road and sports utility vehicles, but Gordon didn't care. He needed to be quick and that was exactly what the Capri promised with its crass power bulge, spoiler and 'go faster' stripe.

Guiding the spaniels onto the back seat, he fell rather than sat into the driver's position and keyed the ignition. The throaty growl of the engine made a nearby Norfolk terrier bark in agitation, and then Gordon was reversing at a pace that displayed every ounce of his current composure – as well as a decent level of respect for the other hill walkers and their animals. He retained this self-restraint until the millisecond he hit the main road, where he called upon all six cylinders and vanished in an aggressive spew of road chippings and noise.

"So sorry," said a voice from the other side of the bulky metal door. "But I'm having a bit of trouble opening this. A nosebleed you see. Only a temporary set-back. Could, er, one of you be so kind as to, ah, give the handle a yank on your side?"

Gordon, flustered but on time, looked about at his fellow troglodytes and wondered if any of them was going to take the lead.

Collectively they formed a loose semicircle around the door, an untidy assortment of bemused tourists – all underdressed for the weather – with Gordon cutting an unfashionable figure in his corduroys and walking boots. The promotion blurb had distinctly mentioned the need to be able bodied and prepared for some stair climbs. He sighed, staring at the wet paving slabs and realising he was going to have to act as envoy for this damp gaggle of explorers who had all parked their brains in neutral.

He hefted his shoulder bag, switched his umbrella to his non dominant hand and stepped up to the door. There was a moment's pause as he surveyed the dented iron portal, wondering if his annoyance would give enough impetus to the heavy looking door. His worries were unfounded though, as the well-greased and oiled mechanisms gave under his grip. With a clunk and an initial groan, the door swung outwards to reveal a man wearing a suit cut in an archaic style. From the high waist of the grey, razor creased trousers, the wooden tie, the pencil striped shirt and waistcoat, Gordon placed the costume somewhere in the late 1930s.

"Again, my apologies." The man – their guide Gordon presumed – pocketed the red handkerchief he had held to his nose and moved into the space beyond, revealing a yellowing corridor lit by weak bulbs behind metal grill covers. Gordon peeked around the corner to see where the man had headed, and then leaned back as the herd instincts of the group took over and they all filed across the threshold without comment.

"Would the last person through mind closing the door please?" The guide's voice was dampened by the number of bodies ambling through the cramped space.

Gordon tightened his lips, collapsed his brolly, stepped into the hallway and hauled the door close behind him. It clunked shut and the sounds of the traffic heavy street dropped almost completely away. At least it was quiet, he thought, and dry. He habitually passed a hand over his beard, smoothing it down with a rain damp hand and used the time to allow his eyes to adjust to the gloomy interior.

The voice of the guide carried well in the cramped space as he began to talk about the area's history and how the Tyburn triple gallows had been located nearby. The tale made for grisly listening, Gordon realised, as well as setting the tone for the tour. So this was going to be more of a London Dungeon than train hobbiest explanation of a station's workings, after all. Still, it might all be of use. He juggled his umbrella across one forearm and rummaged in his bag for his pen and jotter. A further feat of dexterity saw the damp brolly poked into one of the bag's exterior pockets and Gordon primed to take notes.

As the tour guide listed some of the great and not so good who had met their untimely end dangling on the 'Tyburn Tree', the group shuffled into a gloomy ticketing hall that hadn't altered since World War Two. Parchment coloured walls divided by a band of dark brown tiles, archaic signs exclaiming 'TICKETS' or 'TO THE TRAINS', old adverts for products and companies long since gone bankrupt or amalgamated. On top of it all a greasy layer of grime cladding every flat surface. The wife of an Asian couple in front of him pointed at the filth then whispered something in her husband's ear.

Gordon realised that since opening the door he'd been demoted to the back of the group and should really, in a professional capacity, be pushing his way to the front, challenging their grisly guide, getting as much material as possible… But there was something about his ongoing talk of hangings that unsettled him.

"Easy come…" He whispered to himself about the group's fickle approach to his fleeting role as ambassador.

He thought back over his knowledge of London, and its preference for gibbets and nooses, as he allowed the ambience of the station to seep into him. The environment triggered a recollection of the mass execution of Nazi war criminals. Then there was that banker hung with bricks in his pockets under Blackfriars Bridge. Mafia hit, Masonic conspiracy, or a bizarre public suicide? Who knew? He continued to muse, thinking of others. Mark Speight. That was it. That was what he was having trouble with. Just last year, the children's presenter had hanged himself in the rafters of Paddington Station after finding his girlfriend dead in the bath. Natasha Collins. Oh dear. Gordon slumped a little and reached out to fold back the still pliable corner of a poster for Midland Trains. Historic review rather than news was his trade, but it still smarted when the daily and weekly print lines rolled on, leaving forgotten tragedy in its ephemeral wake.

The guide's voice moved up into a more commanding tone, explaining that the station's current power levels meant that the lifts and escalators were out of service. He'd been complaining to management about this for the longest time, but they'd failed to send an engineer to fix it. A few suppressed laughs surfaced from the group at the chaperon's bemused station master act.

He led them to the head of the disused escalators and allowed them to stare down the dim shaft. Sepia propaganda and advertisements lined either side, while a combination of wood and Formica served the purposes aluminium and steel would in any modern station. A distant rumble echoed up from below, cutting through Gordon's contemplation, the weight of decades lifting instantly at the very modern sound of a tube train in motion. He stood puzzling for a second, realising that similar sounds had resonated through this station from the point it joined the labyrinth of tunnels below. Not modern then, more timeless in the context of the suspended animation surrounding them now.

The group looped back upon itself and Gordon caught a glimpse of their guide. He seemed fixated on the featureless floor, avoiding any eye contact despite keeping up a constant stream of chatter about the number of commuters the station was able to service in its prime, the engineering required in its creation in 1907, the shifting business interests that had vied for ownership until the amalgamation of the network as a whole. Gordon scribbled a few notes.

They moved away to a side tunnel that curved back upon itself and led to a concrete, iron and brass spiral staircase. The guide again became more animated as he explained the depth of the station and just how many steps they were about to encounter. He joked that the number wouldn't concern them half as much on the way down as it would on the way back up. Again a murmur of mild amusement.

The thought of the network of tunnels didn't leave him as he descended, his thoughts trying to piece together all the subterranean passages of the capital he was aware of in some topographical fashion. The iconic London Underground map overlaid with the Greenwich foot tunnel under the Thames, the catacombs in Camden and the rumoured pub passages crisscrossing Theatre Land. Wasn't there also supposed to be a secret route that linked the Bank of England to the river? He shivered. Although he was staring down at a bunch of bobbing heads descending a cramped spiral staircase lit by dim, chain-linked bulbs, his thoughts were racing away through the arches below. Tunnels across the whole of the city, but where did they end? How deep did they go? The ancient Roman ones? The secret government ones? He felt insignificant compared to the spaces opening beneath him in his mind. A single termite suddenly being given a macro view of the colony, a chance to comprehend the sheer vastness of the metropolitan mound it inhabited. Just a termite, though. There were no giants down here.

Round and round the spiral went producing a growing sense in Gordon that it would never end, an endless warped rotation heading ever downwards. Then a mother shook him from his brooding by tripping slightly, only to be grabbed by a younger woman who he assumed was her daughter. His concern for them both had no time to escalate as, seconds later, they rounded a final corner and reached the bottom. A flat area curved back into a walkway that was part of a planned flow for pedestrians. Everything was designed to pull the group to the left, but their guide had different ideas. There was a small doorway to the right, shrouded in gloom, and he stepped through it, the murmuring gaggle following single file.

"This," his voice bounced back towards Gordon in the corridor's confines. "Is part of the station that the public never get to see. The offices, conveniences and storage for a constant staff of twenty-three people."

Anterooms opened off the main passageway creating portrait frames onto scene after scene of dilapidated history. Here a storeroom littered with discarded reference books of some sort, there a large tin receptacle that Gordon initially thought was a low and filthy cleaner's sink, but then revealed itself as a bath. He paused, wondering at this. Who would need to bathe down here? Cleaning staff working the tunnels? Their guide hadn't mentioned the station's conversion into one of Winston Churchill's hubs of operation during World War Two, which was strange, as the bath would make more sense in that context.

They wandered into a large low-ceilinged office with ribbed, frosted glass windows that looked out into the corridor they had just filed in from. Again a jarring misplacement of items settled on Gordon as the pointlessness of windows below ground registered. Perhaps they had some kind of psychological effect for those stuck in these rooms all day? Maybe a demarcation of office versus platform staff? He looked to their guide with the intention of enquiring, but the man was bunched against the side wall of the office, gesticulating in a half-hearted manner. His arm movements carried enough universal comprehension to result in the group entering the room and lining up against the opposing wall.

Gordon was the last to enter and took a cue from the final few flaps of the guide's hands to indicate that he should move away from the door and join the others. He shuffled towards the back of the group and stood next to a tall, Scandinavian looking gentlemen who raised his eyebrows in a wry manner. Gordon nodded in awkward acknowledgement and was about to take a breath to ask a question when the guide simply raised a finger to his lips and brought all whispered conversations to an end.

"Ladies and gentlemen..." he began, while still refusing to make any eye contact with those opposite him. Instead he stared resolutely at one, heavy wooden desk next to him, its surface spread with mould-spattered green leather. Whatever the guide lacked in personal interaction, Gordon thought, he more than made up for in melodrama.

"Imagine a bustling metropolitan station at the height of its popularity. Well-tended hanging baskets dangling on brackets around the entrance, regular commuters welcomed by diligent staff. As I said before, this delightful little station was manned by a mere twenty-three people, working in two shift patterns over thirty-one years. And here, good people, we have the nerve centre of the whole operation... The station master's office."

This was the first time that Gordon had a chance to look properly at the strange man in his authentic garb. Polished leather shoes with precision cut, unworn heels. Thin pinstripe jacket with some rail company pin badge positioned on one lapel, his torso covered in a tank top of dull wool – Gordon pictured sleeve braces and cuff links hidden from view. His hair was slicked back, with Brylcreem he assumed, but his eyes held a piercing intensity that sat at odds with the rest of his unassuming attire. He glared at the desk as he continued his monologue.

"A place of order amidst the chaos of rush hours. A rallying point for all of its staff, and yet also the setting of the most tragic story in the life of this humble station."

He's got them now, Gordon thought marvelling at the oratory skills of this diminutive man.

The guide paused, tightening his lips. "So very unfortunate.

220

You see, due to the shortage of staff after the First World War, plus an increase in the size of London and its suburbs, the need for a more rationalised London Underground became a topic of interest. Smaller stations like Down Street could shed their commuters to larger surrounding lines. Meanwhile removing them from the network allowed for a swifter transit of the capital. All makes sense, you see? But the station's closure in 1938 was only the catalyst for a truly terrible sequence of events."

He paused, an anachronistic tableau of sorrow that cut through the tattered background. The grime and spoilage fell away as Gordon filled in the peripheral details. Manila files, tortoise shell beakers, fountain pens, D-shaped blotters, pots of bulldog clips... Office detritus framing the half-imagined scene.

"Closure meant a downsizing of staff, with only a skeleton crew looking after the removal men and engineers reclaiming what they could for other stations nearby.

"Imagine then, if you can, the station master, his..." The guide paused as if struggling with a stutter. "... Wife – who was one of the office secretaries – and one faithful platform attendant who was serving the remainder of his time prior to retirement. That was it. From twenty-three staff down to just three managing a cast of itinerant labourers.

"Regrettably, the relationship between the station master and his wife had taken a turn for the worse over the past couple of years. Maybe it was being in such close proximity for so long that had embittered them each to the other? Maybe it was the uncertainty of the closure that pushed things beyond the pale. Regardless, I'm ashamed to say that their growing animosity began to overwhelm their professionalism.

"The decommissioning was coming to its conclusion, and the station master had planned to take one of his now customary leisurely lunches in Hyde Park – such was his general desire to avoid his wife. The capricious mechanics of fate, however, had other ideas. He had just started on his walk that day but realised that he had forgotten his lunch box – which, I might add – still rests in the locked, deep draw of that very desk."

Here the guide pointed to his left with an accusatory finger. His tone lending something of a courtroom drama to the unfolding scene.

"Cruel happenstance. What started as a moment of simple

absent-mindedness, ended in abject horror. You see the station master's wife had become quite taken with one of the young engineers over the months of reclamation and repurposing, and he with her. This interest had turned amorous, and the station master's long lunches allowed ample time for a mere dalliance to become adulterous.

"When he returned to this low level of the station it became obvious that something was amiss. As you can hear, between the trains there's very little noise down in these parts, and as he reached the bottom of the stairs outside, he distinctly heard something that troubled him deeply.

"What was he to assume? His rising ire told him that the woman in the throes of passion was indeed his wife, but there could be another explanation. Possibly. Something other than the fact their marriage to her was a sham, a farcical thing across all those years. That was the realisation that really tipped the balance for the station master, even before he opened that door and found them in *flagrante delicto* on that very desk. The waste of time. For a man dedicated to the precision and running of schedules, the days and weeks and years of squandered moments hit him like one of the trains racing below.

"A deep, blind rage grasped him then. Such was the feverishness of their coupling that they were unaware of the station master as he entered the room and walked towards the spasming back of the young engineer, pausing only to pick up the large, heavy crystal ashtray that sat on a colleague's desk. It was a wonderfully crafted piece. Several pounds of thick, moulded glass with a tiny matrix of serrated pyramids cut into its base so as to avoid slippage on any surface, no matter how vigorous the stubbing out. It fitted perfectly into the station master's trembling hand.

"The resultant bludgeoning and double murder left the stain you see before you on the desk and, if you look closely, the triangular indentations grouped across the leather mat. However, this is not where the story ends."

The guide, who had been coiled with the tension of his animated account, seemed to slump in upon himself. His head falling forward in a dramatic expression of defeat and depression, several strands of his greased hair half falling across his sweating brow.

He sighed once then said, "Tragedy upon bloody tragedy. Follow me!"

Spinning on his heels he strode from the room. Half the group followed attentively, while some lingered to stare and mutter over the desk's battered surface.

Gordon thought it best to keep up, although his annoyance at the emphasis on melodrama rather than fact was getting under his skin. How the hell was he going to submit a whole article based upon this fairground house of horror?

He stepped back into the corridor where he found the guide led group already walking off to the right. A mild worry about the stragglers behind him was discounted in a second; they weren't his responsibility, and his curiosity had got the better of him once again. A brisk few steps brought Gordon to a wooden door with frosted, wire security glass. He locked back, saw that the rest of the group was now tagging along and pushed his way through.

Steps led down to another, bisecting corridor and, for a moment, the unsettling sense of being alone and adrift in a subterranean system returned – the steps a cascade, this corridor a tributary to the main flow of the train lines further off, their occasional roar flowing back up the channels like the portent of distant rapids. Gordon shuddered and looked first one way and then the other, more disorientated than panicked. Was that muffled chatter off to the left? The noise stopped as soon as he focused on it and then was replaced by the guide's voice bouncing up from the passage to the right.

Half of the splintered tour group waited patiently just around a featureless corner where the corridor widened to double its size. Those behind Gordon caught up with him, and everyone reassembled just in front of wooden double doors.

"The station master's anger," intoned the guide, "ebbed away and he was left stricken with remorse. He walked the short distance you've just covered, picking up a sizeable coil of cabling on route – probably only recently stripped from trunking by the poor engineer he had so brutally done in mere minutes before. He got to this point, and..."

The guide turned his back on them and was in the process of leaning forward to grasp the doors when they both appeared to be shoved open from the other side. Gordon worried that the guide must have caught his hands as the doors swung outwards, but he seemed unaffected. He looked up, half expecting to see someone standing on the other side, but the spacious, circular room beyond was full of rubble, disused machinery but no person at all. It was the oddest thing to witness and Gordon immediately began to replay and rationalise what had just happened as he followed the guide across the threshold.

An archaic wooden step ladder was set up in the centre of the room, where the floor was free from debris, a makeshift noose dangling above it, made from thick wire that might have once been orange. Gordon's line of sight was drawn toward the lowest of a series of heavy cross-beams that traversed the vaulted space above him.

"One of the station's ventilation shafts." The guide dismissed the sheer height of the shaft they were now in with a wave of his hand as he deftly negotiated his way across a mess of industrial concrete and brick.

Huge, ancient and filthy floodlights had been set up behind a battered handrail on a low balcony, but even the power of their beams was beaten down by the volume of blackness above them. The group moved along a narrow walkway that ran the circumference of the room and did their best not to crowd each other as they tried to get a better view of the scene below.

"Wracked with guilt, the blood of his double murder still drying on his hands," the guide continued, placing a foot on the first rung of the ladder, "the station master rigged the method of his own demise in a practical, methodical manner. In his mind he was short circuiting his way to what he assumed was his ultimate fate, for surely he would hang for what he had done."

The guide climbed up the rickety ladder, his unconfident assent eliciting a sense of tension in the group, an uncomprehending intake of breath from a few as he grabbed the noose with both hands.

"Perhaps it might have been a more merciful ending if he had thrown himself in front of a train, one that would have spared those that came after him, discovering each grisly scene as they went." With this the guide placed his head through the noose, craned his neck and tightened the knot above his immaculate collar.

"But you see, that would have affected the service, and he had dedicated the majority of his life to the efficient running of that service. To the conveyance of others. This, however, ladies and gentlemen, was the departure point for that most final of journeys. With the words, 'may God forgive me' he…"

The guide kicked the ladder out from under himself. The bystanders registered his body dropping for an instance. There was a loud slap as the ladder hit the floor, a scream from one member of the group, and the lights went out triggering further gasps and exclamations. In the darkness, the noise of agitated witnesses came to Gordon as his eyes tried and failed to adjust to the abyssal pitch black that now surrounded them. Time stretched into soundscape of uncertain fumblings, no one confident enough of their own location to take a step, but there was a general sense of clutching as those who knew each other huddled together, seeking assurance.

Something clunked somewhere behind them and the floodlights warmed rather than popped back into life. The amber glow left Gordon blinking and adjusting to the return of his vision.

Where their melodramatic guide had apparently just hanged himself, there was no dangling man, no noose, no collapsed ladder. The perfect scene change, everything struck and tucked out of sight in well-coordinated seconds, the magic of macabre theatre. Consummate.

"You have got to be kidding me!" Gordon's exclamation surprised even himself, while those around him looked left and right for some new mysterious horror to unfold.

This display was farcical. He'd come with the serious intention of researching the station but all he'd got form it were a few notes on its history and a crime that may, or may not, be apocryphal.

Any second now, someone would step from behind the scenes and conclude the tour, adding to the sense that he'd been duped, that history was more showbiz rather than fascinating in its own right. He thought of all the leg work he'd now have to do to make the piece engaging, and his frustration tipped over into anger. Not only had this been a waste of time, it had also kept him from the one thing he'd been looking forward to today.

He nudged his way through the mooning group that dutifully waited for whatever was about to happen next and stepped back through the door.

Was that an apologetic, "ladies and gentlemen!" echoing

behind him? He didn't care. All he wanted was to get out of this theme park, to move up and away.

Gordon paused and looked back up the short flight of stairs he'd descended from the offices. Lurid images of the murder played out as soon as he imagined the space beyond, and so he moved forward into unknown territory instead, following the passageway round and down another flight of stairs. An unadorned safety door waited to receiver him. He tried it and was surprised to find it unlocked, opening opened onto the station's platform.

There were dim lights here as well, adding to rather than driving away the dirty colouration. They looped and linked in a chain across the far wall, reminding Gordon of pub gardens and evenings in festival bar tents. To his right, the tunnel mouth was bricked up, a slap-dash affair covered in bleeding mortar that still, somehow, looked solid. To his right, the platform led away much as you would expect from any station, underground or otherwise. The structure was essentially the same, but the surroundings were of a different time, a time of mechanical rather than digital signage, a time of promotions about the sights of London, glamourous cigarette adverts, safety messages that were more humorous, less chastising.

He registered them as he paced past, but a nagging sense of displacement stopped him from investigating further. He'd encountered something very odd, he realised, and recollections of what had just occurred kept tugging at the back of his mind.

Following the ancient passenger routes, Gordon arrived at the bottom of the wooden escalators he had seen earlier from above. There was a low chain with a 'no entry' sign printed on white plastic dangling from it. He found the distinctly modern touch reassuring, and it only barred his path up the escalator in a symbolic manner. He still experienced an odd sensation of trespass as he stepped over it, compounded by the added strangeness of walking up a stationary moving stair. Perhaps the steps weren't spaced correctly, or perhaps his mind had become so conditioned to their expected motion that he unconsciously desired to glide upwards. Either way, the assent was much more difficult than he had imagined, his legs struggling with the uncharacteristic terrain. Another low chain awaited him at the summit and, once that was traversed, he was through the ticket office and pushing the heavy iron door shut behind him in no time at all.

"Absolutely pointless," he said aloud to the uncaring passers-by and the impervious traffic.

The air outside was sodden with drizzle, full of pollution and the smell of frying food, but Gordon breathed deep, thankful to be back on the surface. He popped open his brolly and walked away from the busy roads – blindsiding himself about heading back to Hyde Park tube station and favouring the tree-lined avenues of Green Park instead. Saint James's Park lay beyond, and there was a soothing intimacy to all the ordered greenery. Gordon tried to find renewed vigour in his pace, but while the cacophony of the city dropped to a rumbling hum, the low cloud cover began to feel oppressive. He needed time to process all that had happened, but the ongoing stimulus of this unfamiliar environment kept intruding.

Again and again, he replayed the vivid images of the described double murder, the sheer oddity of the door opening by itself, the speed with which the dangling man, noose and discarded step ladder had vanished. Head down, he scrutinised his memories and, try as he might, he couldn't recall any sound other than those around him in that final blackness. Maybe the adrenaline that had coursed through his body at being plunged into darkness had dulled his senses, but he thought that the opposite was more he case. Fight or flight. A creature of impulse and nothing but sensation in those moments of crises. He shuddered and looked up.

King Charles Street was falling away to his left and he was soon down by the Thames, where the drizzle was even thicker, the clouds even lower. Evidence of heavy construction seemed more prevalent from this vantage point, and the red lights of the cranes gave a defined ceiling to Gordon's compacted world. Dark girder skeletons were just visible beneath their insistent glow, and he pulled his umbrella nearer to his head to avoid their sentinel-like observation.

By the time he reached his intended cut-through just beyond Temple, Gordon found the way blocked by security barriers and lines of people facing towards some activity occurring in the street beyond. He brightened and checked his watch. The Lord Mayor's Show was already underway, but he might still have a chance at catching a glimpse of the effigies. He just needed to find a good viewpoint.

The day so far had been difficult and depressing. He still had scant information on Down Street, but at least his frustration might fuel the much-needed research and let the piece flow before the deadline on Monday morning. Not only that, but there was a chance now he might actually fulfil his one personal goal of the day.

He boosted himself up onto a low wall and clung to the wrought iron railings it supported. Just as his head emerged above the crowd, he was given an excellent view of the approaching procession and there, just being hauled around the corner into Temple Place, were the two wicker giants. He shifted his weight and fumbled in his shoulder bag seeking out his compact digital camera secreted in its depths.

Gog and Magog's design had been, to his mind, watered down, and not just by the drizzle. Sanitised for the child-friendly audience and as nonthreatening as the sportswear-clad individuals that were dragging the tottering figures behind them. But, despite all the beanies, smiles and cheery waves, there was something about the scene that compounded Gordon's sense that today he had somehow become untethered from reality.

One rope-bearded giant carried a pole arm, the other a mace, and both had deep, hollow, unseeing eyes that bore into him as they advanced. With one hand Gordon lifted the camera and began to take shots, hoping that the containment within the small screen acting as a viewfinder might ease his disquiet.

A shield was clutched in the hand of one giant, and on it a phoenix rising from flames that licked its upraised wings. Gordon pushed down thoughts of a virginal Edward Woodward singing hymns from the belly of a burning effigy and found himself overwhelmed by associations once again. His journey into London's underworld, the crushing weight of history down there and now up here, the heraldic symbols crowding in with images of triple gallows, dead celebrities and conspiracy theories. No doubting there was a story somewhere here in all of this monumental mess, but he had no idea how to set things in order.

Gordon dropped down from the wall, annoying those he jostled in his sudden desire to get free, to get out of London and back to his dogs. He skittered from the scene and dodged the traffic until he could look out over the railings at the sluggish Thames. Here, away from all the statues, pageantry, hooky traditions held onto by the ruling class and war memorials, he felt his frustration supplant the growing unease. He'd head home, properly research Down Street and give all of its history the attention it deserved.

Checking his watch, he planned a route back to Liverpool Street Station and set off leaving the ebb and flow of the timeless river behind him.

ICARUS FALL

John Kaiine

For: All of Friedrich Wilhelm Nietzsche's Animals and all us Useless Eaters. Feed well.

And for no reason at all I have begun to weep.
Seamus Heaney. Mossbawn: Omphalos

The simple words of my soul: Why did you lie to me. Redeemed. Innocent. Strangled. Murdering the murderer of being. No dignity and power. *The landscape lies. A known horizon, some longed-for future built on falsehood and deception.*

But that sun sets.

Dawn offers '*O my soul.*' The Gods flickered and glowed.

As white as lies that doves tell. That's how bright it was. Snowblind bright. Brighter. It was written up as bad birth trauma; I saw my records years later, Mine, not my mother's, whatever *that* was. I was birthed into a cage. I was fed pale meat and the remains of past failed Me's.

I, and I alone lived. In time I was told what I was feeling was called survivor's guilt.

I was bathed in anaemic blood. Scrubbed, beaten, raped. That was my precise early childhood. Later, my 'Father', proud, read to me as I sat on his lap. Fed me egg and words. For *whom* he was, he wore a surprisingly cheap woollen suit. He smelt of hair grease, dark tobacco and that never too far away tang of casual sweet sweat violence. He would chew my food and regurgitate it into my little pink mouth between sentences depending on how long the food stayed on his tongue or however long he wanted to savour an end of paragraph word. Or words: The Monster's Child.

Never once knowing commanding is obeying.

I was injected with the liquid dusts of all the broken spines of over-read philosophical volumes. Enemas of Kant and René

Descartes given with force and violence. I took that because of you. And I didn't even know that you existed. Some cultures would call that commitment. Enslavement? Gaudy rings given or not.

I was gently deafened by not the songs of Orpheus.

The wires sprouted from me around year five. They would zizz and spit when pained, curl and glow shine when placated, when I wasn't being educated with cattle prods.

I was taught languages, equations and equators. Burned history and myth and the myth of history into me. Shoots of more wires lithed up and burrowed deeper within my skull, ears and eyes. I transmitted, I received. I saw such landscapes, eternities as jade bridges collapsed under stampedes of Samurai. I watched Ghandi hang himself with his own loin cloth only to be replaced by another bespectacled wretch. I witnessed Nietchsze shit his britches when Einstein got it wrong. I saw Icarus fall. The dinosaurs didn't die, just went macroscopic: Virus's. I spoke Gaelic and Congolese. Knowledge and violence. Poetry and the stripping of heavy armaments. Bolts, breeches, slide. Kipling and Kalashnikovs. Warm dead war poets. Gnomes on the Somme.

All the same in Delta embedded false memory. Words, phrases, Vietnamese gobbledeegooks: 'Copter night flights. Liberated fishing towns. Dry wells. Controlled descents. Breakfasting on napalm. I was a carefully constructed seven years of existence then.

Pre-encoded recognition. Double-blind designs. I was kept in incorrect dream state backgrounded by a murdered Heaven, all white – A Roman white. An alchemical white. *Blutenweiss* it's called: Blood white.

Figures moved there, made of light: Fresh or putrid, they all needed to shine in subtle lowlight. Puccini opera whites.

That was when I first saw you, in a crowd of light, you seemed lost, but I already recognised you.

What was this new landscape of you? A longed for forgotten placebo, the misplaced illusion of Love. Ah, yes. Safety, comfort, trust. Something *Real.*

Something of warmth.

While I slept, dreamt, you, a honied offering said 'I get to practice on you,' as you drilled more cables inexpertly into my skull.

Smiling, new in hidden happiness, with my monitored state I was given critical lures difficult to disentangle – another war scenario. Cognitive conflict. I was parachuted in, instantly learning to tuck and roll, evade the wolves and jump the razor wire. I climbed the lightning blasted oaks and scanned the landscape from above. Assessing the scene, the cacophony of birds and worse all around, I looked down into the valley at an unknown and hostile landscape of a line of lines that was the horizon. Smoke drifting up from a distant town. Some picked apart perspective. Something not-quite-right on that foreign soil. A land washed over by three tides. There, wagons circled in a square, players, peasants, kneeling in the long fields of rice, reciting their declarations of war and their unfinished prayers. And then the rumbling Chinook noise came, the demon screams of F-4 Phantoms. Stale colours of dirty bombs exploded. Monkeys fried. I, as Icarus, fell. The landscape melt from the worst damage of white to grey as gone away.

It was a loose wire that did it. A burnt-out socket.

Encoding ended. Recall, retrieved.

I was an experiment. A weapon gone wrong. One of many down the years. Though they kept me, reversing the recognition programme, My Delta files erased, Echo installed.

Not quite ethereal. A bastard alabaster. I had to descend once more.

A new canvas then. Of Me.

All was a placatory grey. Grey as grief on a good day. Thin shades of you slowly gathered together and there you were in your long pale dress, smiling sweetly, stroking my hand, leaning close, speaking without words – *White paint can be made from little fossilised sea creatures in limestone graves.*

Paint…

Art now. Not war. The Great Noon yet to come.

Monitored in soft focus. Crouched by a quiet riverbank, a thin fire burning on the grass – subdued dust ghosting from making charcoal; roasting bits of willow in an old biscuit tin.

We laughed, as lovers do. Your hair spilling down, all around. Eyes of Treblinka grey. Those lips.

A landscape of longing. Monochrome Monet.

Eternal return.

Many summers I sketched you in precious pigment, in the grey wash of dull afternoons. In dark moments of smile, shadow and the joy.

'I get to practice on you,' you said as you took me, dripping, from your mouth.

Humans are a water-based media. We drowned in one another.

We loved: Passionate, powerful. Gently. Starlight in forest night, frail as butterfly bones glimpsed in candlelight. Dreamlike, we danced on old frost, shone glossy as two perfect pebbles in puddles of dew. My Muse, My Beauty. Portrait after portrait of you. My wires glowing bright illuminating the savage impasto of you. Sonnets and sweet song. My brittle heart awaiting your touch...

And one exquisite dawn the lines blurred. The mind filters expired.

Mastering speech: 'No.'

The working watercolour on the easel, a landscape daubed in runny greys. Greys the body of a bird left three days in the wilderness. Not bad, just unfinished, undone. An overgrown grey of flowerless fields ruinous from lies.

Truth, a few splintered lines on white, scored out by machines.

'No. Please, no.'

The spirit of tragic mistings curdled to fog, I gulped down empty oxygen, choked on romance quarantined. My pain painted heart broke. Nimble numbers fell as rain. Your portrait – Eyes – piss-holes in the snow. Mouth – One in the chamber. A dress of flickering zeros and ones. A forgery painted in someone else's paint.

You faded violent. An imprecise absence. Subliminal programming left only an ashen outline of you, grey as badly cooked goose.

Outnumbered by zero, I fell to my knees screaming without voice.

Another botched experimentation. Art as a weapon.

All of the overworked clichés of love coloured in a liar's palette of grey.

Bad science grey.

Machineries twitched and fidget. Circuitries folded in on themselves. There was an artificial smell of burning metal, the big noise of a gunshot and the landscape was suddenly flat. Me on my back on this slab. Pre-autopsy.

'I get to practice on you,' you said as you made the first post-mortem incision into my chest.

The landscape shifted. Darkened. Deepest darkest fucking liar lover black dark darkness.

As dark as that. And not begun.

The black of the last blood.

Refused any heroic song. No herald of remorse. No immortal laments. No would kill for or be killed marriage. Woe and eternal return. Given a burning, unbound voice.

Ashes. Embers in that flame. No Devil. No God. No true. Ever.

A 'bones be burnt' black.

Bringing chant around the purified fire – *Love when white. Kill when grey. Mourn when black.*

All my truth, like the fake future horizon – so very far away. A sliced up so-called victory served up as an afterthought. And what did the taker take? Scraps for non-existent hounds on so many non-dreamt-of Golden Boats.

(My landscape was the fiction of you. Every waking and sleeping, dreaming programmed thought. Every false second of the wasted years of half trues, lies by omission. Fakery.)

My (You) landscape lied.

Silent/violent: *Words that when they are finally spoken, seem wrong...*

The landscape was and *always* had been the back of my welded shut eyelids. Unseeing. A thing blinded in the womb. Brought to life, 'loved', killed.

But now I thank the imaginary bullet that took me away from the fiction that was the emptiness of you. From the vials and screens in the pretend laboratory where the nightmare of the dream of me was first conceived and rejected as being too expensive and too far-fetched. Away from this dirty, stinking crime scene of life that, like me, never existed.

Why did you lie to me?

The final gift to whatever is my soul. This unfinished prayer answered.

Amen.

A man.

Me.

ABOUT THE AUTHORS

Rose Biggin is a writer and theatre artist living in London. Her short fiction has appeared in *Irregularity* (Jurassic London), *The Book of Poisons* (Egaeus Press), *Soot and Steel: Dark Tales of London* (NewCon Press) and *Creatures: The Legacy of Frankenstein* (Abaddon Books), and made the recommended reading list for *Best of British Fantasy 2019* (NewCon Press). Her first novel, *Wild Time*, is published by Surface Press (2020).

J. E. Bryant has worked as a journalist and PR manager for the past twenty-two years. In that time he has written for publications as diverse as the *Royal Pharmaceutical Journal* and the *Fortean Times*, while also finding time to write in and around a career in video games. His published works to date include stories in *Looking Landwards* (NewCon Press), *Dark in the Day* (Immanion) and *Dark Tales from the Secret War* (Modiphius). When not reading or writing, he can be found cycling the by-roads of Stapleford, a village on the outskirts of Cambridge where he lives with his family.

Emma Coleman is from Northampton and, for that reason alone, supports the local football team, the Cobblers. She spends most days negotiating peace treaties between her four cats, none of whom like each other very much. Apart from football and demented cats, her other loves include collecting early edition H.E. Bates, nature and local music legends, Bauhaus. She also fancies pigeons.

Storm Constantine (12ᵗʰ October 1956 – 14ᵗʰ January 2021) has written stories since she was a small child and first went to school. Before that, she made them up in her head. The first of her ground-breaking Wraeththu trilogy – *The Enchantments of Flesh and Spirit* – was published in 1987, and has been followed by over thirty other books, both fiction and non-fiction, as well as over 100 short stories. Storm has always sought to cross genre boundaries and regards the shaping of language in fiction as a kind of poetry, with its own beauty and rhythm. In 2003, Storm founded Immanion Press, in order to bring her back-catalogue novels (and those of writing friends) back into print.

Nerine Dorman is a South African author and editor of science fiction and fantasy currently living in Cape Town. Her novel *Sing Down the Stars* won Gold for the Sanlam Prize for Youth Literature in 2019, and her YA fantasy novel *Dragon Forged* was a finalist in 2017. Her short story "On the Other Side of the Sea" (Omenana, 2017) was shortlisted for a 2018 Nommo award, and her novella *The Firebird* won a Nommo for "Best Novella" in 2019. She is the curator of the South African Horrorfest Bloody Parchment event and short story competition and is a founding member of the SFF authors' co-operative Skolion.

Cat Hellisen grew up in various South African towns, and now lives in Scotland where she skates, paints, and occasionally writes weird little fictions. Her story "The Worme Bridge" won Short Story Day Africa, and her latest fantasy novel *Bones Like Bridges* plays with class and magic to take on the end of a civilisation.

Andrew Hook is a much published writer in a variety of genres from SF/F/H to crime. His most recent publications are the collection, *Frequencies of Existence* (NewCon Press), and *O For Obscurity, Or, The Story Of N* (Psychofon Records), a biography of The Mysterious N Senada written in collaboration with the San Francisco avant-garde collective known as The Residents. He lives and works in Norwich.

Paul Houghton studied fine art, and then creative writing at UEA, under Malcolm Bradbury and Angela Carter. His first novel won a Society of Authors Betty Trask Award and he has since published stories in magazines and anthologies such as *Panurge, The Fiction Magazine, Cutting Teeth, Mouth, Gutter, You Are Here, Magical* and *Dark in the Day* which he co-edited with Storm Constantine. He is currently working on a second novel and teaching full time at Staffordshire University where he is a senior Lecturer in creative writing.

Fiona McGavin was born and brought up in the Scottish Highlands but now lives in Buckinghamshire with a lot of books and an elderly cat. She is the author of the fantasy trilogy, A Dream and A Lie. Her first collection of short stories, *The Lord of the Looking Glass* was published in 2019.

Sarah Singleton is the author of *The Crow Maiden* (Wildside Press) and eight young adult novels, including *Century*, winner of the Booktrust Teen Award 2005, and *The Amethyst Child*, all published by Simon & Schuster UK. She lives in Wiltshire and is also a journalist and teacher, a keen walker and photographer.

Kari Sperring is the author of two novels (*Living with* Ghosts [DAW 2009] and *The Grass King's Concubine* [DAW 2012], the novella *Serpent* Rose [NewCon Press 2019] and an assortment of short stories. As Kari Maund, she has written and published five books and many articles on Celtic and Viking history and co-authored a book on the history and real people behind her favourite novel, *The Three Musketeers* (with Phil Nanson). She's British and lives in Cambridge, England, with her partner Phil and three very determined cats, who guarantee that everything she writes will have been thoroughly sat upon. Her website is http://www.karisperring.com and you can find her on Facebook.

Paula Wakefield worked as a journalist after graduating from university. Her short stories have appeared in numerous women's magazines over the last few decades. Her genre stories include "The If Game" and "The Fur Boot" in the *Midnight Rose* anthologies, edited by Neil Gaiman, Roz Kaveney and others. She has also appeared in *Interzone* and in the NewCon Press anthology *Noir*. She says that all her work explores love, sex and power – the tales we tell and re-tell to express our desires, regrets and revenge, our loves and losses. Paula is currently communing with the dead for her first novel – part of her PhD project.

Freda Warrington is the author of twenty-three works of fantasy including *A Taste of Blood Wine*, *The Amber Citadel*, *Dark Cathedral* and a short story collection, *Nights of Blood Wine*. She has won Best Novel awards for *Dracula the Undead* and *Elfland*, plus some shortlistings. Freda lives in rural Leicestershire where she's working on a supernatural/psychological thriller thing, allegedly.

ABOUT STORM CONSTANTINE
A Note from the Publisher

The text for this anthology arrived via email in the summer of 2020. It was complete, with page numbers for each story specified in the contents listing, and no introduction; which is... unusual.

Storm was passionate about *Shadows on the Hillside*. Her aim was to craft an anthology featuring stories that take the reader deep into the strangeness of the landscape, where reality flickers like summer's heat. An empty car with a door hanging open by an endless field of wheat; shimmering heat at midsummer, when *something* walks unseen in the sunlight; a sense of presence in the view below you as you reach the crest of a hill and look down upon... a story yet untold.

Shadows on the Hillside is a project Storm had been working on for a couple of years, but sadly she passed away before the book could be published – her absence still something I find hard to acknowledge. I suspect I always will. This has left me with a dilemma. I couldn't release the book without saying something about its editor, yet Storm hadn't wanted it to include an introduction, and I feel duty-bound to honour her wishes. Hence this compromise: an afterword.

Storm Constantine was a special person. An outstanding writer, a creator of other realities and a thoughtful, *intelligent* writer of fictions that reflect the real world while subtly blending spiritual, mystical and historical elements. This statement doesn't even scratch the surface of who Storm was: a warm, generous soul, an invaluable friend, always willing to advise or assist where she could, never too busy for a chat, and ever the first to encourage and support those she felt merited it.

At times I can't help feeling that Storm is still with us, just not in the same room. A phone call away, as she always has been. This volume is published in honour of someone who truly mattered.

– Ian Whates,
Cambridgeshire,
May 2021

ALSO BY STORM CONSTANTINE

SPLINTERS OF TRUTH

Fifteen stories, four of them original to this volume, that transport the reader to richly imagined realms one moment and shine a light on our own world's darkest corners the next. A writer of rare passion, Storm delivers here some of her most accomplished work.

"Storm Constantine is a myth-making Gothic queen. Her stories are poetic, involving, delightful and depraved. I wouldn't swap her for a dozen Anne Rices." – *Neil Gaiman*

"Storm Constantine… is a daring romantic sensualist, as well as a fine storyteller." – *Poppy Z Brite*

"Storm Constantine is a literary fantasist of outstanding power and originality. Her work is rich, idiosyncratic and completely engaging. Her themes have much in common with Philip K Dick – the nature of identify, the nature of reality, the creative power of the human imagination – while her sensibility reminds me of Angela Carter at her most inventive." – *Michael Moorcock*

VISIONARY TONGUE

In the autumn of 1995, Storm Constantine launched *Visionary Tongue*, co-edited by Louise Coquio. Intended as a fiction zine with a difference, they recruited established and successful authors to act as mentors for new writers, several of whom now have successful writing careers of their own. Here is the very best of *Visionary Tongue*. Includes stories by **Tim Lebbon, Jaine Fenn, Fiona McGavin, Justina Robson, Liz Williams, Ian Whates**, and more.

"The visionary tongue speaks. Now listen to its voice." – *Storm Constantine*

ALSO BY CONTRIBUTORS TO THIS VOLUME

The Rose Knot: An Arthurian Tale – Kari Sperring
Kari Sperring, historian and award-winning fantasy author, delivers a powerful story featuring some lesser known members of King Arthur's court. The sons of Lot, the Orkney royal family, with Gaheris taking centre stage amidst sibling tensions that bring unanticipated consequences. A gripping saga of love, infidelity, loyalty, misguided intentions and the price of nobility.

Frequencies of Existence – Andrew Hook
Andrew Hook sees the world through a different lens. He takes often mundane things and coaxes the reader to find strangeness, beauty, and horror in their form; he colours the world in surreal shades and leads the reader down discomforting paths where nothing is quite as it should be. *Frequencies of Existence* features twenty-four of his finest stories, including four that are original to this collection.

Comet Weather – Liz Williams
A tale of four fey sisters, set in modern day London and rural Somerset, that will rekindle your sense of wonder. The Fallow sisters, scattered like the four winds but now drawn back together by their desire to find their mother, who disappeared a year ago. They have help, of course, from the star spirits and the no-longer-living, but such advice tends to be cryptic and is hardly the most dependable of guides.

Learning How to Drown – Cat Hellisen
Cat Hellisen is a South African writer of dark fantasy, with the ability to conjure a vivid sense of 'otherness', casting grounded characters in situations that take a step away from the reality we know. She is the winner of the Short Story Day Africa Prize. This book gathers together seventeen fabulous stories showcasing her finest work to date, including two that appear for the first time.

www.newconpress.co.uk